TRAVELS WITH DIANA HUNTER

9/4/86

DEAR KAREN,

THANKS FOR HELPING
TO BRING DIANA HUNTER
INTO THE HANDS & LAPS OF
EVERYWHERE. MAY
ALL YOUR FANTASIES
COME TRUE. ALL OF
THEM! R. FINE

TRAVELS WITH DIANA HUNTER

by

REGINE SANDS

Lace Publications

Printed in the United States of America

First Edition
First Printing June 1986

Cover design: Michela Griffo
Cover illustration by Laurie Hall

Lace Publications
POB 10037
Denver, CO 80210-0037

Library of Congress Cataloging-in-Publication Data

Sands, Regine, Date–
    Travels with Diana Hunter.

    I. Title.
PS3569.A5197T73   1985   813'.54   86-10449
ISBN 0-917597-07-9

They're eighteen.
They're hot
and pretty.
And they can't wait.
They can't help it.
They elope.

Diana sat perfectly still on the wooden bench waiting less for regular breathing or for reassurance than for Christina. At midnight under the black and blue sky of Lubbock, Texas, she had made her way east towards the center of town, towards the bus station.

On the weathered, slatted bench she sat, lit a cigarette, hoped for patience, took a long drag and a long last look at Main Street.

Christina's Camaro rounded the corner at fantastic speed, raced down Main Street, and stopped practically on a dime in front of Diana, in front of the bus station. She got out of the car, energy surging through her, dress clinging to the swelling curves of her eighteen-year-old body, and moved towards the girl who was driving her crazy with lust or love or whatever the hell it was. With the undaunted confidence of a mature female, she gathered up Diana's bags and swept them into the trunk.

Passion and adventure and flames gripped them both and with one bold stroke Diana grabbed Christina's arm and pulled her close, and hard, and lay an erotic kiss on the girl's lips. Diana was Christina's heroine, her wildest dream, and here she was in the chilly, dusty night air of Lubbock kissing the life out of her. The kiss, that left their strong, young bodies impassioned and yielding, drove them on. Drove Christina to leave her foster family and everything familiar in Texas for the possibility of the incredible with Diana.

The time for upheaval and uprooting was now. There'd be nothing she would not do for Diana. Regardless of the consequences, Christina would never regret this decision, or the inevitable one that would follow four years from now.

And they were carrying on—violently embracing in the pitch black empty street. Not a word was spoken, as it would have been powerless to be heard amidst the noises of their steamy reunion. Diana's hand searched out the full breasts that lay awaiting her touch. Christina pulled Diana towards the alley, to the side of the station. Diana might

1

be able to wait, Christina could not. Christina lifted her dress enough to expose the place that burned most for Diana's touch, leaned back against the brick wall, and forced Diana's hand there.

"Now, Diana, take it now . . . please honey . . ." And with wet kisses and an uncontrollable passion Diana gave Christina what she wanted. Right there in the alley. Christina bore down against the rising tension, her high heels digging into the dirt, pressing her body back against the brick wall and then forward into Diana's. Something powerful was unleashed in Christina, something Diana uncovered, something that only Diana could satisfy.

"Please me, Hunter, for god's sake make me come," Christina cried, demanding her right to be taken. Diana left nothing to the imagination. She took what was rightly hers. Her hands, like her mouth, were everywhere. Her grip on Christina strong and her desire to have her, all encompassing. Christina came with a body-jolting orgasm, and Diana did not move her fingers from inside her. Both damp. Both already hungering for more, for the next time.

They approached the nape of the neck of nirvana and brushed their lips against it on this night. They would never forget the sensation, nor ever stop pursuing it.

Lubbock slept when the girls left town on the open road enroute into the seemingly infinite horizon of possibilities that awaited their arrival. They topped 80 miles an hour; they had much traveling to do together, these two.

The night Diana (impatient by genetic makeup, impulsive by design) eloped with her dream girl, her parents were engrossed in some noisy and probably excellent sex with Audrey, her mother's best friend. They were happily preoccupied; they didn't hear her leave, and had they, they wouldn't have been surprised, as they knew the girl they reared was a pretty wild one.

In the Hunter household, where freedom and adventure were standard fare, Diana was 'on her own' since she matured four years ago, at fourteen. She needed little direction from her parents who believed wholeheartedly in letting her live her life her way. As they had done. They were lecturers on Free Love. This was, after all, the sixties, and this was, they believed, their calling; so how could they deny their most prized possession, their daughter, the same pleasure? They served her well more as nurturing friends than parents.

But despite their openness, Diana planned it so that they
find her note till long after sunup. Long after she would be
north towards anywhere with the blond girl who had chang
thing. Freedom called to the young Hunter lately, and it cou
had completely in Lubbock, nor could it be had without Chri
it had to be had. She couldn't wait for things to take their course, she
decided to risk forcing fate's hand, because with Christina, she knew,
she had nothing to fear. Not a thing.

This girl, who for two years made Diana think of nothing else but
spending every single solitary second with her: by her side, in her
arms, inside her most intimate places. The girl who bore the color of
angels, with her white skin, her sky blue eyes, her honey-colored long
hair, her soft upon soft upon soft body.

As for Christina. A strong and feminine girl like Diana: full of
mischief and wisdom generously beyond her years. She was indepen-
dent and rich with her parents' life insurance money. Smart and quick
and terrific looking. To the naked eye, there was nothing wrong with
this picture.

There is one night in her life, which if you read it now, will tell you
what you need to know about Christina's heritage and the actions
Christina would need to take later in her life. It is this:

She was thirteen years old on the Wednesday night when her next
door neighbor came over to her parents' house to tell her that her
mother and father were executed in Latin America. The woman had
heard it on the news.

At first, Christina didn't believe it, but it didn't take long. Reality
paid a visit to her that night; it had come to crucify her.

She clearly hadn't done anything in her life to deserve this, although
the same couldn't be said for her politically outspoken parents. They
courted danger. They chose it. No one forced them to become spies.
But many people, powerful people in the country, thanked them when
they did. They were brave, these two Russian emigreés, and that heritage they passed along to their only daughter. Courage and dignity in
the face of disaster was indelibly ingrained in her.

They all lived a life of many secrets and that made them even closer
to one another. They were a genuinely intriguing threesome.

Christina was witness to countless midnight candlelight conversations in her living room: foreign visitors, furrowed brows, damp
palms, extreme caution. Her parents' basement always housed at least
one dissident. Christina herself had been transported up the east coast
in a large valise to escape notice, and she had gone thirteen days with
her parents in hiding without food. The Tylers' (nee Luchows') collec-

3

ive courage was larger-than-life; their altruism almost hard to believe; and Christina's moxy, for a girl her age, was nothing short of awe-inspiring. There was nothing ordinary about their lives.

She had been through much. But this news of her parents who were killed in a foreign land, without her, was too much. Their death gave birth to a dark dilemma for Christina which she would do battle with for many years to come: who was she without them?

Specifics, then, of how Diana and Christina met up: back to two years ago; in high school; they're sixteen; very pretty . . .

"I want to get into some trouble . . . come with me!" She stared Christina down. She waited. Christina lifted her purse from beneath her classroom chair, met Diana's eyes and said, "Yes, I'd like that."

They'd be remembered, these, their very first words to one another.

They walked down the school hallway towards the girls bathroom. Door swung open to reveal it empty. They couldn't have been happier: the setting amused them, the privacy beckoned them on.

Cut to the chase . . . much talk passed between them. Clever talk, titillating talk. Neither were strangers to their sexuality as Christina had discovered hers with her philosophy instructor, and Diana with her mother's best friend, Audrey. Both had learned the pleasures of verbal foreplay—well versed already at only sixteen.

During the repartee, Christina thought friends, and Diana, lovers. Both, however, heated up. Then Diana moved up closer to Christina, in fact any closer and she'd have been breath to breath with her. Christina's heart pounded; Diana's breathing, erratic. Both blushed way out of control. Time now, thought Diana, to get to the point.

"The point is this, Christina," Diana said as she took Christina's hand in her own, led her into the bathroom stall, locked the door behind her, turned and whispered to the excited blond right in front of her, "I'm extremely attracted to you, girl, and I'm embarrassed to even tell you how long this has been going on."

Christina smiled. An endearing smile. She didn't dare move a muscle for fear of decreasing the intensity, so said only, "I see."

Diana forged on, "I know it's the civilized way to be your friend first before—"

"Being my lover?"

"Before being intimate with you. Like this for instance . . ."

The girl with the soft lips approached and connected. Christina was perfectly still, felt feverish, felt Diana's arms around her pulling her forward, felt the terribly soft cheeks against her own, smelled the fragrance of a girl this close to her for the first time in her life, felt Diana's tight thighs against her own, felt herself being pushed back against the stall partition, and hands, she felt hands against her waist tightening their grip, hands under her sweatshirt and against her skin, soft hands touching the flesh of her breasts, her back, weakening her, weakening her, and she felt herself surrender. Her eyes closed, her body melted into Diana's, she allowed herself to be kissed this way, a way unlike anything she'd ever experienced. So intense yet so gentle that she felt herself begin to cry with the softness, the slowness, the passion. Few tears; immense feelings. She questioned none of it.

Christina's stomach hurt, her fever rose, her skin flushed, her knees shook, her chest tightened, her thoughts raced during this kiss. It was passion and lust that rocked her insides. She lost her control, and welcomed it.

Finally Diana released her. Christina reeled inside with unfathomable pleasure. The taste of Diana warm on her lips, sweet in her mouth. The beauty of Diana would be an impossible image to shed.

It was this for them: seam-splitting rapture; the perpetual ache.

As for now—three years later, with Lubbock lightyears away, at twenty-one with everything around them gold, every spare moment spent together, they called this thing, that burned red hot between them, Love. Their hearts beat in a confluence of fluid, easy movements, in unison, outrageously in love. Full maturity had come, the heat however had never subsided. In fact, time together brought with it a greater rapture, a steamier throbbing, a more insistent arousal.

Christina, never for an instant, regretted taking flight with Diana, enmeshing her life, her very existence, with hers. As for Diana, she would often ask herself what had she done to deserve such bliss. Clearly not one single second thought arrived unannounced to interrupt their affair, their ongoing fantasy.

One dark thought, however, having to do only with Christina, persisted. She was certain that time with Diana would take care of it. Time served only to magnify it. Christina was losing ground in the battle against the darkness in her. And smelling the scent of her own surrender, she lost precious hope, frequently panicked, but stubbornly refused to share her burden with anyone. Not even Diana.

The two girls attended college in between their inflamed affair— cutting classes, racing home on ten-speeds, side-by-side, barely making it to their sleeping-bag-student-furnished living room to fall into lovemaking with a new bite that one or the other of them thought up in the race home. Passing provocative notes during class, only to spend their break times in a bathroom stall making out. Some things never changed for them.

In their secret sorority of two, on this day, they made love right on the hallway floor as the living room seemed simply too far away. And as for me your subjective, (nascent objective) narrator whose opinions should count for something, I can say their lovemaking was simply this: gorgeous. The sight, the sounds, the smells, the girls.

Later on that day some talk passed between them . . .

"Better?" Diana cooed when they lay still, satisfied.

"Always," Christina admitted against her better judgment.

"Of course, lover . . . you can't help yourself when you're with me."

"You are more right than you know, Diana."

"Meaning?"

"You don't want to hear it, remember—you didn't want anything to do with a serious conversation today," Christina taunted.

"A serious conversation about *me*! I am always up, however, for one about *you*!" Diana laughed.

"That's part of the problem." Christina was clearly not laughing.

"Chrissy, why do you worry yourself over silly thoughts, you pretty thing. Talk to me," implored Diana.

"If I do I know you will just hush the fears away with your—"

"—My assets?!"

"Yes, your beautiful assets, Miss Hunter. Bring them here . . ." Christina beckoned, as she took one of Diana's hard dark nipples in between her puffy lips. And once more today, Christina led them both astray down the wicked and sinful path of pleasure. A road on which they were frequent travelers.

"I've learned a lot from you—" Diana began.

"Please . . . you learned nothing from me that you didn't already know," Christina countered.

6

"I refuse to even acknowledge that statement."

"You refuse to admit how good you are!"

"Christina Tyler!" Diana exclaimed with mock exasperation.

"Diana Hunter!" Christina mocked her mocking lover. "You are almost twenty-two years old. Old enough to sit down and take an honest stock of yourself. You are as close to amazing a woman as I have ever known."

"Miss Tyler," Diana said gently, "did you smoke some of that deadly weed before I got back home tonight?"

Some, she thought, and "None," she replied. ". . . Or at least not enough to impair my judgment . . . When are you going to own up to your assets?"

"When somebody comes along and takes them from me. Why, then, I can look at them objectively and decide which I can handle having, and which I can't."

"The problem is that you *have them* no matter how you work at disguising them, honey."

"It's too much responsibility, baby," she said snuggling up closer to Christina, "and I don't know if I have the energy to do the work."

"You don't have the choice—"

"I have an abundance of choices. I can choose to make nothing of my life if I so desire."

"I disagree," she shot back, pulling away from Diana in an effort to remain the only grave one in the conversation, "you don't have a choice . . . you either move forward and pay the price or you stay stagnant and pay a much dearer price than you can imagine."

"Oh my," Diana teased, "you mean to tell me that you'll leave me if I don't mature?" How ironic. This was the question Christina asked herself about Diana. More times than she cared to recount.

"I'm trying to have a serious conversation about your future, Miss Hunter."

"But I'd rather do something else."

"Tell me what could be more important—"

"Making out . . . with you, baby, . . . come here," Diana said extending her hands and giving Christina one of her better sexy looks and husky 'come hither' voices, "Momma wants to kiss you—just that—nothing else. I promise . . . just kissing, just laying my lips on yours—"

"Don't start with me, Diana."

"If I don't somebody else will."

"Diana, you're making this impossible."

"Good. Maybe now you will leave my future in the hands of destiny where it belongs." Diana was being smart now.

"You always drag destiny into the conversation when you don't want to take the responsibility—"

"—of making a decision that I don't have enough information yet to make!"

"You amuse me, Miss Hunter."

"You torture me, Miss Tyler."

"Communication should not be torture."

"Celibacy is!"

"I didn't know you even knew the meaning of the word."

Diana looked at her watch, calculated and said, "It's been one hour and twenty-six minutes in my new found celibacy. And I think you, the one who speaks so often of responsibility, have an obligation to move forward and please me."

"This makes me wonder if I have cause to worry about you when I'm away from you during the day?"

"Worry isn't the right word, Christina . . . you have cause to . . . consider."

"I always do."

"I know. Which is a good thing. Which is why you're still here!" Now she was being fresh. Diana Hunter's trademark.

"Getting cocky, are we? Well, for a woman who presents such a dynamic facade, Miss Hunter, you lack the serious substance of which great women are made."

After the pause in which Diana was deciding if Christina was telling the truth or just teasing, she picked up just where she left off, as she was a most persistent woman. "Why do you refuse to make love to me, Chrissy?"

"It's not a question of making love . . . we've made love during every spare moment of our time together—"

"Oh, don't you rest on your laurels, Christina."

"I won't if you don't change the topic . . . and if I recall correctly the topic was self-actualization—"

"The topic was sex . . . and I *do* recall correctly," Diana said flippantly, changing the topic.

"Baby, how much longer are you going to wait to do what you were born to do. I worry about you."

"Most sexual inhibitions begin with worry," said Diana refusing to let it rest.

Ignoring her, Christina continued, "You have some very strong talents inside of you whether you choose to discuss them or not. And I want to help—"

"Then touch me now, and stop all this silly talk . . . I want sex tonight, not foreplay."

And with all the conviction of a woman who needed to keep the focus off herself and her problems, Christina implored, "Hear me, baby, it's important. You are not an ordinary woman."

"Christina—"

"Ssssh. Listen to my words, honey. If nothing else, indulge me."

Diana pouted but nodded her approval. And then Diana slowly, softly put her arms around the woman she loved most in the world and kissed her anyway. Christina, despite herself, succumbed.

And there it was, as big as her fear, her love for Diana.

Six months ago Diana's gentle reassurances would have eased her mind; three months ago she might have almost believed them; but now, very little could cool this silent, private desperation Christina Tyler was feeling. Not even Diana Hunter.

In the Grabbag of Life,
She always,
Always,
Reaches for the Bigger
Packages.

Cigarette spent. Diana Hunter, thirty years old and stunning, showered. Packed. The scent in the motel room would take the maid a full eight hours to extinguish.

Diana left the key on the bureau. Grateful for the convenience of the airport motel. Grateful that she had sufficient time to make the next airplane, having missed the prior one. Grateful for the silent exit: the woman had left when Diana was in the shower. Diana lifted her suitcase and attaché in one hand, and stood there. Still.

Something, she thought, there was something left to do. She surveyed the room and nothing left behind. She remained. One thing, something left to do.

She placed her bags on the militarily still-made bed, and went into the pink and black tiled bathroom, caught her reflection in the mirror, leaned back against the wall-to-ceiling sliding glass shower doors, closed her eyes, lifted up her cotton skirt, slid her hand into her white panties and slowly stroked the length of her cunt with her fingers.

She didn't even consider the inconvenience of having to sit on the plane with wet panties for the length of the flight if she masturbated now, she preferred it; what if the person in the next seat on board noted the scent of her pre-takeoff activity . . . all the better; supposing the stewardess confronted her with the fact that she 'knew' what heinous act against God Diana had been up to . . . Yes. Diana could only hope!

Diana felt her already swollen clitoris. Yes, eyes closed, she began to fantasize about her possible encounters on the airplane. Her cunt pulsed, her imagination beckoned, the invitation to fantasize extended itself. She began:

The flight held promise for Diana. She saw the woman in the seat next to hers. The woman in her late thirties: thin, tight, angular, wearing a gray linen suit and a severely tailored silk-soft black blouse. A jet black leather attaché, the color of her pumps and purse, rested on her lap, open.

A "Hello, My Name Is" badge lay inside the attaché. The "Hello, My Name Is" part was blackened out with one thick black marker stroke and on the card was written only the name, 'Miss Tropic.' Miss Tropic. That was all. To the point. Bold. Now came the decisions, Diana calculated, does she or doesn't she look like a Miss Tropic woman. And what are the implications of the heat of that name. And so the silent interchange between them had already taken flight.

Diana noted that this woman was writing on a notepad. What she wrote, Diana couldn't see. She would soon enough, because the woman finished writing, put the pen in the inside pocket of her blazer, folded the note in half and half again, and turning to Diana in one move, handed it to her. The cabin lights turned off, the plane taxied and took off into the black night.

Diana had only to say "Yes." The woman did the rest.

The woman closed her attaché and placed it under her seat and turned again to Diana. Without so much as a self-conscious hesitation, not one doubtful pause, Miss Tropic took Diana's face in her hands and kissed her lightly on the lips with her tongue. Before Diana could bring her tongue out to meet the bold, firm tongue of this woman, Miss Tropic had unbuttoned the top two buttons of Diana's blouse, slipped one hand inside her shirt, and most gently cupped Diana's breast through her camisole. Miss Tropic had a most massaging hand. Carressingly it slid along the outline of Diana's breasts, these long and perfectly manicured hands. A fleeting thought flashed through her mind when Diana saw Miss Tropic's long ruby nails—but it made no difference if the woman was straight or not.

Catching Diana most unaware, Miss Tropic whispered that she wanted to lay her lips on Diana's breasts. Her "beautiful" breasts, is what the woman said. Not surprising. Most women had the same thought when they met Diana. Her breasts were full, large, round and much too much for one set of hands alone to explore. A mouth always fared better.

Miss Tropic's directness was arousing Diana, and she responded to the woman's request (which warranted no response but Diana couldn't remain totally passive) nonverbally: her legs spread apart a slight inch or two. Still ladylike. Still composed. That would soon change.

Diana's breathing though was beginning to give her away. Irregular, heavier, sweet-smelling. She was getting hot. Her legs spread only enough for Miss Tropic's long-nailed, slender fingers to slide up her thigh to her already damp cotton panties. Miss Tropic was pleased at Diana's eager compliance. So was Diana.

Miss Tropic, Diana was certain, would have done what she wanted to do with Diana anyway, with or without her permission. With a woman like Miss Tropic, it was smarter just to do what she was told to do. Like a good girl. And Diana was all for being a good girl. Miss Tropic could expect continued compliance from Diana Hunter.

Miss Tropic returned to stroking Diana's breasts, looking down at her hands on them, desiring them and then looking up to stare into Diana's eyes: a straight, hungry, telling stare. Not asking. With an 'enough-time-has-been-spent' look, Miss Tropic lowered her head and lay her ruby lips on the dark hard nipple of Diana's right breast wetting the camisole. . . . The Rush—

The Rush elicited a low moan in Diana that surprised her but not Miss Tropic. Gently kneading Diana's breasts, kissing her nipples now, first one than the other, kissing, slowly sucking in the silk. Then lifting it to kiss the flesh, slowly, slowly with her parted lips, her smooth tongue.

And yes, there were other people on the airplane. Thankfully, it was a night flight. And no, Miss Tropic was not the type to do *it* under an airplane blanket. And yes, they were watched. Some were too asleep to watch. Some too horrified. Some just too turned on. The sole person watching with focused concentration was the slender, leggy stewardess.

She must have been a California girl. Perfectly Protestant. No more than eighteen. No more than five foot nine. No more than one hundred and ten pounds. Lean, and physically gifted. She stood by Miss Tropic's aisle seat and leaning in against it, she watched and imperceptibly rubbed her thighs back and forth alongside the seat. From time to time she leaned closer over Miss Tropic's seat to watch, to grow more aroused, and she would whisper, or it might even have sounded like a murmur, "Oh yes." And as she grew more excited, "Yes, do that . . . I like that." To Diana, a thrill, the fleeting hope for a ménage a trois. The stewardess would stand straight up again after speaking, to watch. Diana was jaded, already at the ripe age of thirty, but jaded or not, a ménage a trois was one of her most delicious choices, when the choice was offered. Which it was not in this instance.

Miss Tropic placed her hand on Diana's knee and painfully slowly, or so it seemed, moved it up and up the length of Diana's thigh, under her skirt. Diana's skirt barely moved, that is how stealthily this expert hand slid. She could only feel Miss Tropic's soft palm sliding up her thigh to where they both wanted it to rest, tired from its long journey, and at peace.

"No," the stewardess whispered to Miss Tropic, Diana now wondering if they were in this together, "I want to see." Miss Tropic didn't have to turn around to see who was making the request. She knew. Miss Tropic had chosen not to invite the stewardess to join them.

Now Diana saw the name tag on the woman's ample uniformed-covered chest, 'Veronica'. Miss Tropic was to have Diana to herself, for now at least. Veronica was waiting impatiently for an invitation. Too polite, and not assertive enough (anyone paled in comparison to Miss Tropic), she remained a not-too-silent partner.

But Miss Tropic did turn to her. She said calmly and cooly, with almost a deliberate ease, "What is it that you want to see, Veronica?" (This question seemed natural enough to those who didn't question Miss Tropic like I did, knowing full well Miss T. knew the answer to it before asking.)

Veronica replied, trying very hard to maintain some semblance of control, as she was *only* eighteen, "I want to see you put your hand in her panties." Speaking slowly, her trembling voice continued on admirably with its request, "I want to watch your fingers rub her pussy, and I want to watch her come."

Always one who tried to accommodate every woman's wishes (especially when they coincided with her own), Diana joined in the conversation with, "Let her, Miss Tropic," after all, permission had to be granted from a woman like Miss T., "I want Veronica to watch," she asked turning to Veronica. When no response came, Diana continued, "It's okay, doll, you can watch me. I want you to. I'll spread my legs wider for you so you can watch me come."

Miss Tropic turned to Diana with a 'you-did-very-well' look on her face and smiled an experienced smile. Superior. Diana had done well, and she was pleased.

"Lift up, I want to slip your skirt up to your waist," Miss Tropic said, and true to her word Diana complied for Veronica's benefit, spreading her legs apart. Her clitoris was pulsing noticeably, her panties damp through and through and Miss Tropic could sense Diana's wet. Miss Tropic was pleased.

Skirt lifted, in full view were Diana's panties hugging her round, soft hips. A flattering sight. Miss Tropic noted that Diana looked just like she hoped she would. Veronica, too, was grateful. And Diana could have come right then and there, but she knew better than to hurry a woman like Miss Tropic.

"Pull your panties down so Veronica can see. She wants to watch and I want you to show her everything." What a deep melifluous voice Miss T. had—her words measured, weighed, exact.

Diana did as she was told. She slipped her panties down her hips, down her thighs, calves, ankles and off. Not knowing what else to do with them, she handed them to Miss Tropic.

"You are so good," Miss Tropic whispered to Diana with a seductive hint of a smile. It was intensifying this heat of hers, as it seemed that Miss Tropic knew exactly what turned Diana on.

Legs spread for Veronica, Diana awaited further instructions from the woman in charge. Miss Tropic pushed the button on the armrest of Diana's seat and it reclined back. Diana was almost laying flat, bare-legged, nude from the waist down except for her high-heeled, open-toe pumps. Red alligator pumps. Miss Tropic lifted the armrest between her seat and Diana's and pushed it back flush, out of the way. No obstacles, no distractions now, as Miss Tropic had work to do.

"Now spread your legs wider for me, honey, like I know you can. Like you want to. Spread them very wide, darling, so Veronica can watch." Miss Tropic's hands on her thighs, parting them, helping Diana to obey. Miss Tropic placed her hand right on top of Diana's grateful cunt. Massaging. The young married couple two rows back heard Diana's moan. Diana, to say the least, was intoxicated. The closer Miss Tropic's fingers came to the threshold of her wet recesses, the harder she throbbed there. Veronica was motionless. Miss Tropic made longer and longer strokes up the length of Diana's cunt. Miss T. had no intention of penetrating Diana: Diana had every expectation that she would. Diana grew hotter with anticipation, with the touch, with the strokes, with the look of the ruby nails on her this way.

Veronica was not hiding the fact that she was going to come herself at any moment. She had lifted her dress up discreetly, as befits a woman in the proud position of stewardess, and was gently masturbating herself in the dark aisle, facing the two women. Diana was certain to come shortly herself with this vision in front of her. Veronica's eyes closed, her teeth slightly biting her thick lower lip, her breasts slightly moving, and her hands rubbing her own wet pussy. Miss Tropic, once again, was pleased.

Still stroking, gently at first, but now more firmly. Regularly, rhythmically, steadily and more firmly, purposefully and more firmly, watching Diana's every move.

Watching Miss Tropic watching her watch her: Diana was aroused in triplicate. Yes . . .

Miss Tropic instructed Diana: "Come, now. It is time for you to come. Let go now, little darling." With this Miss Tropic lowered her head to Diana's cunt, kissing her there, and whispering to her in between the gentle wet kisses, "Come . . . You want to . . . I know you want to . . . And you have to now for me . . ." Miss Tropic's beautiful hands on each of Diana's thighs holding them apart, with Veronica watching, and Miss Tropic's wet lips, throaty voice, full tongue upon her now . . . on her lap . . . between her thighs . . .

Diana came.

Her orgasm must have lasted a bit of time, for in that time Veronica had knelt down, lifted Miss Tropic's skirt up from the rear, and no panties to contend with, slid her more than wet

14

fingers inside of Miss Tropic. Oh God, Yes! This was the scene Diana opened her eyes to, not knowing even that she had closed her eyes when the orgasm overcame her. The look of this sent bliss-filled tremors up her spine, as she watched Veronica tongue Miss Tropic, lick her, taste her from behind. The sight was unmatched: Miss Tropic in her crisp linen suit being taken from behind by Veronica. Kneeling in the aisle with her face gently pressed against Miss Tropic's bottom. Miss Tropic was groaning, and not in her usual measured and controlled way.

"Please me, Veronica, I know that you've wanted to . . . Come, sweet thing, do it to me." Miss Tropic began breathing harder and continued with her instructions, "Yes, Veronica, that's right, yes, please me . . ." And Miss Tropic cooed other things that neither Veronica nor Diana could hear. She was seducing herself with her own words, her own voice.

Diana still laying still, turned to her side and let Miss Tropic's head rest in her lap, with "Lay your head in my lap, Miss Tropic, and let me hold you." And Miss Tropic obeyed—both giving and receiving instructions well, this woman. And while Veronica with her perpetually wet fingers kissed and tongued Miss Tropic's bottom, Diana caressed and stroked Miss Tropic's hair, her shoulders, her back. Her hands were everywhere arousing, arousing.

Miss Tropic came violently and Veronica did not so much as ease up penetrating her, but continued to do it to her more firmly. Veronica knew Miss Tropic would not ask her to stop even though she might have wanted to. Miss Tropic reveled in the hard fuck and the smooth grace of Diana's hands, and told them both so. And before long, Miss Tropic shuddered with the second coming.

"Good," she said, the sound resonating from her most wet and swollen lips that were buried in Diana's wet and fragrant lap. And all were pleased . . .

Coming as no surprise to me, Diana came at the exact moment she fantasized Miss Tropic's final parting word, "Good." Without the passion of the orgasm with her tropical woman friend in her imagination, but with enough knee-weakening force to sate her temporarily.

Diana opened her eyes and found the hotel housekeeper, a blond girl of no more than twenty, leaning against the closed bathroom door, watching her. The girl had been watching Diana masturbate. This was a delightful surprise. Sometime during her semi-conscious state of fantasizing, the girl apparently entered the bathroom, shut and locked the door behind her, leaned back against the door, and not more than seven feet away from Diana masturbating, watched. Oh, most definitely, yes!

"What is your name, little one?" Diana asked.

"Whatever you'd like to call me," from the girl, told Diana everything she needed to know for now. Her name might have been Veronica. Or Christina.

And with less time now than before; and the next and last plane taking her to the University of Arizona where she would begin a one year contract as visiting lecturer with full professorial status, at a salary that was downright handsome; and a cool seat waiting for her hot bottom to warm; and so very many women, and only two-thirds of her life left to go. Where, oh where, does one even begin, Diana Hunter wondered as she approached the girl.

Fire in the Philistine eyes
compels my approach.
Absent caution.
Who is to blame
for the charred remains?

In a spacious Tel Aviv penthouse apartment, Jade waited impatiently
for Simone to come home. She was late. Again. Jade expected her to
be—she always was when Jade wanted her most to be on time. It wasn't
that she did it purposely, as Simone always put Jade's needs before her
own. She sings long after the two hour show should be over; she drinks
too much when others insist that she join them for just 'one more'; she
never cancels a show or taping session when she is sick; and she never
stops at a party until every last person has left or until she falls down
too exhausted to move. She lives the consummate torch singer's life—

17

burning the candle at all available ends. Never saying "No."

Tonight, Simone Boulange was singing in two back-to-back shows, all the while hoping that Jade would remember it was their anniversary. She decided to only have one or two drinks after the show, get gorgeous in a get-laid kind of gown, put Jade's anniversary gift in her purse (it was in the safe during the show), jump in her Fiat (a past gift from Jade), and race home wet in anticipation of the lovemaking, the fucking, that would be rough and sweet, until the sun came up. The show she was giving tonight was better than most as the drama going on between her legs heightened the singing. The audience couldn't have been wilder with appreciation. Jade watched Simone's first show, dashed home to prepare for the climax of the day while Simone sang on through the midnight show. Both girls aroused with what they knew would be an evening together to remember, to say the very, very least.

It was three years since they met in Israel, six weeks after Jade fled Switzerland in an attempt to avoid her fate, to avoid falling in love with 'that' woman, to outsmart her destiny. Again, as always, poetic justice had the last gentle laugh.

With candles lit, the meal baking, her body primed, Jade reclined on the couch for some reminiscing: not a sentimental woman, this was a novel little experience for her.

"Yes, Miss Boulange, you are 'that' woman," Jade thought, "and you have altered the course of my life. I am crazy in love with you, girl," she smiled closing her eyes. Warming, she thought back to that night of their meeting . . . oh heaven it was that night:

. . . At a bar known for its strong drinks, creative conversation and easy lays, they met. Jade had finished rehearsal for the dinner theater comedy to premiere that weekend. She had worked hard and needed a bit of help letting go. She came for the drink, not the company, as she was not lonely, just too tight to go back to the apartment and call it a night.

Simone had no desire to unwind tonight: she yearned to be totally unwound, which meant totally drunk. She had no intentions of drinking like the lady she wasn't and never pretended to be. No one ever mistook her for a lady, as she was something else, something more intense than that. She'd worked hard, she told herself with her usual, predictable, uninspired rationale, and earned this reward.

And she did work hard. That was true. She had two songs in the number one spot on the Israeli music charts in the past year. A first. She had the rough, tortured voice that attracted listeners who needed purging from their own troubles, their own pain, their own emotional crises.

Simone Boulange sang of struggle, she sang of sacrifice, of the dark side of living and loving and losing. And of winning, winning big when all odds are lined up waiting for you to fail. Hers was the voice of Israel's struggle. She lost herself in her music, in the songs laden with intensity for a Nation known for its intensity. She sang of sheer will—the will to survive. The Nation and the woman were in love with one another. The people loved her, worshipped her. Revered this woman who ached to be happy for more than a few hours at a time. She searched long and hard for the missing pieces in her life, whatever they were, that would make her content, make her sit still and just relax, make her feel whole. But her unhappiness intensified her singing all the more, making her even more successful, making her answer more elusive, her search more exasperating.

Jade, on her second and final straight tequila, was sitting back more comfortably now, watching the woman across the room more openly. She was unwinding, her mission completed, and soon she would be leaving the bar. Alone. Content in her newfound celibacy since arriving in Israel . . .

Jade got up to check the food and the time. The food was nearly ready for Simone's return; Jade entirely ready for it. So where was she? And because this was the norm for Simone, not the exception, Jade returned worry-free to the couch to continue:

. . . Since the second Jade had spotted Simone, her curiosity could not rest. The woman was surrounded by a genuinely adoring crowd. Lots of drinking, talking, laughing, noise. Jade tried to imagine what the woman's occupation might be to warrant such worshipping admirers: a poetess, a lecturer, a musician, a cult leader?

The woman had coarse, heavy, too-thick black hair pulled back severely into a ponytail, bound with a leather lace from the top to bottom. Her bound tail fell short by only a few inches of reaching the small of her back. She was darker than most Israelis, black almost, making her sharp green eyes all the more piercing. Large green eyes that were, without question, alarmingly inviting, vulnerable, frightened, powerful. Her laughing, her joining in didn't juxtapose well with her furrowed brow and apparent intensity.

Here was a woman, Jade sensed, who was begging for relief. From what, she wondered, release from what? From Jade's table she stared at this mystery, putting together some accurate assumptions about her. The deep clef on the woman's chin called out to Jade. If she were to kiss this woman it would be right there on her chin, running her tongue along the line of her clef.

Israel's artistic crowd called this bar their second home. It was a mixed crowd of young teens and very old talented men and women, gay, straight and all the other possibilities in between, and Jade began wondering whether this woman might be a lesbian.

Simone was wearing one of her more exotic performance outfits. An honest-to-goodness leopard skin top that fell two immodest inches below her ass in the back and front in a V shape. The sides of this poncho skin were tied loosely together with black leather laces, the same used to bind her hair. Around her waist, a thick black rope belt was wrapped four or five times, knotted in the back. She was half-naked and reeked of sexuality. To Jade, she looked like an Israeli Jane, of the Tarzan and Jane variety, wearing what could not be mistaken for anything but high-heeled-come-fuck-me black snakeskin boots.

There was nothing lighthearted about this woman—she was seriously sexual. You could not help but notice her. A sexual amazon. And it hit Jade that maybe the woman had just come from a show, or a performance, or the jungle.

Men found Simone devastating. She surpassed even their own private fantasies. She was a marathon girl, wearing out her men very early in the evening. Accepting her fate, she took to having two men at a time. And this seemed to work well. When done, almost as much as she enjoyed having them have her, she enjoyed watching them fuck. One another. The image she presented and her sexual tastes were one and the same.

Now Simone, tired of the conversation, on her fourth neat scotch, began scavenging the room and stopped at the sight of Jade, the woman in the room who didn't seem to be caught up in the frenzy of last call for drinks, or drugs, or sex. This woman sat composed. A detached coolness about her. And striking: a tall and beautiful woman.

The rest of the world washed white, as Simone focused in on her. Who was she waiting for, Simone tried imagining. Intrigued, she stood watching this woman at the corner table who sat and watched her. The excitement began at this instant when nothing else in the universe mattered anymore. Unflinching at the thought of a lesbian encounter, it would be Simone's first, her feelings were unbelievably strong.

Already Simone was staring with a sense of ownership at this woman; the woman who sensed a certain danger in the inevitable encounter. A certain power, a certain violence yielded a powerful pull for Jade towards this stranger. Neither moved, neither stopped staring, neither ignoring the passion, the surge swelling up in both their bodies . . .

Jade was off the couch again, time checking. "You're late, bitch woman!" Christ, she hated waiting for Simone sometimes. She opened the velvet box which held inside an emerald and diamond necklace and earrings. Not nearly enough to give Simone in exchange for what Simone had given her in these three years.

Life with Simone Boulange was fire. More painful than pleasurable sometimes. She was a heartwrenching performer on stage and off, a smoldering tempestuous woman. A woman who did anything, anywhere, anytime she felt like it. Always hot, always ready to fuck, and Jade always willing to have it, to give it.

How different a woman she was with Simone, she thought, remembering their first night together when she was bound and fucked time and time again by Simone who was loving, passionate, and violent, demanding nothing short of complete submission. Something Jade had never done before, giving over her power, her will, her self entirely to another woman's control. And with Simone she did it, wanted to do it willingly, eagerly yearning for Simone's scalding lips, her pressing hands, her full body taking, taking from her what it wished. That night she couldn't give enough to Simone. Craving it with her, this fire-eating, fire-fucking amazon who with one move threatened to violate her. It was sex with the devil that night, heathen sex, extraordinary sex the likes of which she had never imagined. She wished Simone were here now. She returned to the couch to recall the final act of that life-changing night:

. . . Simone made her way to it, the corner table, standing now in front of the woman, leaning over her, her breasts pushing the tight leopard skin insistently to be released, almost eye to eye with the woman sitting.

She asked, "Perhaps you can tell me what I am doing here?"
An earthy voice, from the throat, rough, French. There was a wild passion Jade sensed that was already close to being released from this woman, from herself. Jade wanted the woman to drag

her outside, on the ground, and have her immediately—it was that hot between them. This was so unlike Jade Desmonde to think such things.

The woman's Israeli brashness, aggressiveness came to claim something, to claim Jade. Jade's look told her already it was hers for the asking.

"Doing in the bar, or at my table?"

"Since when is this table yours, my American Friend?" Simone continued, ". . . It belongs to the club, so I claim it as my own."

"If you want it," Jade countered, "I will be generous and share it with you."

"No, the table is mine, and I will allow you to share it with me."

"I—"

"And, you will share this night with me, beautiful woman."

"If I choose—"

". . . And your pleasures."

"Here?" Jade teased.

"If I please," Simone responded, sitting down.

"Who are you?"

"I am a wandering Jew, Jade Desmonde, traveling—running away—from a woman who I did not want to fall in love with in Switzerland."

"What makes you certain she isn't in Tel Aviv?"

"What leads you to believe she is?"

"Ahhh," Simone grinned, touching Jade's cheek, "I know the woman," now pulling Jade towards her, her hand behind Jade's neck, and then kissing her full on the lips. Open mouth, hot tongue deep in Jade's mouth, taking. Jade grabbed and held this woman's thick bound hair in a tight fist. Jade allowed herself to be kissed. The fire in this woman was real, the pressure strong, the pull was immense and Jade moved into it.

"You see . . . I am the woman's earthly messenger," Simone whispered, releasing Jade, "And she wants to have you tonight. She wants to explore you."

"She must ask first," Jade instructed, still reeling from the kiss.

"I am here, that is enough. It is her way of asking. And she wants this: to offer you as a sacrifice—if you are not afraid of the pain."

"I am not afraid of anything. Tell her . . . I burn with the desire for her. Tell her I am honored."

"You shall be well received and well pleased. I will see to it."
Simone finished her drink in a swallow, took Jade by the hand
and left the bar. Her Lotus tore out into the night with the two not
talking, not touching, just Simone trying to control the wild thing
inside her from moment to precarious moment until it was time
to let it out. It took all her energy. Jade sat awaiting her fate.

The Lotus hugged the road deeper and deeper into the black
night, into the dark unknown. Jade was shivering from the chill
night air, from the scorching energy that Simone's body emitted.
Even, rhythmic breathing was impossible now . . .

The telephone call came. Dead on Arrival. Simone Boulange had
crashed head on with a concrete wall. How, was impossible to discern.
Not even the Goddess could save her most beloved and gifted child who
sang the songs for all of her children of Israel. The Nation mourned.
None more profoundly than Jade Desmonde.

Spiritwild,
breathlessly chasing,
desirous of all things.
My soul hungers so,
and you tell me
your breasts are dry.

On the evening of her twenty-second birthday, six years after falling
in Love with Diana, and two months after deciding what it was she
must do, Christina disappeared.

What seemed to be an average day for Diana, turned out to be a
nightfall filled with tortured despair. The handwritten letter Christina
left explained everything, and explained nothing. Diana refused to be-

lieve the words written anyway, even if they were true. She made up her own truths. Chose to believe what she wanted to believe. For the first time in her life, Diana was hysterical, which for her was a silent screaming. And the letter:

> My Dearest Love,
>
> I am leaving, darling. Know that it is not you, nothing you have done or said or ever could do or say, that makes me go. I must go now, must separate myself from you now, this evening, this hour. There is traveling I have to do to reach something which I cannot seem to capture, or even understand yet. I am not saying I am seeking to find myself. I am saying I love you with everything that I have to give. More than . . .
>
> Please, please always know that I love you more than the God that created me. For all lifetimes,
>
> Christina

Diana read the note twice. She headed for the liquor. She took the first of many drinks that evening, and offered only the first one in a toast to Christina, the toast that would be her last instant of sanity, grace and perspective before the ground would cave in around her: "To my elusive lover . . . You will be with me forever, darling . . . Oh God, it was simply Grand." And beneath the words her heart was clearly breaking.

Diana refused to believe a word of the note. It was beyond belief that Christina had left her, yet the fact remained as impossible as it was, that she was gone. That night she burned the note in anger at herself for making Christina leave her. She burned the note before the time for burning it was right. For when she tried to recall what she had read on that wild and monstrous night, she couldn't. She couldn't even remember that Christina had said she loved her more than God—which was unimaginable. She didn't remember what would have eased her pain, or brought her back to reality a bit sooner, or erase the blame, which was the worst of it all. The onslaught of self-punishment began that evening.

Time went by, long stretches of time, and Christina didn't call or write. Or anything. The letter was to be her final explanation, and now Diana did not even have the comfort of understanding why. Now, nothing in her life made sense.

She tried to fill the space that Christina left. One woman wasn't enough to fill the void, so Diana found two. And the more anonymous

24

women she found, the far shorter still they fell. Christina's impact on her life made itself known in every moment, in every thing, and in every way, and Diana's toxic rage towards herself brewed to the boiling point. Self-forgiveness was out of the question.

Self-loathing turned to self-destruction. She chose women who smelled her masochism from across the room, and used it to their advantage. Diana attended to the mental pain and left the realm of the physical to others more capable than she. What on God's earth had she done to make Christina leave her this way?

And what was it about Christina that would make her so remarkably unmatched by other women? Her body—a splendid body—could be found. It was nothing physical, as physical as Christina's looks that would keep Diana so tied.

It was a gentleness about her, a loving kindness for all the people she entertained in her life. There was no judgment, no intolerance, no dark side. She was a good, good soul. A fine specimen, that perhaps the Goddess Herself was pleased with. She was not perfect, and far enough away for comfort from being a saint; but, there was a warm, easy and almost spiritual aura about her. It beckoned people forward, strangers even. So it was not uncommon to find her always talking to someone somewhere. It was becoming on her.

And as for her serious insecurities they were well hidden, especially tucked away out of sight. That was Christina's secret. Even from the woman she loved most—Diana . . .

". . . I'd love to know what makes your wheels spin so quickly tonight," Diana asked.

"You'd always love to know everything if you had your way."

"If I don't ask questions, how can you expect me to learn?"

"Could there possibly be anything about me yet that you don't already know!"

"I'm sure there are skeletons in your closet that you hide even from me, sweet thing." There she was being extra cute again, that Diana.

"None that would better the situation by being spoken."

Diana glared. "Meaning what—you're not going to tell me?"

"Some things are better—"

"—Left unsaid! Oh goodie, a cliché, just in time!"

"I'm being serious." Christina wasn't entirely.

"You're about to be evasive."

"A girl like me needs some privacy, some things to be entirely her own."

25

"If one believes that you are as sick as your secrets—"

"I don't believe that way, if you recall," she said too sweetly as she was about to get a rise out of Diana.

"You almost did . . . I *almost* had you believing that last weekend," Diana smiled.

"That doesn't count, silly. Almost marrying you but not quite is a far cry from being married to you; besides, only secrets I keep from myself are sick, not the ones I choose to keep from others." Gently spoken.

"You're wrong."

"You're wrong," said Diana, mocking through her laughter.

"You're wrong," loving through her mocking.

"No,—" Then Christina pushed Diana on the couch with her hand a bit tightly around her lover's throat and laid on her a kiss that was worthy of commemorating.

Christina Tyler was nothing if not a sensational kisser. The girl was versatile. And unless you've ever had an excrutiatingly exquisite kiss, you really don't know how good, really good that makes things inside of your body feel, where all things good and wet are conceived.

"What did I do to deserved that?" Diana asked softly coming up for air.

"You were a bad girl—you were probing."

"And that was my punishment?" Diana asked, thinking more, more.

"It's called positive reinforcement in reverse."

"You'll make some therapist."

"I'll make some patient," she whispered letting her thoughts drift . . .

And no one who knew them as a couple could say. Christina was an exemplary model of a closed-mouth woman. She had left no clues. The letter was gone, Christina was gone, and Diana's life, it seemed to her, was as good as over.

Personal phone calls went unanswered until inevitably the phone stopped ringing. "Good," thought Diana, "more time to think. To think." She quit her job as a speechwriter and found one requiring pitifully little mental attention. "Good," she planned, she would not have to think on the job about anything else but the one missing key: What had she done, what had she done to make Christina leave her? The more she reviewed their years together, the more determined she was to find something, anything, the key to explaining it all. She just did not believe she deserved to rest until she did.

26

An entire six months passed like this in isolation from human contact. Another six months before she forgave herself for her still unknown crime against Christina forcing her to leave. And she stopped, finally, trying to track Christina down. Christina had vanished. Period. Diana gave up . . .

". . . At the heart of it, baby, is that you're afraid."

"You always say that—that fear is at the bottom of everything," Diana responded with noticeably pouting lips.

"Because, darling, it is. For a fact. Tell me this is not true—you're either afraid of not getting what you want, or losing what you have?" Christina waited.

"Well—"

"No well's. This isn't a multiple choice. Now choose, true or false, Diana."

"In theory, I agree—"

"Then it's true then?"

"But in reality, I guess if I'm *forced* to choose it would be true too."

"You always choose, Diana; about everything in your life, every day is nothing more than a series of choices."

"It's tiring," Diana said laying her head on Christina's shoulder.

"For all of us!" she whispered stroking Diana's back, and repeated, "For all of us," tenderly.

"But knowing the universe of people is tired doesn't make me any less tired."

"Knowing that you are at the helm of it all, of your entire life, makes you less tired," Christina whispered. Diana thought how tired that thought alone made her. But Christina grew excited with the possibilities. An endless array of them made her feel courageous and anxious both. The good girl and the bad girl in her smiled for two completely different reasons.

Going into her second year after Christina's disappearance, on the threshold of it, on New Year's Eve, she gave herself permission to find a quiet space to lay her head down and rest. She quieted the internal riot, the persistent blame-placing voices. She found within herself a gentle compassion. She was weary and needed comforting and had removed all the people, the friends from her life who could have provided her with it. She stopped beating herself the night she ushered in this New Year, for she was just too exhausted to continue . . .

27

"What scares you, lover?" Diana asked.

"Most? Most is the fear of not measuring up."

"In whose judgmental eyes?"

"My own . . . And yours."

"You couldn't be so foolish as to worry about measuring up in my eyes. I adore you. You can do no wrong, honey. I mean it. I'm so crazy in love with you that it will take years for me to put down my rose colored glasses when it comes to you."

And Diana just spoke the truth, no matter how irrelevant it was to the heart of the matter.

The process of healing herself in all the broken places began the following morning, when she gave up and came to learn that that was called "letting go."

Followed, then, by the search for happiness without Christina, if it could possibly be had again.

It is how you sugared me
with your smile.
It is how you ravaged my spirit
with your eyes.
It is how you creamed me
with your desire.
But, it is the taste of you
I miss most.

Jade Desmonde returned to the States within the week. Plagued still with the fragrance of Simone, she took very odd jobs from one coast to another, finally settling on Washington, D.C. Less out of choice than sheer exhaustion. There is only so much running in everyone, and Jade ran out, temporarily.

At thirty-two she wondered if it was indeed time to settle down to a real job with real money, real responsibility, real opportunity and real escapism potential. Jade had stopped running, but not escaping. Getting lost in a high pressure, high demand job was the only foolproof way.

Communicast, a multi-national marketing firm, hired her as Director of New Business Acquisitions. The escape plan was a huge success: she lost herself in a seventeen-hour workday and a meager six hours sleep a night at a furnished hotel room across the street from her office. It was all she could do to stay strung together from moment to moment to moment.

And her love for Simone grew more, not less, intense with time. Her passion, to one last time, just once, see Simone, touch her was her only prayer at night before she fell into a restless sleep. It was curious that she prayed to a God she no longer believed in, and more, that she listened intently for an answer to her prayers. She spoke her request clearly to be sure that Whomever was listening could understand the exact nature of her wish. Nightly she lay in bed listening with all her heart for the one serene "Yes" that she was certain would eventually come in one of God's more benevolent and merciful moments. Just to see Simone once more. Just once.

She moved into each day hardly living, just moving from one step to the next. Jade Desmonde was a woman in waiting, for the Yes, the Yes, which must come. Day in and day out she paced out her day, ate her meals, did her work, made the motions until night when she could privately concentrate on asking and asking again.

As all seemingly black situations have a white counterpart; and as all things do happen for a reason, no matter how obtuse; and as the greatest growth comes not necessarily from pleasure, but pain, destiny's next strategic move was played out cleverly this way:

After nine successful months, Jade was fired without so much as a warning. Had she given in to her boss' continual requests for a private tete a tete and 'whatever else came naturally' she would still have been employed. It wasn't the loss of the job that threw her into a panic, but the loss of a more expedient escape route. Severance pay in portfolio, and both in hand, she made a clean exit. No time to pause. Another geographical followed.

Within two weeks she was living in Arizona, maybe the warm climate would soothe the chill, warm the longing that persisted still. Jade applied for an interview as an Executive Assistant to Diana Hunter,

Visiting Lecturer, Honorary Professor at Scottsdale University. At one third the salary, twice the work and only a twelve month guaranteed contract.

Jade met the Personnel Officer in charge of interviews. She was undecided. She was introduced to her future windowless cubicle, work assignments, colleagues. And still undecided. Then she was introduced to her future employer, Miss Hunter. Indecision liquified at the sight of her. They both went into Miss Hunter's office to talk about all the things that wouldn't make the slightest bit of difference to Jade's decision to accept the position. This is what was said, anyway, just for the record:

"I get paid a lot of money to speak my mind, Miss Desmonde." This was the way Diana explained her profession to Jade. And I would like to take this pause in their conversation to provide a little clearer picture of Miss Hunter. Allow me this small digression as I want you to know Diana as well as I do . . .

Not boastful, not cocky, Diana was just a woman who appreciated those qualities about herself that were worth appreciating. The woman liked herself. A lot. She was an easy woman to talk to, easy to be with and easy to like. People were attracted to her because she was able to find the good in them; she made them feel good about themselves. She wore her femaleness and sexuality and charm well, all wrapped in a cool, fluid, gentle, strong and savvy package. She amused herself constantly, and that is what she liked best about herself—her smooth, sharp and smart sense of humor. She is the woman who wears a perpetual hint of a smile on her face almost always. Entertaining, easily entertained, spirited, awake and alive. She was a handful of good trouble for anyone who had the energy to take her on. And finally, it's important to keep in mind that Diana Hunter always meant well.

"It's most amazing, really, to be paid for speaking in public about my personal philosophy about the art of creative living. What surprises me is why more people wouldn't want to be in this business of public speaking—getting paid good money to speak their minds."

"Most people," responded Jade in her best interviewee tone of voice, "are petrified to even *stand up* in front of a group of people, let alone speak."

"Most people," Miss Hunter italicized, "are afraid, period."

Jade thought a moment on this one, and responded, "I am always disappointed, although I grow more used to it, that there are so few strong people around." Jade didn't count herself among the strong ones anymore.

"There's an inherent fear of being strong . . . the strong ones usually are tested more frequently than the weak, as they have the ability to withstand, and the resiliency to bend rather than break. The strong have the strength to learn and recover and move on. Most people crack at the slightest hint of pressure in their lives."

"I agree. Although there comes a time when that one major pressure, or test, strains even the strongest person's ability to withstand, breaking them into pieces they barely have the energy to pick up and put back together again."

Thoughts of Christina and Simone swelled to fill the silent pause between them.

Interesting, Jade noted, that images of Simone almost stopped with the sight of Diana Hunter: the blue-on-blue eyes, the dimple in her chin, the full round lips, the beautiful hands. Jade was determined to have this job regardless of Miss Hunter's wishes. This was Jade Desmonde's way when she set her sights on something that she wanted.

Diana moved from the philosophical to the pragmatic as, after all, this was an interview: "Let me ask you the obvious question and get it out of the way. Why, Miss Desmonde, would you work in an underling position for me, for hardly any pay to speak of, in an embarrassingly tiny cubicle outside my office, with little chance of renewing your contract when mine is up next year. Most interviewers would dismiss you and your resumé instantly as being ludicrously overqualified."

"But you wouldn't. And didn't . . . and won't. I am *here*, which leads me to conclude that my respect for you, as well as your work, continues to be warranted." Jade had read some of Diana's work and heard her interviewed on radio back in D.C. Keep in mind that Jade was not the type of woman to resort to flattering Diana. This was not flattery—her admiration of Diana and her work—it was merely a strict statement of truth.

"Meaning?" asked Diana Hunter, always open to flattery.

"Meaning, you are not threatened by an assistant who might have something to teach her employer."

As far as Miss Hunter was concerned this woman was hired. But the interview had taken less than ten minutes and she was not yet ready to release Jade: "What kinds of things can you—"

"Can you expect to learn?"

"Yes. Other than the obvious."

"The obvious?" Jade questioned.

"Humility!! When I find myself outshined by my Assistant!" They shared a laugh.

"You have my word, Miss Hunter, that I will do my best to harness my brilliance when we are in the company of your colleagues."

Diana was not entirely sure if Jade was being clever or just fresh.

Jade continued, "Anything else you want to add to what you will learn from me, or now would you like *me* to answer your question?"

Now Diana knew. "You are awfully fresh for a woman who wants what I have to offer. You should work towards being a bit more ingratiating."

"For ingratiating you should call Katherine Gibbs; for clever, and one hopes amazing from time to time, you will be happy with me."

Diana believed her implicitly.

"Anything else to say in your defense before you leave me to decide your fate?"

"You *have* already decided, Miss Hunter."

Confident to a fault this Miss Desmonde, thought Diana, moving now to the personal domain from the formal. She was about to stray way out of bounds. She couldn't help herself, as Jade had this one coming to her: "How long since you've been slapped for being fresh, Miss Desmonde . . . I'm curious."

When Jade pushed the image of Simone aside, she met Diana's eyes and with the gentlest voice replied, "Too long, Miss Hunter, too long." There was no missing the pain in her voice.

The interview was over. They each knew everything they needed to know about the other. For now.

Jade Desmonde, Executive Assistant to Diana Hunter, began work at 8:15 the following morning.

Diana and Jade shared similar philosophies about life. This was not why Diana hired her. Jade was almost beyond belief in intelligence, some might say touched with genius. This played a big, big part but still wasn't the reason Diana hired her. Don't get me wrong, it was a phenomenally powerful contributor to why Jade got the job, but still, if we want to be brutally honest about Diana, it wasn't the reason that instantly propelled her into hiring Jade.

It was this: Jade Desmonde was a ravishing, striking, statuesque amazon beauty. Her looks hit you with the force of a physical blow, or at least they did Diana. A gorgeous, almost six foot tall woman with broad shoulders, shining blond highlights in her heavy brunette hair, full-breasted, long, long legs that . . . need I continued . . .?

In Diana's more honest moments she would come to admit the truth: brains, shmains, this woman looked like a goddess. Miss Desmonde's looks alone guaranteed to wet Diana's perpetually damp panties morning after predictable morning. And what is wrong with that, thought Diana coming to her own defense. An assistant should not only be competent and bright, but equally as key, she should be exceedingly easy on your eyes.

To give Diana the benefit of the doubt, Jade Desmonde *did* have a sterling professional and personal background. It's important that you get a glimpse of it in order to fully appreciate this woman. As for my own professional and personal background—well, it is at this very moment retreating to another room to whimper privately, shamed in comparison with the incomparable achievements accrued in Jade's compact life.

At sixteen, while Diana was falling hopelessly in love with a woman named Christina Tyler, Jade Desmonde was instrumental in obtaining the funding, property and personnel to staff the first Home for the Homeless Women her state of Texas had ever seen, let alone heard of. There were many shelters for homeless men, but they were too frightening, too violent for most women. Too afraid to use the State run facilities, most women chose the streets and ended up face-to-face with violence anyway. It was a lose-lose proposition for them. The State stood its ground and refused to fund a shelter just for women. Jade went to the private sector to amass the monies needed.

"Desmonde's Open Door," as it was later affectionately named in her honor, now operates in over ten states, hers being the prototype of all the others, accommodating thousands of street, battered and neglected women yearly. This was Jade's most cherished of accomplishments. If she had died the night she put the first Home in place, it would have been without any regrets.

At nineteen, through the expert grantwriting skills she was richly endowed with, she procured a five hundred thousand dollar grant for the tiny child abuse crisis center. "Loving Friends Center" used to operate out of an empty storefront, with one black rotary telephone, staffed by volunteer housewives and psychology students from the neighboring University. That is how it was when she signed up to help in ". . . any way that she could." The grant and her management skills changed all that.

When Jade last visited the original "Loving Friends" it took her a whole day to meet the staff, tour the facilities and marvel at the sophisticated 24-hour-a-day hotline telephone reporting system available to help abused children. With her lobbying skills, child abuse went from being a hushed up family affair to one of State-wide attention. She gathered, with the help of staff members, cratefuls of educational materials written and published by the Center for distribution worldwide. This was only ten years after she left her mark on the original shabby crisis center storefront when she was nineteen. (*Nineteen!* Can you imagine?)

A well-deserved bit of traveling followed. With her own and her parents' money—they dabbled in oil—she traveled and ended up studying in Europe, later settling for a full summer in Switzerland to do nothing but swim, sleep and dine on multiply-delighted and delightful Scandinavian women. Jade Desmonde had quite the way with the women, and it was not just her looks that attracted them. It was her way. Her way with them.

Then, something unexpected happened. Something Jade didn't want, didn't need, didn't plan for. On a rain-drenched night where the brittle icy air cuts skin like tiny razors, she sat in an abandoned villa with friends. She was drinking too much, indulging in mood changers too much, and experimenting sexually in a way that only liquor gives one license to do; taking her turn performing and being a part of the aroused and receptive audience.

The talk turned to sex and the sex turned to talk again. This time of the psychic—the Tarot cards were spread and read.

The message for Jade that evening was that she would soon meet a woman who would alter the course of her life, alter each minute facet of it from the moment of their first meeting. Jade requested a second reading, and again the card of the woman appeared, more distinctly this time. And then Jade demanded a third reading. By its completion she was convinced. The cards never lied to her before. So when these cards spoke of a passion without restraint, expressions of violent emotions unleased, a confluence of pleasure and pain so biting, a bond so strong that only God or death could break apart, Jade was nothing short of terrified.

She wasn't about to get tied down to any woman, let alone a fucking crazy fire-eating amazon, as the cards portended. Jade took the warning seriously. So seriously, in fact, that she had packed and was enroute to Tel Aviv, Israel, by the end of the month. On the Israeli Sabbath morning, Jade arrived in Israel leaving 'that' woman somewhere behind on the slopes in Switzerland searching for her.

It's only when I find
a carbon copy of myself
that I start to notice
all the typographical errors.

Diana had more than her share of goodies to be grateful, if not thrilled about. Being invited as Guest Lecturer at the School of Communications in Scottsdale University was a remarkable prize. Not only would this enhance her credentials going forward, this would give her a year to lecture, to write, to publish and to use the talented research fellows at the University to help her crank out the work at a salary that was not only handsome, it was positively gorgeous.

She had become quite well known in the past five years. Public speaking fees improving from $100 to $1,000 per lecture, when she wasn't speaking gratis for one good cause or another, much to her accountant's dismay. Seven hundred fifty dollars per diem to consult to corporate CEO's and Executives, and having the stamp of approval on almost all that she would publish in the future. Her success was sweet and lucrative—a winning combination.

How ironic that it all began with the tragedy of Christina's disappearance. How can something so good come from something so bad? The first year just holding herself together from one end of the day to the other was cause enough for celebration. Not falling apart on her job was praiseworthy. But after that pitch black year, after that was when she put her feet down, tentatively at first, on the path that would lead her to this, to her successes. Her search for a permanent happiness and wholeness took her up and down the east coast in search of help, teachers, mentors. And she found that when you do knock, there is always someone on the other side eager to assist. She ate self-help groups whole, read voraciously, and spent most nights talking endlessly to people who seemed to have a firm handle on this "happiness" business. There wasn't a positive living theory propounded that she had not read, not a spiritual treatise written that she hadn't noted, studied, memorized. Her life became the research table upon which all hypotheses on the Art of Living were laid out to be tried, tested, utilized.

There was an interesting correlation happening as well: the more she was taught the more opportunities arose for her to share the newly-found information with others. For each skill she acquired and included in her own personal repetoire, there was a person who approached to have her teach it to them, too. The principle of giving and receiving was in action in Diana's life. The more she searched, the more she sought to grow and expand, the more she felt compelled to pass the words and the lessons along. It was only a matter of time until her one-on-one teachings grew. By the time she was twenty-eight she was called on, often, to present lectures to Universities, High Schools, Corporate Meetings and Conferences. The audiences grew from ten-fold to a hundredfold. Not confident enough yet to write a book, she wrote papers and got them published by anyone who showed interest. Mostly Research Journals. She created and edited the "Creative Living" newsletter, which at last count made its way into the welcoming arms of 1.1 million subscribers.

And to think, it all started with the pain, her twenty-second year, the year of the scorching pain. Still there was no doubt in her mind that she would trade all that she had gained in the years since Christina left, just to have her back. To this moment in time, in her thirtieth year, she still wanted her back more than anything in the world.

There was a brisk knock on the door. This was a serious door knocking. It sounded important, and Diana was not in the mood for a more-than-a-second interruption. This knock was definitely an I-have-something-we-need-to-discuss one. Poor Diana, always the victim of someone else's poor timing. She stood, pushing away from her desk enroute to the mirror to arrange, fix and check that all was looking at it was supposed to. Her afterglow, that certain smile and flush, was incongruent to a woman working; although, most appropriate for a woman having just masturbated. Oh, how Diana loved to masturbate in her office when she was working late—her private reward at the end of a difficult day—her little weakness.

Diana opened the door to the sight of Mrs. Whitney Leighton III, who stepped forward, passed Diana and walked straight to the middle of the office. She walked with the gravity of a Dean of a School of Economics. This slightly plump woman did not let her roundness stop her from dressing well—in expensive uniforms of one sort or another; a perfect match to her no nonsense personality and right-to-the-point conversational skills. Rich, well-fed and cute in a 1950's sort of way. Immaculately manicured. Mrs. Leighton's most glaring liability was that she was seriously unfriendly. Which left people with little personal information about her—free to fill in the blank spaces. Which brings us back to Diana, who at this very instant was doing that same thing.

Diana thought Mrs. Leighton actually looked like a woman who had two Ph.D.'s. Ice cold. Diana had met women like her before: women, who full of life had their fires put out, unexpectedly. Wet was left. Then cold set in with the bitterness of the experience. Then, the ice formed: thin crusted ice laying on the surface of the emotions. With time, thick slabs of impenetrable ice. Was this, Diana conjectured, what happened to Whitney Leighton III? If it wasn't, Diana made a pretty admirable stab at it.

Mrs. Leighton had taken the liberty of walking to the closet bar and pouring herself a brandy, "I saw yours on your desk and knew it was the right idea."

"I am delighted you feel free to help yourself," Diana responded like the good hostess, trying to accept the fact that this woman who she hardly knew was not going to be leaving her office any time soon. She relaxed and eased into the oncoming interchange.

Diana's graciousness made Whitney smile, and this was no simple task for her. It had been a long time between smiles and her lips took some time to remember exactly what a smile felt like. Diana noted her white, evenly spaced teeth and thin, precision-sharp lips—designed with talking, not kissing, in mind. Be nice, Diana told herself, but it was difficult for her to be nice under the circumstances. She was certain that this was no social call. Whitney was the bearer of some kind of bad news, and Diana wished she'd just get it out of the way and be done with it. Whitney was working up to it. She walked back towards Diana, leaned back against the corner of her desk, lifted her glass of brandy in response to Diana's raised glass and listened to Diana toast:

"To the President's new economic development proposal. Grant it the fortitude to survive the trials and tribulations to befall it in the halls of the House and Senate." Whitney smiled easily now as they both stood smoothly sizing each other up, figuring, or trying to, who the woman each was dealing with was. They were getting a feel for one another.

"I don't want to take up too much of your time—"

Whitney got interrupted in middle of her lie by Diana who was about to start her own. "Please don't begin with an apology for my time, I am always glad to see you under any circumstances," she said. And if this fell short of qualifying for being a lie than we can just say it was a violent exaggeration.

"How nice of you to say that, Diana." Whitney said in all sincerity. Oh, not that she didn't doubt the veracity of Diana's words, because she did, but that she appreciated good manners. Manners were everything to her, still the rich daughter of a rich family from Connecticut. She continued, "Unfortunately I was elected as the messenger of what I know you will refer to as 'ill tidings,'—"

Whitney spoke on as Diana repeated vehemently "I knew it! I knew it!" silently damning the news to hell without even hearing what it was.

Whitney noted the flagging attention, "Before you kill the messenger—"

"I wouldn't—"

"Oh, you might when you hear what the news is, so don't back yourself in to any promises you won't want to keep . . . As that frightful saying goes, I have some good news and bad news." This was a newly acquired skill for Whitney: using clichés. Allisone taught her that: how to use clichés, how to relax and kick back, how to feel her feelings. She learned who the real Whitney Leighton III really was. This Allisone taught her a lot of things.

Whitney continued, "The bad news is that your presence is requested at the next bi-monthly party at Dean Thaxton's house. We all know that you are not a permanent fellow of the University, but because your reputation precedes you, Miss Hunter," Whitney said, not above an occasional bit of friendly sarcasm herself, "you are granted the rare privilege of joining us."

No, no, no! If there is a God in heaven, how can you allow this to happen to me??—Diana's thoughts were already racing, but she stood there calmly and smiled and nodded and let Whitney continue.

"The good news, my dear colleague, is that I have concocted a foolproof alibi which will excuse me from attending this ridiculous and *mandatory* engagement. Mind you, I do not doubt Dean Thaxton's wisdom in holding these events at her house to bring the faculty members together . . . like a family; but I do object to them being mandatory."

"What I want to know is where *my* good news is now that I have heard yours."

"There is no more news to go around, my esteemed comrade. You have heard it all," Whitney answered, growing more playful.

Diana refused to be amused even though Whitney was doing her best. Instead she shot a sickeningly enthusiastic smile, not lost on Mrs. Leighton, and responded, "I couldn't be more delighted. Honored in fact, and overwhelmed. Overwhelmed with joy!" Diana the dramatic martyr. "And I can only hope that you find it within your heart to let me use your foolproof alibi the next time I am invited to attend this mandatory brouhaha."

"And there *will* be another one, of that you can be certain—"

"I know—the alibi, the alibi Whitney, can you help me?"

"But then . . . you will owe me one," Whitney said slyly. Playfully.

"I can live with that," Diana smiled.

"But you don't know what payment I might devise."

"I'm willing to take the risk."

"Then let's toast to it—" Whitney began.

"Allow me," Diana offered, raising her glass a bit, "—to my . . . indebtedness."

The thought of decimating a perfectly good Saturday evening made Diana queasy and she told Whitney so. Whitney said she understood having attended more parties than Diana, and therefore having a lot firmer grounds to base her opinion on. They commiserated, and Diana promised not to hold the bad news against the messenger. What started between them as stiff cordiality transformed into genuine enjoyment of one another's company, and they told each other so. Then their talk turned to other things; however, nothing private enough to warrant heading for a good woman-to-woman talk on the couch. And where did Whitney's stapled-to-her-side husband fit in to all of this Diana wanted to know—and said nothing. They didn't know each other well enough yet: this interchange held promise, but it was too soon to tell if they could be friends.

"I'll be sure to come by your office and fill you in on what you missed at the party," Diana said.

Whitney, at the door about to leave, turned and took a risk: "The grapevine has it that you're looking for a couple of hundred students for some research study you are planning. I'd be happy to make mine available to you, if you'd like."

"I will be in your office next Thursday morning at ten to make the arrangements. I'm most appreciative, Whitney."

Whitney smiled, something she did a lot of this evening with Diana, she noted. She knew the conflicts in timing and scheduling that this would cause her and her students. It was a sacrifice—it was worth it.

What Diana did not know was that sacrifice was practically a way of life for Whitney. She did it with ease. This was one, however, that Whitney would enjoy immensely, for reasons she herself didn't even know yet.

A Seasonal Affair

Winter eyes
Make Summer heat
Spring
Between my thighs.
I Fall hard for you.

"Whitney?" This was the third time Whitney Leighton was not responding to the man calling her name, and the fourth time in a bar in
her life. One of these tacky, cramped singles dance halls, where if you
put your mind to it and pay careful attention to the clientele and not the
setting, you might just get lucky and find someone interesting among
the crowd. Or so she was told. The chances are slim, her two friends
admitted, but the choices so few in Connecticut that one should feel
compelled to at least try. Whitney was trying tonight at the behest of
her two close friends, both named Edward, who insisted that a woman
like her should "Get out more," "Not work so hard," "Cut Loose."
Meaning, of course, "Get Laid." To Whitney there was no such thing
as working *too* hard or taking things *too* seriously. She hoped to find
someone reasonably intelligent to pass the evening with, to appease her
friends. Tomorrow, she planned, she could return to her isolated, but
familiar lifestyle in peace. And why her friends always insisted that
they knew what was best for her, she couldn't imagine, but tonight she
took their advice and found herself at "Freestyle," where at least, the
clientele was over thirty. At least that, as she couldn't pretend to have
anything in common with anyone younger and less solemn than she
about life. At thirty-four, she was a model forty-five year old.

The ironic part of this is that for the last twenty or so minutes
Whitney was completely unable to stop staring. It had already become
obvious to both Edwards, and they soon left her at the bar to pursue
their own company for the evening, leaving her to the wiles of the man
next to her, who had told her his name was Ted, or Tom. He was really
putting his best foot forward with her, making an admirable effort to
pick her up. For the fourth exasperated time he called her name, and
after she didn't respond and still seemed to be staring at someone
across the bar, he gave up and decided to only order himself a drink,

figuring it was cheaper that way. Assuaging his hurt feelings he searched the room for who might be less challenging to bowl over with his charms. For the record, this guy, his name was Tom, was charming; Whitney would have enjoyed his company had she just paid him a little more attention.

Whitney had been staring at someone across the bar, this was true; she was comprehensively preoccupied. Spellbound. She tried to relax, make conversation with Ted or Tom, but finally, not being able to help herself, she gave into it and let herself stare and be consumed. She found her companion for the evening.

Congratulations, Whitney. The small problem was that this someone was a woman.

She began to build up her case, fact by fact, pro's and con's: one, she found other women attractive in her life, didn't most women notice other women; two, of course it was odd to be staring at a woman in a heterosexual bar of all places, but the woman *was* pretty; three, the stranger was obviously aware she was being watched, and apparently did not seem to mind. And weren't women always evaluating other women, looking at them, at what they wore, at their style, at their carriage—well, didn't they? But, Whitney had to admit, at least to herself, that she was not picking up fashion tips from this woman, she was staring. And Whitney was not an impulsive woman, she was conservative to a fault, and a creature of habit to say the least, so it surprised her all the more to be feeling this way towards a woman. She felt good and confused. So she ordered another gin and tonic to fortify herself, to give herself time to think this one out—should she go up to her. The stranger seemed to be with her girlfriends.

She drank, long past the point of sipping in the evening. How could someone like me—a rich, old money rich, woman with a bearing that bespeaks so well of my heritage—have these kinds of feelings for a woman? Where did they come from? She'd never even thought of being with another woman, even in her fantasies. Ever. But, she had to acknowledge, that it did feel natural enough. And would making love with a woman mean I am a lesbian? That question went unanswered, as she didn't quite know how to answer it. Plus, she didn't care *what* the implications were, she only knew what she was feeling, and her feelings were real, and this woman was very pretty, and Whitney wanted to touch her. To hell with what it means or doesn't mean, Whitney, you'll have time enough later to sort all the questions out, is what I say, right now you have work to do. That is my unsolicited advice to her.

Before approaching, she took one last long look at the stranger: she was a small-framed woman, some would call her petite, dressed to accentuate her better features—a modest, short skirt hugged her lean hips and thighs, a loose white angora top, heels that gave her a 2-3 inch headstart, seamed black stockings, and wavy hair swept back from her face with two jeweled hair combs. This was nothing short of a vision to Whitney. Her insides went wild—butterflies slamming themselves against her intestine walls—and Whitney froze.

This was Whitney who was, to date, a calm, controlled, unshakable woman—nothing good or bad moved her as this stranger did. She never lost her calm at her brother's funeral, the brother who took his own life by washing down a bottle of pills with a bottle of gin. She was cool as a cucumber when she received the Presidential Certificate of Honor for proposing a progressive economic development plan saving a third world neighboring country, and a U.S. ally, millions upon millions of dollars in the coming decade. Nothing shook this woman until the sight of this simple little woman whose name she didn't even know.

Suddenly Whitney wanted to know everything about her; wanted to hold her in her arms and feel her, and tell her things that she never told anybody in her life. Her secrets, all her secrets. Whitney the intellectual was *feeling* tonight. Her intuition leading her by the hand and introducing her to her feelings. So this is what this feeling business felt like, she reveled. She couldn't tell you *what* she was feeling, but she knew she was feeling . . . because it felt warm and gentle, not sterile like the thoughts that stirred in her laboratory-like mind. She couldn't stop the now open floodgates of feelings. They all surfaced. Confidentiality or not, risking her job or not, she did not want to stop.

The stranger was paying as much attention to Whitney now as she was to her. In fact the woman had a hard time not noticing her. There was talk, it seems, that passed between these two women since they first laid eyes on one another. And, *finally*, Whitney the unmovable moved towards the stranger. Not knowing what it was she was going to say, hoping enroute for some last minute inspiration . . .

"You and I must talk," Whitney said to the woman, who was even prettier than the dim lighting had led her to believe. A clear young complexion, and this woman was way under thirty years old.

"I believe you're right," the stranger responded, turning then to her circle of friends and excusing herself to follow Whitney to the entrance and out of the bar and down the block to an empty doorway at the corner of Magistrate and Bank Streets. Whitney turned then to set her eyes upon this woman who had her mesmerized.

"I see I caught your fancy tonight," the stranger began, smiling, as this was the last thing she expected this evening herself.

"My name is Whitney Leighton III, and I can't take my eyes off of you," Whitney confessed not taking her eyes off of her.

"I am Allisone Dupont," smirking gently at Whitney's formality and extending her hand. Whitney seized the opportunity to hold her hand. Allisone liked this older woman. "I'm surprised you waited as long as you did to come get me, Miss Leighton," still poking easy fun, "but I'm glad you finally broke down and came over to me. You would have been home in bed by the time I got the courage to say hello to you."

"I've never done anything like this," Whitney confessed, "I swear to you, this is not a line, I've never approached a woman in my life."

"Well, good, that makes it all the more surprising then. I'm awfully glad you did. I think you made the right decision!"

"Being approached by a woman didn't surprise you at all, I see," Whitney prodded.

"Being approached never surprises me . . . what does, is when I'm not!" Allisone was telling the truth, not bragging.

"You mean people find you so irresistible they can't help themselves—" Whitney said with sarcasm not lost on Allisone.

"Don't take that to mean I'm patting myself on the back or—"

"I don't—"

"But yes, I guess guys do find me pretty enough to want to meet."

"And women?" asked Whitney knowing this woman was still a girl compared to herself.

"Only twice. A girl in the college library once started with me, and a girl, or, really, a woman, the other time." Intimacy was already around them.

"When was that?"

"Also in college . . . she was my teacher . . . Chemistry, and a lot older than I was."

"Did you date either of these women, I mean did you pursue—"

"Both . . . I dated both of them for a while." Whitney wondered if dating them included sleeping with them. "Didn't it work out?" Whitney, with her seemingly endless list of questions asked.

"That depends on what you mean by work out."

"I mean, if it worked out you probably wouldn't be here, at a bar, tonight if you were still seeing them. Would it?"

"I still see my girlfriend from college. She's a lot of fun to be with . . . you'd like her."

Allisone's casualness frightened her. Whitney reminded herself that she was the only one over thirty in this intimate group of two. But Allisone was holding her own. Whitney continued, "And your teacher?"

"That's over now. She wanted something more than I was willing to give—she wanted a forever after, and I guess I wanted a here and now."

43

Allisone felt like she answered enough questions, "What exactly is it you want to find out with all of your questions, Miss Leighton III— what you are dealing with or what you're about to get yourself into?"

They laughed, diminishing the tension and urgency by a degree or two.

"I'm *already* into it," Whitney smiled, "and I've been into it, into you, since I laid eyes on you inside the bar."

Now that Whitney began to speak honestly, Allisone wanted to light a cigarette and put some smoke between them. Whitney took the lighter from her hand and lit the girl's cigarette for her. Their eyes met and held above the flame.

"I know . . . I kind of have that same feeling about you. And I want you to know that I'm not playing a game with you, although—," Allisone smiled and squirmed, "I have been known to do things like that, but not with girls . . . um, with women. So you have reason to ask, ask me anything. Go ahead."

The difference in their ages was both apparent and appealing.

"Thank you for your candidness. Let me offer some of my own." Whitney chose her words cautiously, and began, "My intentions towards you are not entirely honorable—."

"Gosh, I hope not . . . I wouldn't have followed you outside if I thought they were—"

"What!"

"A woman doesn't stare at another woman like that if her intentions are honorable. And I know that was hard for you to admit, so now I thank *you* for your honesty." And she put her hand on Whitney's shoulder, reached up and kissed her quietly on the lips. The sweetest, simplest little kiss.

Whitney had never been kissed on the lips by a woman before, not in a sexual way; the flesh on her back rose, and her nipples grew erect almost instantly with the flash of the physical, the sexual. Her body had never responded to a kiss like this before from a man. As to the implications, as to what this meant about her heterosexuality, she didn't even venture to guess anymore that evening.

"That was my first kiss," she admitted.

"Ever!"

"Ever, by a woman," Whitney said and fell again into staring, a hopelessly juvenile infatuated kind of a stare.

"Well, if that's the case, please don't think that that's the best kissing I can do—."

"I am unable to think clearly at all at this moment—."

"Good, then it's a start." And by the way Allisone was dressed

Whitney believed that she *could* do better kissing than that, better probably than anyone she had ever been with.

"I'm seriously attracted to you, Allisone, and I don't know why, and I don't know what it means, and . . . I don't know why I'm so nervous with you."

This was Allisone's first glimpse of the vulnerable side of Whitney, which very few people who knew her well ever saw. Allisone found it a welcome change from the stiff, rich formality. She took Whitney's hands in her own. "Don't be afraid," she said, the one now who was older and wiser in these matters, "I promise not to hurt you." Whitney let her take the lead, let her comfort.

Allisone continued, "I know I don't have the best track record or anything, and I know I'm young," slowly caressing Whitney's hands in her own, "but I wouldn't be out here if I didn't want to be with you very much. I wouldn't go any further with you if I didn't want you as much as you seem to want me. You do, don't you?"

"Yes," like a schoolgirl, "yes, I do!"

"Good, then let's both not be afraid. I'm sure you won't hurt me, and I promise that I'll take good care of you," she said with a wink, "And I bet you good money, Miss Leighton, that I am probably going to be very, very good for you." Whitney received her second stirring kiss on the lips, this time putting her hands up to Allisone's face and gently pulling her closer. Allisone was whispering, "Don't be afraid, Miss Leighton, I'll be easy with you . . ."

At this moment, Whitney wasn't afraid of anything anymore. All she knew was that she wanted Allisone with a fury she had never known before. All Whitney's supposedly dormant sexuality rose to the occasion, all the years of social dating, sleeping with men from time to time, seemed nothing next to her feelings towards Allisone. She wanted to have her like the teacher wanted to have her: forever after. She wanted to hold her and take care of her and be taken care of by this girl who made her knees shake for the first time in her life.

So, this one chance meeting, this one chance evening, overwhelmed with emotion, overpowered by sexual arousal, Whitney allowed Allisone to lead her to her car, to her home, to her bed, into her arms. This first night was the sweetest lovemaking Whitney could imagine ever having. And Allisone was no youngster: she was a capable teacher, a passionate lover, a wonderful emotional provider. The freshness of Allisone melted the sharp edges, warmed the cool exterior, and moved Whitney, for the first time in her life, to let her feelings take center stage in her life—to express themselves, to be heard . . . to dance.

Easy come.

Diana hated social functions. Hated academic social functions. Hated the mandatory bi-monthly heterosexual academic social functions most of all. She had never been to a single one before, basing her opinion on sheer conjecture only. She hated this one before she even arrived. That's the spirit, Diana.

She searched the room for someone to blame, not being able to blame, in all good conscience, Whitney. There was little wisdom, too, in blaming Dean Thaxton, who she had just spent close to thirty minutes chatting amicably with, and came to find out that she wasn't altogether a bad egg either. Her motives for turning the faculty into a family were admirable, her intentions good. The road to hell is paved with good intentions, Diana thought to herself, slipping in and out of the living and dining rooms making the required superficial contact.

The talk, the boisterous talk buzzed in her ears. The inevitable headache arrived. The headache that predictably followed the drunk talk, superficial stabs at intimacy, the heavy-hung smoke that permeated the air and her clothes. A sound like an "ugh" grumbled in her throat. She was not happy. She refused to take part in the feigned revelry—not Diana, she was no hypocrite. She would just pretend to be following, and instead watch, that was her game plan for the evening. This would be nothing more than a spectator sport tonight.

There wasn't a single interesting person there to talk to; not one kindred spirit. She was surrounded by the noise of petty talk, petty jabs, petty academicians.

Considering how attractive, awfully attractive, Diana was, it was a blessing that the faculty wives were not intimidated by her. Surprising that they did not give her a hard time, a group cold shoulder. They sensed that she was not going to be a threat by exhibiting interest in their slightly balding, slightly perspiring, slightly inadequate, prized husbands. The pipe-touting professors with their condescending attitudes gave her mental heartburn, if there is such a thing. Had they been clever, bright, witty, challenging, *anything*, she would have forgiven them their superior attitudes. But these professors were stale, and their uninspired dryness left her longing for the great outdoors. She re-

46

minded herself not to hold ill feelings towards all academicians just because of this one poorly represented group.

An interminable ninety minutes later she had made her rounds methodically, expediently. Her work completed in record time—this was the key, as the party was nearing its peak. The peak approached in direct correlation to the quantity of liquor consumed. The more the nascent alcoholic group drank, the louder and more lewd it became: the uptight, loosening up; the loose ones, searching for prey. At this preclimactic moment, when the stiff politeness was gone, and the in-house dirty academia jokes and puns began, Diana made a sharp exit. There was only so much a woman could take of such ribaldry, and Diana's cup was running over.

She assumed her most ingratiating posture while lying through her teeth to the hostess about how she, "simply adored the party . . . was ever so sorry she had to leave early . . . how anxious she was, not to mention honored, to come back again." All perfectly socially acceptable fibbing.

Relief set in when she stepped outside the front door and closed it behind her. Ahh. But, she would get that very married woman who refused to change a syllable of her maiden name—Mrs. Whitney Leighton III—for this! Relax, it's over, she told herself. Diana didn't have to see one more pair of oxblood loafers; breathe in the exhaled smoke of one more tweed-blazered, elbow-patched, pipe-smoking instructor; listen to one more fabricated rumor about an instructor who chose not to attend the party. She felt stained, and stood waiting for the chilled night air to cleanse her of the smell of this social obligation. That was when she noted the woman leaning against her car.

She looked across the courtyard to where her car was parked, the car that was calling her to come, take it home to where they both belonged, when she saw her. Squinting, she could see more clearly that it was more like a girl than a woman leaning against her leased Saab. The fire-engine red color made the well-tanned bronze skin of this girl stand out all the more strikingly. If only I had my camera, Diana thought, eyeing the shot. Titling it perhaps, "Waiting in the Courtyard," or "After the Prom," or "Young Girl Waiting for Hunter." Diana was not above self-flattery.

The girl leaned on the hood of the car, her round bottom resting on the cold red steel. Who was she? Certainly not a faculty wife. A neighbor, a student, perhaps? The girl looked a lot like Charlene Tilton in her better days. Diana gathered up her confidence and charm, and approached. Whomever she was, she was pretty, looked bored, was waiting for something to happen. A dismal expectation to hold fast to in the sterile heart of the Arizona suburb. Or maybe not, maybe she was waiting for someone. Certain that they already had their boredom in common, Diana moved more resolutely to the car, her curiosity piqued. Diana heard her calling, found her purpose for the evening, pursued her new found goal while walking towards her car pretending not to notice the girl at all. Even the ever-cool Diana Hunter was shy . . . in a smart-aleck kind of way.

The girl saw Diana approaching. Diana made a mental note of this. She watched her coming closer; again noted. She was boldly staring right at Diana, a fact which Diana not only noted but memorized. Oh good, she thought, the game was taking shape. Diana approached slowly now, seemingly uninterested, and took a seat leaning on the hood, next to her. Both radiated the calm of those comfortable, not to mention confident, with their good looks and ability to please if given the chance. Women can be so endearing when they play like this.

The girl's eyes, still staring, flickered, like a thought striking, an idea registering. Not more than fifteen silent seconds passed before Diana said, "Comfortable?" By now Diana figured that the girl proba-bly realized that this was her car, or maybe not, so she decided to enlighten her. "Saabs are even more comfortable to sit in when you're inside of them." Now Diana was sure that the girl knew. Diana thought back: was she this bold when she was that young?

The girl, still staring, said and rose with a start, "I'm sorry."

For what? Diana thought, for being the only event that sparked my interest all evening. She said, however, this: "No, don't be, please you're welcome to sit. Join me," and she motioned for her to take her assigned seat again.

She never once stopped staring. Not so much into Diana's eyes now, but at her face. Her eyes watching Diana's lips as she spoke, taking in the shape of her face, the white glint of her teeth in the blue night, tracing the line of her hair with her eyes, from the top of her head down to below her shoulders.

Diana wondered how the girl felt about auburn. The girl was taking in all the details. The girl had yet another flicker in her eyes and brought her gaze once again up to meet Diana's head on . . . What was she thinking? And who the heck was she?

Whatever calm and sophisticated facade Diana had attempted to muster and present was slowly melting. The girl was warming her with her eyes. Diana started to feel herself disquieted inside; the girl's bold-ness, and blondness, unnerving her a bit. She was growing excited by the mystery, as well as the girl.

As far as Diana knew, no young woman in her right mind would behave this way unless of course she was trying to pick someone up—preposterous! Not in a faculty party courtyard, in suburbia! Diana kept forgetting that she wasn't in Dupont Circle, she was in Scottsdale, Arizona, and that fantasies of women picking her up right and left were less than likely out west. She warned herself to behave. Then she warned herself a second time, good and hard—to be sure it would take.

The girl never did join her on the hood of the car as Diana had requested. She merely stood, still, standing in front of her watching, eternally watching, and now smoking. Long draws; long exhales. How sexy this young thing was.

"I'm Lila," and with that Lila sat down next to Diana. I mean right next to her, and Diana felt her naked arm touching hers. Soft, round arms, young arms.

"Hello Lila," Diana replied in kind, "I am—"

"I know who you are . . . I saw you inside. I was sitting on top of the stairs watching you all talking and drinking. You didn't do much of either, though. You just seemed bored by the whole thing," Lila offered.

Diana's first thought, paranoid as it was, was how many other people noticed how bored she was inside. Her second thought was of Lila. She saw her now more as a comrade, a perceptive little woman, another faculty party runaway like herself. Heterosexual, no doubt, but a delightful surprise nonetheless. Diana picked up the ball: "You know who I am, but I am still waiting to find out who you belong to." Still aware of Lila's arm rubbing gently against hers as she lifted her cigarette to her mouth from time to time.

Lila looked away, and put it this way, "Let's just say that I'm on good terms with Dean Thaxton," and changed the topic quickly, ". . . who, as you well know is responsible for this evening's entertainment."

"To put it loosely—"

"Very loosely! You have her to thank for this," she said pointing to the large colonial home.

"And you, little Lila," growing braver, "were the coward. You didn't even have the guts to come downstairs and brave it out firsthand." Shooting a self-conscious look at Lila's body.

My oasis in the dry Arizona desert, thought Diana. In tight, worn denims, tapered at the ankles, sling back sandals and a revealing white cotton tee, Lila looked the student. Diana saw the erect nipples under the shirt, the firm legs, the small pretty hands, not to mention the long,

long blond hair that fell down her back. And turquois-colored eyes. Diana was willing to wager that she was quite the promiscuous girl. Still in the dark about Lila's motives and identity, she remained cautiously aroused.

"I'm no coward. I just have enough sense to enjoy my privacy. Like you . . . you know, I kind of wish you had been sitting on the top of the stairs with me, watching. It was altogether much more fun up there. Maybe next time I'll give you a formal invitation to join me."

Of course, Diana thought, she had the luxury of not attending, not having to—so who was she? And how did she know the Dean? A girlfriend of the daughter of the Dean? This was confusing: Lila was teasing her, wooing her, playing a little flirtatious game with her, and all the time Diana was wondering if Lila could tell just how much she was enjoying their interchange. She did her best to maintain her cool, despite the fact that her own nipples were now erect, and despite the fact that she told her anxious breasts to control themselves, as this woman next to her was just a girl, a girl just out looking for some kind of trouble tonight.

"Would you accept the invitation?" Lila asked.

Diana was hoping that Lila would be quiet long enough for her to just sit and stare down at her legs, so she could imagine what it would be like to be touching them. Diana wanted, right then and there, this moment, to throw caution to the dry Arizona wind, to run her fingers across the insides of her thighs. And this was most definitely getting out of hand, and Diana grew nervous, telling herself to get a hold of herself. Retrieving past caution thrown prematurely to the wind, she replied stiffly, "Probably not." Diana went back and forth: approaching and recoiling from her. Danger, she sensed danger in this episode, and added, "No, I have a responsibility to attend these functions as part of my job—"

"Please don't be so formal with me. I didn't mean to make you angry, Diana." She spoke Diana's name as if she was quite comfortable with having said it numerous times.

Who is this woman spurring me on, Diana kept wondering? "I'm not angry, Lila—"

"Do I make you uncomfortable? Because if I do I can leave. I really didn't mean to. I mean . . . that is the last thing I want you to—"

"No truly, I am not uncomfortable. I just feel, rightly so, that I don't know who you even are. Let me present this scenario to you: I leave the party only to find you leaning against my car, seemingly waiting for me, as if you planned this whole thing before I ever arrived at the party tonight!"

"I did."

She did? questioned Diana silently, sensing trouble.

"I did . . . I've been waiting out here for you for the past half hour. Waiting real impatiently, Diana, if you must know. I saw that you were about to leave the party, and I really wanted to meet you. Talk to you."

"What about?" Diana asked, feeling a chill now, growing more stimulated with the sound of the girl's voice, watching her brush her hair from her face sensuously, calculatingly. Oh, Diana didn't know the half of Lila's charms.

Caution dictated that Diana rearrange her position on the car so their arms were no longer touching, which she did, and she looked out into the horizon somewhere. To cool herself down. Diana, getting more nervous about this planned interlude, knowing that her interest was inviting trouble, wondering if the little Lila was using it to her advantage. She was. Wondering about how nice Lila's small hands would feel on her own breasts, which were still obstinately calling out to be touched.

"I wanted to know if you were going to be doing anything after the party?"

If I am wrong, and this is *not* a come-on, Diana thought, then I'm getting out of the business of dating girls . . . This girl *is* putting the make on me, right outside the faculty party! And Diana was right. And she backed off.

"Don't most people go home tired, and go to bed," already knowing this word 'bed' was the wrong choice, "after parties . . . or at least that's what people I know do."

"Well, if a party is really a party, which this one was not, then I agree, you'd be too tired to do anything *but* go home and go to bed," Lila confirmed, lingering on that last word playfully, not about to give Diana a break. "But," she continued, "this event couldn't have turned into a party, in the true sense of the word, no matter how drunk everyone got."

She was accurate, Diana gave her that.

"Why didn't you drink like everyone else?" Lila asked.

"I didn't want to waste good liquor," Diana answered.

Both laughed.

"Well?" Lila asked, waiting.

What am I supposed to do, thought Diana, invite her back to my apartment for drinks and some lovemaking, so she can spill all about her teenage identity crisis, or sign up for my course and be assured of an A? Diana sincerely didn't know exactly what Lila wanted from her, or what she was supposed to say. What do I *want* to say, Diana asked herself. She wanted to tell her how pretty she thought she was. But this was off limits.

"What are your plans after this party . . . I have to know?" Lila prodded.

"Why do you have to know?" Diana teased, knowing that she was going to pay for this.

"Because . . . I have to know the right thing to say to you, in just the right way, so you'll want to spend some time with me. Tonight, I hope."

Diana couldn't believe her ears—this girl had nothing whatsoever to lose—and there was more:

"Do you think I'm pretty?" Lila asked.

This was too much, Diana thought, this girl wasn't wasting a second. And, even though it was beside the point, Diana did think she was pretty, and wanted to kiss her on the lips.

Lila, reading her mind, parted her lips, to expose the slightest glimpse of her tongue, making Diana more uncomfortable. Discomfort, then silence.

Lila's breasts were small and firm, and Diana wanted to cup her hands over them. How dare she wear something this provocative, the little slut, Diana vented silently. Diana knew Lila knew that Diana was hooked, interested; here Lila was now facing her lifting one leg on the fender of the car. How much more can I take from this calculating and manipulative girl, Diana asked herself, still watching the lips, the thighs. Then losing all control she answered, "Yes, I think you are lovely, Lila."

It was all over now. It was finished—her career, everything. Diana saw scenes of her life flash before her eyes. Having just committed professional suicide, unholy dread gripped her. And yet, something told her that it was all right. All right to stay with her; to let her woo her with her words; to allow all this to play itself out.

Grasping onto her last shred of sensibility Diana told her, "I find all girls your age lovely. That is why I enjoy teaching. All girls and boys," Diana continued laying it on, "who aren't hardened yet by life, are wonderful and fresh. It's a pleasure to teach uninhibited people like yourself." Lila's social upbringing prevented her from telling Diana that she was full of shit. Diana knew that Lila sensed she was bluffing, their eyes still locked, knowing, the both of them, that Diana couldn't hold out much longer.

Feeling trapped, Diana stood, got her car keys out of her handbag and looked at Lila for the final time, "I've really got to go now. It has been very nice talking with you. Refreshing." Refreshing? Diana admonished herself for being a fake. But, oh, how safe she felt once again. She raised her hand for a polite handshake. Lila stood full face in front of her. Her breasts pert, firm. Shorter than Diana by a few inches, so Diana would have to bend her head slightly down in order to kiss her . . . which was the way Diana was dying to say goodnight to her. Diana's hand extended, waiting. It was shaking imperceptibly, and before she could withdraw it, Lila extended hers, took Diana's hand. This was killing Diana as she warned herself not to lose it now in the home stretch, a few seconds more and she would be home free. Lila applied a gentle pressure once, twice and then released it. Her knees were not as steady as she had hoped. Hold on Diana, one more minute to go, sixty measly seconds. Diana turned, walked around the side of her car, opened the car door, got in and shut and locked it behind her. Frantically cool. She started the engine and looked up at Lila who had followed her to the driver's side, and knelt down to the window.

Against her judgment, her better judgment long gone now, Diana rolled down her window to look at Lila. Lila leaned in, her face so close Diana could almost feel her breath. God knows they both wanted the same thing. One would swear that Lila was about to kiss Diana at that instant. It was agony for the driver sitting so still, so prim. Lila smelled of youth—Diana could almost taste is.

A trace of moisture between her thighs called attention to itself—Diana just had to hold on. Wanting Lila so much this way; Lila's look beckoning her, lips wet for her, and Diana's body responding in kind.

"Diana, I want to be with you tonight," Lila said, coming as to surprise to either of them.

Of course, Diana debated, she had nothing to lose and I do. I do, she repeated hopelessly attempting to convince herself. Alarm bells rang in Diana's head, jail cell doors slammed, and Diana was filled with misgivings and trepidation and excitement.

Further, Lila added, "Let me come with you," not even noting the double entendre. Not pleading, not whining, just stating the facts. Diana wanted her to come and wanted to come with her. She wanted to press her lips against Lila's and draw her tongue into her mouth. She wanted to suck the breath from her.

Diana grew furious that she could not control her own thoughts. I have other women in my life, she argued, I'm not lonely for companionship. I'm probably ten years her senior, I'm too old, she's too young, this whole thing is too dangerous! That's it! It was finally settled. Thank goodness it was over. Diana knew she was leaving alone, and praised herself for winning the battle over her primitive urges. She was heartily self-congratulatory.

Then she told Lila to get in the car. Before regaining her senses they were driving out of the courtyard. What have I done? What have I done! she thought. Mortified, horrified, driving straight into the clutches of dread.

They didn't speak. Diana concentrated intensely on her driving as if it were her first time behind the wheel of a car. Lila, silent, in her bucket seat, hands folded on her lap, sat staring straight ahead. Pleased.

It would be a forty minute drive back to Diana's house. Did Lila's mother know that she would be out for the evening? Again, alarm bells tolling in Diana's head. Did her mother expect her home? Apprehension growing at an alarming rate. She decided to ask an important question, "Who exactly do you belong to, Lila?"

Lila, knowing the jig was up, responded, "I'm Dean Thaxton's daughter. I'm home for the weekend on break until Monday. I attend Wellesley College in Massachusetts."

The face of death reared its ugly head in Diana's rear view mirror, and she swerved to the side of the road stepping hard on her brakes. It would soon be time for the eulogy—Diana's eulogy.

"Look!—" Diana said turning to Lila.

"I live at the butler's cottage behind my mother's house," Lila appealed, "so no one knows my comings and goings, and I only came to the party to meet you, Diana, and ever since the semester began my mother talked so much about you that finally I looked up your picture in the college newspaper to see what all the fuss was about, and then I knew I *had* to meet you. I just had to. My mother thinks you are a beautiful and bright workaholic, and she likes you. And so do I . . . a lot. And you can't really blame me . . ." And the more Lila defended herself and her motives, the more nervously excited Diana grew.

This time arousal was one step ahead of anxiety, and Diana pulled the car back on the road.

Lila's hand was warm on her thigh as they approached Diana's house.

Do you remember the time
I followed you, and
signed up to be whatever
you needed me to be, and hungrily
dined on your words, and
lined up with all the others
where you could find me by number?

This particular sunrise was designed with Diana in mind. The color of daybreak, the smell of daybreak held promise. Its brilliance called out to her to come. Its morning song woke her from her sleep, took her hand and led her to her terrace. She could feel its warmth through the sliding glass doors even before she opened them. At five in the morning, Sunday, when her neighbors slept, the town slept, Lila slept, Diana experienced one of the most beautiful sunrises imaginable. It was her morning gift. Acknowledging the Source, she offered a silent 'thank you.'

At this precise moment in time, all the events both externally and internally were as they should be in her life. Perfect. Her life was in order. She was walking on the proper path, at the proper time at the proper speed. It was all, all right. The serenity, the peace that swelled within her affirmed the rightness of her thoughts, her choices. The calm was always with her as her internal barometer of her progress.

Diana was exactly on time in her life. Who she is was in perfect harmony with who she wanted to be, was supposed to be. She had no one to share these thoughts with so she returned to the Source, for a private communion. The white light she called on in her meditation coupled with the rising heat of the sun warmed her into a welcomed semi-conscious state of release . . .

Lila stirred. She made that throaty satisfied noise that women make when they are unable to verbalize what they want . . . the "Yes, I like it, I want more" sound. Lila, only half awake, already sounding for more. Precocious, promiscuous, predictable. Unused to waiting too long between the asking and receiving, Lila's impatient arm, hand, fingers searched out in the bed for the bearer of some of the most pleasurable sexual gifts she'd ever received. The gift giver of the previous night was nowhere to be found in bed, as she opened her eyes and almost pouted with disappointment. Distraught, with no one there to welcome into her arms, she left the bed to explore. She was in a welcoming mood, her body purring.

Turning the corner in the hallway, she had to go no further. She spotted the woman, who had made love to her so expertly last night, illuminated by the first signs of this most radiant sunrise. Even Lila noted the exceptionally beautiful dawn, leaning against the wall and staring at it, and at Diana. Lila was at it again—staring—and now breathing deeply, trying to dissipate some of the intensity she felt in her chest. The energy in the house was overwhelming, or whatever it was that felt this strong. Exhaling deeply, trying to relax, let go, maintain some modicom of calm. She turned and went to shower, more to buy some thinking time, then wishing to wash clean the lingering scent of the night before. She washed reluctantly, and thought.

She needed time to sort out the strong feelings she felt towards Diana, a woman she only just met. Feelings too strong for comfort. Trying to separate her physical attraction to her from her emotional one, her sexual from her mental one. Did it make any difference from where the attractions came, but just, that they existed and demanded interpretation. Turning the hot water off, she stood courageously in the stream of ice cold water, bringing with it the needed clarity. Ah, now she could think . . . she reminded herself that she was never serious about any lover, any woman, ever. She was the type to search out and capture playmates, spending equal amounts of time discarding them as attaining them. Her pattern of relationships with women was this: search, find, conquer and release. Somehow, she sensed this was not to be the case with Diana. Her pattern was going to be broken, as this thing with Diana was serious, she feared. But, she rationalized, she was in control, always had been, she would just refuse to let this affair get too heavy, she would remain playfully detached as always. Her game plan laid out for the morning—showering, dressing and splitting.

Exiting the shower she felt better already. When love would happen, she thought, she would be the one holding the reins in her clenched fists. She'd dictate when the time was right for her to fall in love with someone, she envisioned. She'd hold the all-powerful position in her victorious, self-controlled heart; she would decide, make all the moves, all the right moves. Her dilemma resolved, she toweled down and dressed.

Rational intellectualization is all well and good; but, they're quite the waste of time when up against pure emotions. Lila was raw emotion last night. Her feelings ruled, her body complied and her intellect was told, in no uncertain terms, to get lost. Her heart and mind battled over who would be master this morning, back and forth, back and forth. Her intellect arguing that the timing wasn't right, Diana was too old for her, telling her she shouldn't waste her time possessed by some smothering older woman who was brittle and aging. It said to her, she was too young, too energetic to settle down. A playmate maybe, it said, but not a lover. Keep it light her intellect advised. However, try as it might, all logical arguments were rendered anemic by the fact that Diana would make the perfect long term lover, her heart countered. Diana was tender, beautiful, creative, feminine—a perfect match. Now, Lila was more determined than ever to dress and leave before it was too late: before her heart called the shots.

Hurry, her mind instructed, hurry and go before your heart leads you to make the biggest mistake of your life. Leave now! her mind directed, before you say anything. Before you, god forbid, expose yourself. More than anything, Lila hated to be vulnerable, or even worse, to appear to be so. And over and over she told herself she must leave this house now because her emotions were growing more insistent, more clear. Having to stay, even if she didn't utter a sound, would be too hard, for how could she stare at Diana and not want to express her feelings. She wasn't in the mood for complications at this young age. Hurry!

So, knowing what she had to do, she walked straight onto the balcony and leaned out over the railing, looking down. Like the alcoholic insisting that she just wants 'one more,' so, too, Lila rationalized that she just would see Diana, just *see*, one more time, and then that would be enough, and she would go and she would be satisfied and that would be that.

There, leaning with her back to Diana she struck one of her extremely seductive poses and waited. Poised, she let the warm breeze do what it did best—sweep her long hair gently back off her neck. Lila made some sight.

Diana was nobody's fool: she noted the entrance, the pose, the silence and the anticipation. She matched silence with silence; she would wait and see what Lila had in mind for her this morning. It seemed to Diana that this Lila made a life's work of playing little harmless games.

For a while nothing was said. Diana watched Lila do her posing, teasing routine. Lila was not about to turn around and face Diana, as the total visual effect would be shattered. So Diana got to watch in peace: the thighs, the legs, the round bottom challenging you not to touch, the body that was so playful and grateful last night. Lila's early morning game-playing spurred Diana on. Knowing how much this would incite Lila, she did it anyway to force Lila's hand: she picked up a magazine from the wrought iron table and began absently thumbing through it.

Lila's sixth sense reported to her that she was no longer the center of attention, so she turned around, reached for her cigarettes, lit one, took a painfully long drag, exhaled and stood facing Diana, but not looking at her. The silly little game was taking shape and Diana was confused as to its meaning, but no less amused. After all, she reminded herself, Lila was only nineteen. The pose Lila struck this second time was even more alluring: legs spread, arms holding the railing on either side of her body, cigarette smoking, breeze blowing, hair dancing.

This attitude of Lila's kept Diana distant. Exactly the antithesis of what Lila hoped to achieve. Diana thought this would be a perfectly normal, fun-loving morning-after, and had no idea in the world what Lila was up to there on the balcony, silent and seductive and almost sad.

Lila, on the other hand was swelling with words she dared not begin to speak. She couldn't afford to expose herself. The words mounted in her chest and she consciously continued to choke them back. How much longer could she hold out, she wondered, this not talking was driving her crazy.

Realizing that Lila's scene was not about to abate, Diana grew content watching this girl who primped, pranced and posed in front of her in the place of communicating what was really on her mind. She assumed that Lila would speak when she was good and ready, so Diana sat smiling, staring. She felt much older than nineteen this morning, if this is what nineteen-year-old's did in the place of open communication.

It was Lila's style to watch and be watched from afar, having practiced so often in the mirror to be sure she got her look right, that cool, easy detached look. She wasn't cool, or easy or detached right now. Her feelings surged on the brink of articulation. But what would she say, she asked herself, and why didn't she just leave as she planned to do. She gave in and broke the silence, and could have left the instant her lips began moving with the words that almost spoke themselves, but it was too late now:

"How do you feel about this pretty, young girl—" and just as she was about to place the question mark at the end of that sentence, she sucked in her breath, summoned her energy enough to change the course of the sentence midway, "—calling a cab home, now?" Complete. Not bad, could be worse she told herself, and raced into the den without waiting for Diana to respond. Placing a call to the taxi service, she was grateful for the surprising swelling of hidden strength that got her out of the balcony jam.

Diana remained on the terrace for now, giving Lila some space. Diana wasn't exactly sure what was going on yet.

Calling to her from the terrace after a few minutes, she asked, "Want to talk, little girl?" She was not being condescending, it was just her way, this "little girl" business.

Lila, still searching for the much sought after composure, said, "Not now, Diana . . . please, maybe later." Lila had a great deal of work facing her in the next few minutes: could she still hold out, not say anything she would be sorry for later? Restraint was key. And she needed space.

"Are you just going to leave me without a word, just like that!"

"Just like that. For now," Lila answered in the midst of trying to forgive herself for her loss of control, trying not to allow herself to walk back out on to the terrace, and trying to accept the fact that she better not see Diana anymore.

That was Diana's last question to Lila. She wasn't a woman of force. Lila signaled for her to stay away, so she did, even though she wanted to tell her that whatever it was that was bothering her now, was okay. Not to worry, to relax and enjoy the Sunday with her.

The taxicab arrived within the silent quarter hour. Lila's exit was clean but by no means final, Diana intuited. And Lila didn't even give Diana the time to say how much she enjoyed last night with her, as it was fun. And it was fun—nothing more, nothing less for her, just fun. That is what Lila could not handle hearing—the fact that it was casual for Diana. Because it was anything but that for her.

In Your Honor, Diana Hunter,
the Gathering of Women will
take place after Dark, on
the Twenty Sixth,
Nine Grace Terrace.

The invitation arrived last night by private courier. Boy tipped, door shut, envelope opened, it read like a poem. No signature, no return address and how in her right mind could she not accept? What a novel little tease this handwritten and delivered invitation was, she was thinking. What an imagination this anonymous suitor has. And wouldn't Diana just love to meet up with this woman in a dark alley, she fantasized. And how long would it be until this mystery host made themselves known? And how long would she be kept in the dark? And she hadn't a clue as to who would do such a thing for her. Reading the invite just one final time, and slipping it into her portfolio, and getting all happy about this spontaneous adventure in her life, she tried once again this evening to get back to the business at hand that she was being paid well to do—grading papers.

She was the cause of her own trouble, as she was the one to insist that her students write these mammoth papers that would take forever to read and grade. "Communication Obstacles in a Narcisstic Society." What in the world ever possessed her, she wondered, and could just slap herself for requesting such craziness? She had a book to write, a lecture to prepare, better, more important things to do than grade papers. But the nasty deed done, tonight she was supposed to provide her red-letter commentaries to these austere, folder-encased compositions that literally lay on her desk perspiring with anticipation.

Was it her fault she wasn't in the mood for this kind of work tonight, she thought, glaring at the pile of papers that were practically hyperventilating in front of her? After all, she debated, I've been working weekends and holidays, I owe it to myself to relax, don't I? She was working up towards granting herself permission to masturbate behind her locked office door; instead, she was busily adding up all the uneventful desert nights when she had to slip off dry panties in the pursuit of success, in the name of work.

And young Diana Hunter was an amazing workaholic. With a zealot's alacrity she pursued her research to the exclusion, oftentimes, of sleeping and eating. Writing precluded the time, as well, for just plain fun. Oh, yes, some might say, "Now she has carried this writing and speaking thing too far." But for the most part, since she arrived in Arizona, she spent most of her time eating, reading, sleeping and masturbating to research, reading, listening to lecturers, listening to tapes of lecturers more accomplished than she, designing her research study, preparing her upcoming lecture, creating the outline for her first book. Some women have children; some, plants; some, pets. Diana, her research. Diana, her dry panties. Diana, her memories. The best of which were all of Christina. She often wondered where she was, what she was doing and with whom. And most important, if she was happy. God, she loved her so.

After what turned out to be ten full minutes of internal debating, Diana proclaimed that, "Yes! Yes, I do," granting herself the permission to do it, the hard earned right to do it. As for me, your friendly narrator/voyeur, I gave her my blessings long ago, telling her to do it, knock herself out . . . but she had to work this one out for herself. So, there she sat: breathing in langorously of the upcoming promising moments.

Promising: Her university office furnished to her taste in black and red laquer, door locked, after hours, staff gone, Rachmaninoff on the stereo, legs up and resting/teasing on the top of her desk.

More Promising: Her panties dangerously nearing dampness.

Most Promising: The scent of her own sexual arousal taunting her to give herself completely to this moment.

The thought of the mysterious party invitation flashed, but she was busy welcoming the fragrance of her excitement—it, drawing her more deeply into the abandon. Diana parted her legs a bit. She loved the fragrance that she gave birth to when aroused. The taste, when passed from a lover's lips to her own, pleased her as well—often, to no end.

Still the literary discourses, each at least twenty pages long, simultaneously and politely cleared their throats. They had to be graded by Friday, and the only way they could possibly be completed in time was by reading them one by one for three hours every evening from tonight until Thursday. Laying her fingers of her right hand underneath her skirt, between her thighs, and against her moister recesses was the obvious choice; but how, pray tell, could she explain the delay to her nervously-awaiting-their-grades students on Friday. She couldn't tell the truth. One point herewith awarded to grading the damn papers.

Diana parted her legs a respectable amount, enough to make a difference, enough to make a strong case for masturbating, as the cool air felt good against her there. Two points awarded here.

Well, she told herself, it wouldn't hurt to just touch myself once, just to see if I am even wet at all yet. This! From the woman of perpetual wetness! The rationalization went something like this: If I find that I am dry, then I will willingly go back to grading the papers now; and if I find myself wet, then what choice do I have other than to yield to nature's call?

Lazily her slow hand drifted down to her skirt's edge to lift it up above her knees, inch it up her thighs, exposing now her hair that was almost the color of dark strawberry blond. She warmed at the sight of her own body which she worked so assiduously on at the gym for the past five years. She knew what it wanted, hearing the silent whisperings of her own sexuality. With the feminine ease innate to all women, she slid the hand between her thighs to discover, softly, tenderly.

Slow hand arousing her, she closed her eyes and began an enchanted release into fantasy and orgasm . . .

Until a better thought stopped her! And Diana knew just the woman. You'll have to wait only a little longer, she explained sweetly to her body, because I know just the woman who will make it worth your wait.

Carefully she gathered her papers which she would deal with at a later time, the later the better, and left her office.

"What keeps you here so late?" questioned Diana, locking her office door, knowing very well that she hadn't generated that much work for Jade this week.

"The obvious," she responded pointing to the pile of papers, making Diana doubt the actual amount of her workload.

"When do you have time to play, Jade?" Diana asked without, for once, a hidden agenda.

"It depends on the object of desire, and how persuasively it calls to me."

Diana felt shaky. Where was her composure off to at this time of night? Why did Jade always have this effect on her? She was the boss, she was in charge; and yet, the nearness of Jade, just the sense of her presence made her stop. Diana couldn't help but notice that memories of Christina also stopped when she was in Jade's presence. No woman was stronger than thoughts of Christina. No woman she had ever met. She was pulled towards Jade and there was no denying that. What was worse: she found herself making extra work for herself to do so that she could be nearer to Jade after hours while Jade worked on the other side of the door. Just to be near her was enough some of the times. And when they perchance stood next to one another, less than a foot apart, words escaped her, and it was all she could do to stare at her, or maybe incite Jade into a verbal sparring match. To get a rise out of her, to make her feel as off guard as she did, perhaps. Whatever it was between them had already taken some kind of amorphous shape, and had already begun to alter their behavior, their thoughts.

"Let me ask you something, Miss Hunter," Jade said. And still Miss Hunter rather than Diana after all this time. "Do you really find playmates of your caliber, or do you usually end up settling . . . like, tonight for instance . . . for less?"

"First, I find your perceptiveness disquieting, and second, I know you are about to make a maudlin point here, one which will force me to think about things that I don't wish to think about and which will throw the proverbial damper on my evening. Unless, of course, that is precisely your objective."

She was right; Jade was about to give her a stern "why settle for less" lecturette, but decided instead to say, "You don't need to hear it, Miss Hunter, you know the answer already."

"And you feel that if you don't find people who inspire, why bother with less. Right?"

"Right."

"Sometimes bothering is an improvement over solitude."

"I disagree," Jade shot back, "it's an insult to it."

Whew! This was one serious girl. And Diana lost herself for the moment in trying to visualize what Jade's home life must be like. How could it be that attractive, considering she spent most all her time working, working, working. It must be private, intense, stark, challenging, and lonely. Or maybe not. Maybe Jade was telling the truth . . . keeping her life clean while she waited for the woman she sensed would come into her life. Eventually. But, oh, how impatient Diana Hunter was with matters of this sort. Wait? Who could wait when the voice from her loins called to her?

And then she began wondering who it might be that Jade was waiting for in her life. Diana didn't dare for one moment think it was her, even though that is what she was thinking, and what her heart told her. Seriously entertaining this thought would change the whole course of her evening. Not to mention her life. It would complicate it she told herself. Tonight she wanted something simple, something easy, something hot and sexual with another woman. Jade would demand, or at the very least, expect something so much more than that, and she wasn't sure she was prepared to handle it. Not only tonight, but in general. It *was* what she wanted whether she knew it yet or not.

Jade turned back to her work. The dialogue, as far as she was concerned, was over. The perfunctory "goodnight" was understood, not spoken.

The scent of arousal, the scent of the hunt remained in the air long after Diana parted. Jade lit a cigarette, smiled and took note of it.

I imagine
sand castle days
and windy nights
when I imagine
us forever.

Eight years passed for Whitney and Allisone. Love letters, candelit dinners, drive-in necking, open road and back seat adolescent petting, and promises of forever-afters passed between them for the first six years. The differences in their ages, now 43 and 31, mattered little. They had much to learn from one another, especially Whitney who grew relaxed, excited and younger.

They cloistered themselves away in their bliss, focusing only on each other: each willing hostages of the other.

The latter two years of the eight found them married—although, not to each other. Allisone was wedded body and soul now to her thousand-dollar-a-week cocaine habit after Whitney took her vows to her ninety-hour-a-week job as Economic Consultant to the Americo-European Think Tank, headquartered in Great Britain.

Was this any way to live or love, Whitney would rumble on her endless transcontinental flights? But what can I do to change things, short of leaving my post? Whitney worked excrutiatingly hard all her life towards professional success; success did not come easy to Whitney, but it did come. So, Whitney tried to ignite each rare moment she spent with Allisone: lavishing her with gifts, indulging her every whim, even supporting Allisone's recent cocaine habit. Of course, Whitney figured, when my post as consultant is over in a few short years, Allisone will put down the drugs. She was dead certain Allisone would put down the drugs. It's just a poor substitute for me when I'm away from home, she rationalized.

This was Whitney, the eternal optimist. Love had dramatically changed her, as she never used to be so positive, open or spontaneous. This love business was probably the single finest cataclysmic event in her entire life. It affected every area of her personality: loosening her, freeing her, enabling her to give, give, give. And to think, that before Allisone, her few polite relationships with men were interesting, at best, compared to the life-changing thrills that love with Allisone brought. She was one thankful woman.

Because of the delicate public nature of Whitney's post, their love affair began and remained clandestine. At first the secrecy served to intensify their time together. After six years it ceased to sit well with Allisone. Loneliness in these last twenty-four months became a way of life for Allisone now that Whitney attained national recognition. Sure, she was proud of her for her brilliance and her amazing nonstop work ethic until it began robbing them of their precious, sheltered time together.

To Allisone, who made an art form of living off her parents' inheritance until Whitney insisted on supporting her, work was irrelevant, at best, inconsequential. Always surprised at how seriously Whitney took her work, always playfully chastising her for it, especially since Whitney had more old family money than she could even spend in two lifetimes. "What is your problem," was Allisone's still unanswered question, "why work so hard when we already have everything we need and want?"

The last job of Whitney's changed everything. Allisone was left alone for long stretches of time—not days anymore, but weeks, and once or twice, months. She had no friends to fall back on for companionship or even conversation to break up the monotony of her days alone. There was only so much shopping and reading a person could do. Easily bored by nature, she tired of all distractions. Allisone didn't want friends, she wanted Whitney. And nothing short of that would do.

Intercontinental travel took Whitney and her cabinet member colleagues to Paris, to Belgium, to London, and eventually Allisone ran out of constructive ways to fill her time. "Why can't Whitney just settle down and be happy with me, be married? How can Whitney expect me to just sit still and wait and wait just for the few moments, as good as they sometimes are, when she arrives home, between trips?" Recently, making love to Whitney meant Allisone had to wait in line for her turn. Wait for the few hours with a jet-lagged lover who pretended not to be exhausted.

She was tired of making tired love with a tired lover, so she changed partners: she began making love to the white dust. It became, for her, the attentive constant companion that Whitney used to be.

She never expected to get hooked—just even.

She got hooked. Her money rapidly disappeared in those two years, before her appetite was sated, so she began making her way into Whitney's money. Of course, Whitney gave Allisone all the money she wanted, to buy pretty things, Whitney thought, as Allisone was still a pretty woman, and occasionally to buy cocaine to keep her from feeling too lonely.

For Whitney, this was her first time in love. And she fell in love hard and blind. Like Allisone. And because no one knew them as a couple, or knew Whitney was even married to anything but her career, no one could warn Whitney of what was to come.

In fact, Whitney was so exhaustively blind when it came to her lover, "the woman could do no wrong," that when Allisone confronted her with her demand for two hundred thousand dollars not to tell the press about their lesbian marriage, Whitney was amused. It took a tremendous amount of convincing, and Allisone was desperately persuasive, as addicts grow to be, to convince Whitney that the woman she was eternally devoted to was blackmailing her to support her habit.

At month's end, just shy of their ninth anniversary, Whitney turned over the money to Allisone, along with their house, the two cars and the deeds to their jointly owned summer cottages. And a note:

Like zebra stripes your contrasts are. Your fire and ice soothe and burn, hurt and heal. Scald me tonight, Allisone.

At this, Whitney's request, they made love that evening one last time, ravaging one another with a passion long since forgotten and abandoned. It was the end of a chapter for Allisone; it was the end of the volume for Whitney.

When Whitney moved out west to apply for the much acclaimed position of Dean of the School of Economics at Scottsdale University, she also turned over her most precious possession—her lesbianism. She arrived in Arizona as Whitney Leighton III, certified heterosexual. She swore, her first evening in her new home, ceremoniously with her hand on her never-opened bible, never to allow herself to love anyone again. She meant, a woman.

And to stay true to her oath she married Harold Stillwell after one month in Arizona, and a two week courtship. He was a professor at the school, and her insurance. She could never love him, and his presence would insure her of never being free to love, and then be devastated again by a woman.

Whitney made one concession, a goodwill gesture: she changed the Miss to Mrs. for Harold. She would always remain Whitney Leighton III.

Harold fused himself to her side from the moment, at the alter, when he eagerly barked, as this was too good to be true for him, "I do," sealing it with the hot wax of finality.

I give you license
to drive me wild.

Diana was on her knees in front of Maria Lanning, and between her legs. Maria in her cool blue leather computer room chair waited and watched, as hers was not to do, but to comply. Diana, in her severely cut tailored skirt hugging her thighs for dear life, her wine colored high heels, her loosely hung silk blouse exposing the tops of her large breasts, leaned her head towards the most hot and demanding part of Maria's body. Maria could see the exposed breasts: dark on dark nipples, erect, touching the silk material of the blouse—making their point. A three inch chain link gold collar lay masterfully around the neck of its owner, with thick gold cuffs on each of Diana's wrists. They too made their point even more clearly. There was nothing ambiguous about this female, Maria thought smiling to herself, knowing that Diana had every intention of getting what she came for.

Diana's purse and blazer lay on the coffee table by a six inch thick manuscript. Maria recalled that Diana came to pick up the rough draft of her book that she had word-processed for her. Diana shared a cigarette, coffee and talk of the book on the couch with her.

It was some time after that when the winds changed: Maria went to her desk, opened her top drawer to compute the bill for the Word Processing Center time, was halfway through the onerous chore and turned around to find Diana leaning over then lowering herself to her knees beside her chair. Maria shifted to face Diana head on. Without permission, knowing it would be granted, Diana slipped Maria's skirt up and over her legs and up around her hips. Slowly. Diana was not surprised at not seeing panties; she had expected as much, as Maria's scent on the couch was too fragrant to have been concealed by panties. Maria lay back in her chair yielding control and exhaling a deep down pleasurable sigh. "Yes," she said to Miss Hunter, and generously parted her legs. Most generously. Diana offered a "thank you" and was pleased with the sight that was more delicious than she had imagined.

Maria closed her eyes and felt a gentle tongue touch her pussy. A kiss. Then another. Again a slow, so slow tongue licking lips, then the insides of her thighs. Licking and alternately kissing and sucking in quickly the lips with lips, saliva meshed with come. Diana's lips growing more assertive, not asking but telling, not teasing but taking, licking the moisture between the thighs.

Reclining further into her chair, melting into the ambiance of the moment, the calm sensations and anticipating what was to come, Maria flushed. She waited on that precipice, her breath missing beats . . . holding and holding her breath, making her heart beat harder and faster, with Diana tasting, kissing and making those wonderful sounds of pleasure that only comes from the uninhibited giving of pleasure.

Soft-sucking and cool breathing. Diana's tongue now, "Oh, yes" sighed Maria, to the tongue that made its way into her. Filling her, in and out again until the fingers replaced the tongue inside of her. Two then three fingers made Maria wince unexpectedly. Then four caused Maria to stiffen and relax, saying, "I am not ready, Diana."

"I am," Diana said, establishing the rules. The huntress set the parameters.

Maria was losing the gentle calm of the moment, her body without consent was beginning to stir, her pelvis responding to the fullness inside her by undulating, saying, 'Yes, I want to feel this way, I want to give myself to it.' Maria knew not to ask, not to say anything; what she wanted to say was "Do it, Diana, just do it right and do it hard." Her body was taut, lifting off the chair a few inches to meet the insistent fingers, lifting so the woman on her knees could watch to see how good she was making Maria feel.

Diana's long elusive fingers moved deliberately in and out; when out to purposely graze the center of Maria's fire; and gently exhaling cool air to soothe and incite, rubbing, knowing how, exactly how to do it. Maria, eyes closed, furrowed brow now, clenched her teeth, jaw stiff, knowing what was to follow and why and counting the seconds until the yes . . .

Then, unexpectedly the winds changed. Again. Diana grabbed Maria's thighs suddenly, with a pressure to leave bruises, and spread her legs even wider apart. Diana bared down harder still. Passion turned to pain in Maria's face. Ownership in her eyes as Diana stared hard at Maria's legs, her pussy, her frightened look. She was smiling and hurting Maria, just enough. 'It is mine for the taking,' Diana's face said to Maria awaiting the new rules, growing more aroused, growing now afraid. Diana was hurting her, pulling her skirt further back and up her body; the clothes annoying her, but left on.

"Sorry," Maria said on cue, knowing that she was only to help and take instructions.

Diana made her move, wetting her fingers inside of Maria only to move them down and under, searching and finding and without warning penetrating, no, driving into Maria. Maria's body convulsed once, jaws slammed shut, her back rigid against the leather of the chair, instantly damp, afraid at how aroused she was growing in response to the pain. She leaned into it, her body saying 'More,' 'Don't stop before it's done, let me have the pain you want to give to me.' Her body, her moves, urging Diana on, not to stop, please not to stop. Already, though, she had asked too much, assuming that she had a say, and Diana noting this, withdrew her fingers from inside of her, and told her to sit upright in her chair with her legs spread wide.

Maria's passion accelerated as she watched Diana's planning eyes, examining eyes. She waited; the waiting creating tension; the tension, intensity; the intensity, arousal. She wanted it now, Right Now, but she had to wait for Diana. Her breath quickening, the feeling strong, skirt up, legs spread with Diana's hands easily sliding up and down her thighs, her calves.

Examined in detail Maria was, exposed like this, feeling the pulsing between her own legs, wanting it, and not being able to move, and trying hard to regulate her breathing, trying to quiet the impatience, almost the anger welling up inside of her at having to wait this long, not being able to ask for it.

All was silent in the room; Maria nervous with this woman who had yet to make her next move. Red and swollen and Maria didn't want to wait any longer. She didn't have to. Diana lifted both of Maria's hands and placed them deliberately, fingers in place, on her pussy showing Maria what she must now do.

No, no, Maria thought, no, and she tried to pull her hands away, but Diana having anticipated her refusal, held fast to Maria's wrists, held them in the place where she wanted them to be, and grew angry that Maria would resist. Her anger tightened her grip.

"*Now!*," Diana demanded in a soft voice, but Maria was insistent, and she would not have it, not this way. And she struggled to free her hands from Diana's, feeling the angered woman's nails digging in. Diana was furious and she grasped Maria's wrists, cruelly, pushing Maria back into her chair, putting her weight into holding her there, never yet letting go of the wrists, the wrists that were growing red with the pain.

Maria struggled, tugged her arms, squirmed to get free, the throbbing in her wrists telling her to lay back and obey, as they hurt a lot now.

"I will watch you, Maria, and you *will* do what I ask," Diana shot at her, displeased. Extremely displeased.

Maria breathed more rapidly, intensely aroused with the confluence of pain and pleasure and fear and injury. And she didn't want to masturbate herself with Diana watching, didn't want to and rebelled further. She jerked her arms trying to wriggle her wrists free with her legs still on either side of Diana. Pulling and pushing Diana in order to free herself, she grunted with force meeting force.

Both women were determined to have their way. Power struggled to usurp power.

Maria said, "I won't, you can't make me, let me go!" and Diana didn't let go but tightened the death grip. Maria knew now that Diana was the stronger of the two, was growing angry, would hurt her. And the pain in her hands increased and she couldn't for the life of her break free.

In one sudden move, Diana twisted Maria's wrists to the side, creating the burning on the flesh, hurting her to the point that Maria cried out a quick scream, too unexpected to muffle it. Her wrists were in such great pain that when Diana pushed her back into her chair, she relented.

The ache was acute, as was her arousal. Her face was flushed, her entire body damp from the struggle, her eyes watering with Diana's added pressure to her wrists. It hurt and it was her own fault. Maria understood, as the sweat turned to tears and the tears to crying. Her eyes shut fast to stop it.

Then came the sudden, tempestuous, stinging full-handed slap across her face. The blow slapped her head to the side, disheveled her hair, left her crying.

"Now you will listen, Maria, and do it my way," Diana commanded. Maria stifled even the thought of making another sound, forced back her tears, submitted. It was her own fault.

Diana's searing stare read displeasure. "We'll have no more of this doll, I warn you."

Maria surrendered to Diana. Diana took her hands and again placed them on her exposed pussy for the final time. Maria's cheek throbbed as did her cunt, and her hands were not even free to wipe the tears from her face.

"Now you will do it for me because this is the way I want it," Diana said to her obedient concubine.

And Maria did as she was told. She masturbated herself—for Diana—in front of her, with Diana watching everything. And yes, yes, Maria took only seconds to come with an orgasm made more potent with the pain pulsing on her red cheek, red wrists. Eyes opened she watched Diana watch her come, afraid to close her eyes for fear of another slap, unexpected and painful. Fear of it arousing her further. She watched Diana; she watched her own hands arouse. Maria was making herself rise to climax a second time before even descending from the first, her fingers surprised with how very wet she was, how very wet the leather chair under her was, knowing how wet Diana must be. She closed her eyes, moaning under the pressure of this second orgasm.

"Very nice," was all Diana said.

When Maria's lips were pastel pink again, when her breathing was regular, when her eyes were opened, Diana moved Maria's hands from her cunt and lovingly, tenderly kissed each of her wet fingers.

Diana stood, lifted the shaky Maria from her chair and kissed her full on the lips. A deep, wet passionate kiss, whispering, "You did well, doll." Maria knew she had.

Business to complete: Diana wrote out a check, Maria took it, Diana took her purse and blazer leaving the manuscript. That can be had later—Maria could only have been had on this night, in this way, like

this, once.
Both pleased, they parted.

I am used to rugs
being pulled out
from under me
so often,
I now choose
to walk on
bare floors.

In the posh private hospital for eleven months, force-fed and counseled every day of the week, every week of the eleven months, confined
for anorexia nervosa, Monica Peters spent the eighteenth year of her
life. At twenty-four, she refers to herself as a 'reformed' skeleton. She
smiles when she recalls those days; she smiles, but she never laughs
about them. And she never forgets.

An eerie gray light of the morning foreshadowed things to come.
Monica took no note. She was consumed in the novelty of eating breakfast. After five years and two months, the thrill of eating still hadn't
subsided.

At five foot nine, one hundred and twenty eight pounds, bright, doe-
eyed and gregarious, no one could've guessed at her past affliction.
Who could have imagined a ninety-pound woman refusing to sleep in

order to exercise off imaginary pounds she swore she put on. A woman who followed each meal in a hunched position over the toilet driving frenzied fingers down her throat. A woman whose sole goal seemed to be not to eat. Anything.

But she did have an appetite, a voracious one, for the feelings that came from not eating. The feelings of ultimate power and control over her parents, feelings of achievement over her own bodily needs, the quintessential feeling of superiority and victory. She honed her self-will raw: it was sick living and remarkably pleasurable.

It was ten in the morning when Monica stood face to face with her family's estate. The house was an impressively grand showplace. Massive. Immaculate. Perfect. Housing, one was led to believe, the perfect family. The real live Donna Reed show family. Some people, however, witnessed the events behind the facade. Some, the targets of it. One, was Monica. You have to know her history to appreciate Monica Peters. Appreciation soon turns to admiration once her story is told.

All Monica knew was that her parents left word with her roommate that they must see her. No explanation, as usual. Her parents were creatures of habit, doing what they did, whether it worked or it didn't, because they always did it that way. Predictable. To their advantage, they had a flair for the dramatic and banked on the power, and impact of it. True to form, they laid out this morning scene that was about to take place so carefully, so as to ensure its inevitable success. Timing and script in place, they waited for their daughter's arrival.

Monica sensed a thick suspicious air about her as she entered the house. The maid, a new one again, ushered her into the sitting room to wait. The set, calculatingly designed, yielded its desired effect: oppressive and intimidating, on everyone but Monica. She did feel, though, she had a strong feeling, that this was going to be a supreme waste of time. As all their battles were. To her, anyway.

The curtain lifts. Lights dim. The scene begins:

We are introduced to an unusually exaggerated amount of tension and an added measure of solemnity. We can't see these players, but we know them by their smell. Monica was still. Enter Barbie and Ken. They take their seats on the couch on either side, flanking their daughter. Barbie begins, a might high pitch and anxious for an opening line, her emotions overriding the control practiced in rehearsal: "How is it that you never told us of your . . . abnormality?"

Monica was fast furious trying to decipher this first clue. What was her mother talking about? Adrenalin already pumping through her sharpened senses. At twenty-four the challenge of this game with her parents excited her; however, it was not a game as a child in this house. Monica said nothing.

Her silence was Ken's cue, "How is it that we were the last to know of this lifestyle of yours?"

This was too easy—the word lifestyle gave it away. The game already over in Monica's mind, she was preparing to leave. She knew, of course, they were referring to her lesbianism. She never told her parents about it, this was true, but she never told her parents anything. They never earned the right to share in any part of her life. Certainly not in this, the most personal part, the part of her she treasured most. Barbie and Ken, allegedly the most perfect of perfect parents in the community, spent most of their time trying to undermine her from the time she was eight. They made their intentions perfectly clear, so she learned to keep her thoughts and especially her lifestyle to herself. Even as a child, she could sense danger in them.

From the time Monica's body and mind began forming, her parents had trouble with her ordinariness, her obvious lack of female sexual appeal, her lack of ambition and the quick sharp tongue. They were ashamed of her kind heart, gentle soul and good nature. She was their inferior by-product for all their community to see. They simply did not like the daughter that they, together, had created.

Barbie and Ken, not happy with the end result, wanted to remake their daughter into their own image. They tried and tried to get her to be what they wanted her to be, and she continued to refuse their offers for small physical alterations, hair coloring, speech lessons, nose job, European Finishing Schools, et. al. When their teenage daughter did not yield, did not allow them to call the shots in her own life, they wanted little more to do with this girl they rarely called their daughter. They made it known that they cared little for her, that she embarrassed them, that she disappointed them as their only child.

Oh, she was meaty prey for their predatory instincts. And she was slowly being asphyxiated by parents obsessed with methodically tearing her down from the inside out—emotionally and mentally. Eventually, they calculated, she would have to buckle under the pressure and give in. They banked on it. Certain that her constitution was too weak to survive the emotional battering longer than say a year or two. Then, weakened to the point of desperation for their love and affection, they planned, she would be ready to acquiesce. That's when they'd step in and begin the remodeling, to make her into the showpiece for their elite Boston community to point to with envy.

They underestimated Monica's strength, her will, her determination.

Anorexia nervosa was her weapon of choice. She chose it and wielded it with the precision of a skilled warrior. It didn't start consciously at first, as she began not eating out of depression, anger, fear, loneliness. Then not eating turned into a punishment of her parents. Then her parents took note. Then the race was on. Then she crossed the line, and the disease itself began calling the shots.

Within three months she had Babs and Ken figuratively on their knees; within five months, literally so. Within eight she had them by the balls. All they wanted, for god's sake, they told one another, was to make her into the beautiful, cultured, selfish, rich elitist like themselves. Was that too much to ask? How could such influential and revered persons like themselves be expected to settle for a normal, healthy, regular, nice, gawky teenager that Monica turned out to be. It wasn't enough for them, and they shouldn't have to settle for less, they argued. Not with all their money. And they were outraged at their powerlessness.

That, though, was all history. Monica moved out of the house at nineteen when she was discharged from the hospital. Since that time to the present she saw her parents only a half dozen times in the past years.

"We're waiting for an explanation young lady, and I don't think it would be wise of you to keep us waiting too long," Barbie warned. Ken shook his head in agreement, clenching and unclenching his jaw. She had seen him look like this before. Monica looked from one parent to the other, as each took their turn speaking, like a spectator at a tennis match. This was too much. How dare they presume that I should feel compelled to feel anything for them, she demanded silently. Be cool, she counseled herself, you don't have to play into this and you don't have to get angry.

She gave in to the urge to smile and said, "Short of the doctors in the hospital, I don't owe anybody anything, and I owe less than nothing to the two of you." She could have stood and made her exit. That was all she wanted to say, except for this, "How Dare You!"

"How dare *us*!" How dare us?!" he repeated. Here we go again he was thinking. Once more Monica usurped their spotlight, stepping on his lines by not taking her cues properly, and refusing to, for once, do something his way. She did it to them again, he thought. Goddamn it, goddamn it! He was quiet, but the veins in his neck were beginning to swell, bulging over his shirt collar.

"How dare US! What do you expect people will think of the kind of father I was to you, you turning out a lesbian. They'll think—"

Barbie finished the thought, "—that we're bad parents, didn't do our job, that you turned out this way because of us. And lord knows that we . . ."

Barbie continued to mouth the words but Monica was too busy thinking to pay attention. Of course, she was not surprised, it was their pride that was hurt, it was what others would think of them that always came first with them. They could be nasty people and hateful parents, and that was okay just as long as nobody knew. Just as long as it was their little secret. Monica tuned back into this:

"—We can have you committed, you know, and we intend to do just that if you force us to."

Barbie jumped in and backed Ken up. "And won't that suit you and your girlfriend just fine." Ken was now working himself up into a self-righteous fit. Barbie continued: "Those unnatural things you do with girls—"

Ken's turn. "—This is a sickening turn of events, Monica, sickening and embarrassing, not to mention disgusting. How in god's good name could you do this to your parents?"

Monica was growing angry at their easy reference to God, never ever mentioned in this house before this morning. But it didn't matter; she wasn't listening anyway. She was like stone. The anger she felt, superficial. The more her parents said, the louder they got, the wilder the fire in their eyes, the closer they got to releasing their energy physically, the more like stone she became.

And again, "I'm talking to you . . . how could you do this to your own parents? We gave you everything for christsakes!" Her mother's hysteria rising.

Ken tried to explain the situation, "You are killing your mother. She's not strong enough to live this thing down. The humiliation, the—"

"—the SHAME. Shaming us," Barbie blurted out on the verge of tears, "in front of our family and friends. How do you expect us to ever walk down the street with any dignity? You . . . whore!"

"Can't you see what it's doing to her, it's just too much for your mother to handle." He was repeating himself.

Stone.

"How dare you do this to us. You can't expect to live like this and get away with it. People like you pay for this kind of behavior. Read your bible. It will tell you that people like you never go unpunished, and neither will you—"

"—They pay, Monica, they pay." This from Barbie.

"And eventually, they change their sick ways, and so—"

"So will you, I promise you—"

Stone.

Ken was getting carried away, "And just because we're your parents and we have to love you, and take care of you, don't think—"

"—for one second that we won't do everything in our power to help you change."

Stone.

Ken elaborated on the details: "We hired the best detective to find out how you were and what you have been doing, because we never see you anymore, and then we find out what you *are* from a detective! From a stranger! So now we will get the best help for you, the best shrinks, the best . . . whatever it takes, the best . . ."

Monica had enough entertainment for one morning. She stood up to leave and Ken grabbed her arm with both his hands and squeezed with surprising ferocity. No one humiliates Ken. Ever. He was angry enough to hurt her. She had seen that look in his face before, and now, at this moment, she recalled when it was. Visions of Ken, in a fit of rage, kicking her terrier to death on their front lawn flashed before her eyes. She was thirteen and she watched the only thing on this earth that was ever nice to her, being kicked to death. Monica was unafraid then, and now. Stone.

"You sit here, young lady, and listen to your father."

"You listen good to what I'm telling you. And if you so much as move—" he choked with such fury, borne of wounded pride, he couldn't manage to find the words anymore.

Their diatribe ended within the hour. Timing, as always, was key to Barbie and Ken and this situation had to be dealt with before their lunch guests arrived. Monica was not extended an invitation, but she was given instructions. It was Ken who articulated them for her: "You're going back to your apartment right now and pack up all your belongings. Here—," he produced a business card from his vest pocket, "—is the telephone number of the movers. You're to call them, and they will move your possessions here within 24 hours. It's already paid for. When you're done, you're coming right back in this house to live, where you belong. If you aren't back by Friday, we'll have the whole fucking police force tailing you. They'll find you no matter where you go." Leaving the best for last, he continued, "And if you decide to run away, I'll get you back here and lock you in your room, and I swear to you," his voice lowering and slowing for intensity, "I will help you change, I swear you're going to change under our guidance, and you're going to get on with your life in the normal way like everyone else's daughter."

Flashback to thirteen and the terrier. Ken was Serious. Barbie Silent. Monica stone.

Barbie and Ken had played out all their trump cards years and years ago. Monica was immune. This was too easy, too predictable. The impact of their threats was nil. At eighteen, when she lost a year of her life to anorexia nervosa, from that moment that she left the hospital on, the cords were severed. When she left the hospital and looked in the mirror she liked the reflection: she liked herself, the way she acted, her choices, her friends, her smarts, her courage, and her kindhearted way with people. Monica, for the first time in her life, without the anger or resentment plaguing her, was introduced to Monica. And she liked her a lot. She was not inferior to anyone anymore; she was not an embarrassment; not a stain on anyone's family tree. She had no family and had no regrets and had no past. Finally, finally she took herself in her own arms and welcomed herself, nursed herself, loved herself back to health.

After she left her parents' house that morning, before the guests arrived, she packed her bags and left Boston. In fact, she left the East Coast entirely. She never once returned, never turned back either to see if she was being followed. It didn't matter. Nothing mattered anymore. She had herself, her best friend in the world, and that was enough. More than enough. Life began on the plane to the warm, gentle desert plains of Arizona at sundown that evening.

An "Amen" was in order.

The push.
The pull.

They walked down the steps of the building together after work. It was the first time that both left work simultaneously. Usually Jade worked on long after Diana headed home. Sometimes it made Diana feel guilty for working Jade so hard; sometimes she felt sorry for Jade; and sometimes, like tonight, it made her feel excited. Excited because here were two dynamic women (she didn't hesitate to call herself that from time to time) working for a just and grand cause. How could they not succeed?

Tonight was such a night for Diana—grateful, powerful and full of energy.

"What would interest you?" she asked leaving the options wide open.

"In my lifetime or in this evening?" Jade asked.

"Take your time to consider the former, and share it with me later. What interests me now, Jade, is what interests you for this evening."

"A walk . . . with you . . . around campus would suit me."

"It's yours, my celebrated colleague. It is long past due for you and I to stroll and to, perhaps if we are lucky, get to know something about one another." Diana hoped so.

"We do know *some* things about one another."

"Few . . . too few to even count between women like us," Diana smiled.

"Everything counts between women like you and me, Miss Hunter. Nothing is irrelevant or inconsequential, nothing."

"You'd like to think so."

"On the contrary, I know so," Jade responded gravely.

"How can you be so sure that what you see happening or not happening between us merits attention?" Diana said turning to Jade.

"Because, Miss Hunter, we both are women who pay an inordinate amount of attention to detail, so why should our situation warrant any less than that?"

Jade was correct. Their talk had preceded their stroll; it was as it should be between them. The campus grounds extended their welcoming arms to these two bright women of the night.

When the official stroll began, Diana had the opening line: "What is surprising is how much *is* happening between us when we've spoken so little. This is quite the silent affair we are having."

"Is it *that* peculiar?" Jade asked.

"To me it is." Diana was first and foremost a communicator, a talker.

"Perhaps we don't know yet what it is we want to say to one another."

"The feelings are there—," Diana began.

"But they are not yet ready to be articulated."

"I am ready—"

"*They* aren't" Jade advised. "Give them time, they'll let you know when it is time for them to speak out."

"My feelings for a woman were never shy before," Diana admitted.

"This is different." Oh, Jade had so very much she wanted to share with Diana all of a sudden.

How long it had been since Jade jumped into this thing called Life. Since Simone died, she avoided it at all costs. However, since she first met Diana, she had been making gestures towards reawakening to life. Noticeable gestures. Her pull towards Diana overpowering her pull towards the memory of Simone, her impossible wish to be with her.

When Jade returned to the conversation, Diana was saying: "Which is why we are walking together tonight. It was time for some words to be spoken. We couldn't not speak anymore!" Then Diana was quiet for a moment and continued with, "When we are together, you have an awfully strong power over me."

"Ah, you've noticed," Jade laughed.

"Don't tease me, I'll fire you . . ." Diana threatened.

"Don't threaten me, I'll quit."

"You would too, wouldn't you?"

"You know I would."

"Your strength unnerves me," Diana, the extra-open one, admitted.

"I know. And you haven't seen the half of it yet . . . neither have I these last few years. I've been running away—"

"—As if you could."

"I not only could, I did. And did a good job of it."

"That's what frightens people away from you." Diana stopped, and turned towards Jade.

"But not you," Jade lowered her voice and continued, "and *your* response is all I care about."

There, it was said.

"I don't need a sparring partner, I need a lover." Oh, the touch of Christina was upon her and gone in a moment. One day Diana Hunter *would* let go of Christina. And then there'd be some free space inside her for the Goddess to work Her magic. And then Diana would wonder what in the heck took her so long to let go—just let go and trust the Goddess in the first place?

"You need a match *and* a mate, Boss. You need everything."

"Which means that I'll wait until the woman with everything appears. I'll have to." Diana wasn't certain whether sarcasm was called for or not.

Jade stared Diana down and said, "Your problem is that you genuinely, in your heart, believe that if you try hard enough, you will attain perfection."

"That's my goal!"

"Jesus Christ wasn't perfect."

"Maybe he wasn't trying hard enough," Diana said adorably. And then said, "Do you know, Jade, that everything I say somehow has something to do with you? And me?" That came right out of Diana, of its own accord; she didn't even know that's what she was thinking.

Autumn on the campus was prettiest of all the seasons. The earthy colors made all pretenses uncomfortably inappropriate. What was spoken between friends and lovers on the campus during Autumn was all truth.

And what to do now that her feelings for Jade had begun to crystallize? And how to answer Jade's question: "What are you prepared to offer me?"

Yes, Diana enjoyed Jade's company. This woman's sexuality called to her often; her air of detachment from all things less than important attracted her; her convictions, her strength, her power were like magnets. Diana, who wanted her very badly indeed, said,

"I don't know what it will be worth to me."

Tenderly, Jade replied, "You lie, Miss Hunter, you know exactly what it will be worth. The fact is, you're not prepared to make an offer. *You are afraid—*"

"I'll admit to that only with certain disclaimers—"

"—And furthermore you are willing to settle for affairs in the place of true love!"

In a poor attempt to defend herself Diana said, "Affairs of the flesh count for some—"

"*Nothing*, Miss Hunter. And don't insult my intelligence please."

Diana wanted to have Jade right then and there. "I admit I am settling for less. Sue me."

"I prefer to wait."

"There is no reward in celibacy, Miss Desmonde."

"There is no reward in superficiality."

"There is no comfort in either," Diana barely whispered. And for the first time that entire evening, Jade agreed with her.

You have appeared to me
countless times.
Visions of you
bring moisture to my parched lips.

Amidst computer printouts, creased clothing and cold pizza, sat
Whitney and Monica. It was home to Monica, it was a test for Whitney.
The cramped graduate quarters were trying Whitney's nerves, for one
so concerned with status and appearances, and she was proud of herself
for staying. She had good reason to.

As promised, Whitney provided Diana with her two hundred economic students as research subjects to test out certain theories of the
way people deal with crises in their lives, overcome obstacles, and
handle trauma, emotionally and mentally.

Naturally, Whitney was concerned with the success of the project,
and could think of nothing else for days since Monica called her to tell
her the project was nearing completion. It was only natural to want to
work shoulder-to-shoulder with Monica Peters, the statistics wizard of
the University, Diana's prized helper, for six hours straight without
break. What woman in her right mind wouldn't want to be locked into a
twenty-by-thirty foot room with a research assistant only an arms
length away at any given moment?

Whitney's denial system was such that she actually believed that her
new found love of academic research had nothing whatsoever to do
with her feelings for Monica. The feelings were pressed down so deep
that even Whitney couldn't have articulated them. Or short of that,
acknowledge them. If she could have, she would never had allowed
herself permission to so much as enter this tiny room with Monica for
what she knew would be a long evening alone.

Monica possessed a pure one track mind, which was a tremendous
asset in her line of business. When she focused on her research it was
only that that she put her mind to. Assiduously. Workaholism wasn't a
foreign word to her vocabulary, and for her yielded certain advantages.
Not the least of which was avoiding emotional entanglements; the trav-
esty with her parents left scars on her that she couldn't begin yet to
imagine. She kept her relationships light and breezy and especially
non-committal. She claimed it was her free-spirited approach to life;

others more perceptive understood it was the result of her past familial relations.

She had long ago let go of her family; however, it persisted with its damaging, albeit subtle, side effects. However benign her problems with intimacy were, they still existed, and would need to be dealt with by Monica eventually. All this was going through my mind, not Monica's, as she was gleefully absorbed in her work that was strewn over the floor, the bed, the desk and other assorted and sundry places all within a short arms length from where she and Whitney now sat on the floor.

They were working on finding a statistical error somewhere in the printouts, and after two hours of conscientious effort it was still nowhere to be found. Monica persisted; Whitney relented. Whitney's professional skills lay in other areas: detail work was not her forte, preferring instead broad-stroked thinking, strategic planning, innovative conceptualizing, leaving the details and clean up work to others. Like the Monica's of the world who could sit for hours at a stretch contentedly staring and figuring statistical minutiae.

All semblance of patience left Whitney. "I quit, my dear," she said, causing Monica to jump, her concentration and the silence aborted.

"You can't," implored Monica, not wanting to lose her partner so soon.

"I can and I will," Whitney added with determination, smiling and kicking off her pumps. Slowly, one at a time.

Separated from her work momentarily, Monica had a moment to take a look at this woman sitting on the floor across from her. It gave her a thrill to see a woman like Mrs. Whitney Leighton III displaced like this in her tiny studio, student-class, and seemingly perfectly at ease amidst the mess. Glancing at her watch, she said, "It's late, that's true . . . but I am anything but tired."

"I didn't say that I was tired—"

"Then why stop?" questioned Monica not conceiving of the notion that one could stop working before exhaustion set in.

"Because I have had enough. I stop when I've had enough."

"I don't!" Monica said flippantly. So, the first double entendre of the evening emerged on the scene and positioned itself between them in the space where the tension would be momentarily.

"I have seniority, little one, and I'm not above pulling rank," Whitney herself flip, "and when I say stop, we stop, not because we have to, but because I want to!"

"So, we're looking for a fight are we?" Monica quipped, "Well that's another story then . . ."

Their staring at one another now did nothing to decrease the rising tension. Whitney's personal jousting would cost her, of this she was certain, but at this present moment flirting with a woman was what she wanted most. Even needed. It had been so long since Allisone.

"If you make the rules, then at least let me set the conditions: You don't pack up your things and leave just yet."

"I have no intentions of leaving."

"Then maybe I mean," Monica added, "you don't run away."

A perceptive little woman, thought Whitney, as barely a hundred words ever passed between them since Diana introduced them to one another at the onset of the project. But Monica was nothing if not perceptive, maybe not about herself, but always one step ahead of her companions. It was this built-in keen eye for details that was her foundation of survival growing up with her parents.

Whitney still recovering tried to salvage the ruins of her obviously transparent facade by remarking, "I never run away from anything." A lie.

"Call it what you will, but every woman alive," Monica said with soft sarcasm, "walks swiftly away from something at one time or another in her life."

"Not me," insisted Whitney defensively.

"As you wish. I have, many times . . . left the scene of many crimes—to survive. I don't see it as a sign of weakness anymore, anything that helps you cope through a crisis is a positive choice—"

Trying to veer the conversation away from truthtelling, Whitney interrupted, "—Diana should have included a profile of you in her research study—"

"You're changing the topic, Mrs. Leighton . . . It's not so frightening to admit that we are all doing the best we can, including running away when something is too painful to deal with. To me, it takes courage to throw your hands up and admit defeat even if it is only temporarily."

"A pleasant theory, Monica, but hardly a foundation upon which to base your life—"

"Neither is your macho attitude about bearing up, beating down the opposition and forging on, Mrs. Leighton."

"It beats running away with your tail between your legs, to go find shelter to lick your wounds—"

"If that's what it takes until you regroup and get your strength together again, then what's so wrong with that?"

"It appears cowardly—"

"Appearances count for nothing in the scheme of things," interjected the now excited Monica.

Both women were getting lost in the heat of the conversation, both committed to getting their point across, getting the other to agree. One woman, still not realizing that running away was precisely what she had been doing for some time. It was already growing clearer to Monica— Whitney's denial—and she was pushing, and she couldn't help it as she was already feeling things for this woman. She was already caring for her.

And what in the hell did Whitney think living with Harold was all about if not running away, she thought, growing ashamed. The last year of her life was a sham, she thought, a farce, and this Monica is absolutely right. I am too darn concerned about appearances, she said chastising herself.

"You must admit that appearances are important—" Whitney said talking through her denial.

"Bullshit . . . excuse my language—"

"It's imperative that we concern ourselves with the look of the things we do—"

"Bullshit . . . excuse my language again, but you are making me angry. It's hard enough just getting through your life in one piece without having to always check your reflection in the mirror to be sure you're doing it fashionably—"

"I am not referring to fashion, I am referring to dignity," she rebutted, her temper beginning to smoke.

"Ah, dignity . . . To me, surviving is a dignified endeavor in and of itself, without all the trimmings!" Monica had spent her childhood surviving—she knew what she was talking about. They were both staring at each other again, as boxers in a ring might do, sizing the competition up before striking out again.

Monica slammed another one to Whitney. "I'm even willing to bet that this whole heated discussion is nothing more than you avoiding getting close to me." As if Monica was one to lecture on intimacy.

For that second, Whitney trusted Monica for her clarity, her honesty, her chutzpah. This was the first real conversation Whitney had had with another woman since Allisone, and it was important. Minutes passed; with it, the pretenses. Whitney couldn't leave now if she had even wanted to: she was riveted to the floor with immovable iron studs of desire.

It had been so long since Allisone laid tiny kisses along the length of her throat. So long since she allowed herself to smell the scent of a woman this close. And then there was her Oath. And how would it feel, she thought indulging herself, to run her fingertips along the insides of Monica's thighs and watch her close her eyes and exhale with pleasure. Ah, to please a woman; to be pleased by one. Or just to kiss a woman's lips, gently; to lay her body next to Monica's, and wrap this woman in her arms. The scent of Monica, the scent of Monica and the Oath.

Whitney was paralyzed with the coupling of fear and desire; Monica sat watching, far from understanding the implications of Whitney's silent debate.

"So am I right or am I right, Mrs. Leighton?"

"About?"

"About your not wanting to get close to me," Monica repeated, noting that Whitney was as stubborn as she was. She liked that. She liked Mrs. Whitney Leighton III with all of her rich finery, her wealthy trappings, because inside was a strong and vulnerable woman dying to break out. Monica wanted to make love to that woman inside. Tonight.

"Don't rush me, I'm thinking," Whitney teased as best she could under the circumstances, stalling for time.

And in the few seconds of silence, thoughts shot through Whitney's mind like wildfire: giving in to Monica would mean diving into the dangerous waters of her past, taking the ultimate risk; was she ready or was it too soon; would she ever be ready; was it all worth the touch, the caress, the loving of one woman for one night? The part of her that hadn't held a woman close since Allisone, was banking on the fact that this one night would have no negative consequences. But could she be sure this was the right choice? And no one came forward with a guarantee. Whitney was on her own without the proverbial net.

"Say yes, Whitney," Monica said in a sensitive hushed voice, and moved slowly towards her. And closer still, kneeling in front of Whitney now, staring straight into her eyes. She put the palm of her hand up to Whitney's cheek and repeated, "Say yes."

The touch sent a trail of heat from Whitney's cheek to her heart, which already was saying yes, yes! Heat that Whitney hadn't felt in such a long time it made her want to cry. It made her eyes moisten, and Monica had no idea what her personal battle was all about. Whitney had forgotten it was possible again to feel happy, to feel. Her insides laid wasting for so long, her softness parched, her sexuality bankrupt.

Short of begging God for the courage to make the right decision, she didn't know who to go to. Her heart led her to Monica; Monica's arms led her to the bed.

She made love to Whitney, who was on the verge of tears of pleasure that entire evening, with the tenderness and sweetness that always could be found between two loving women loving one another.

Rapid breathing,
Flashing pulses.

Political incorrectness was running rampant. Lesbians were being politically incorrect all over the place, and no one was invited to this party who could or would want to stop such goings on.

Such was the party with no name, and no hostess, that some unknown woman threw in honor of Diana Hunter.

At first, the question really on all the women's minds was 'Who was hosting this extravagant soirée?' But with no name on the mailbox, no clues scattered up the asphalt driveway, no notes pasted on the stucco walls of this rented Mexican style home, the women settled in and admitted defeat, and pretended they really weren't burning with curiosity and went so far as to say that they didn't really care who She was. Really! Eventually, they began to do what came most naturally: all were here looking for trouble.

Voices, voices, women's voices filled the house. Voices came in whispers, in agitated spurts, self-conscious introductions, seductive invitations, insecure proposals, joyous exclamations melting all into the voice of Woman.

Wondering if she was being watched, her movements meticulously charted, Diana pulled up in front of the party house and got out of her Saab, and there, lit a cigarette leaning against her car summoning her energy. She was mobilizing her powers of perception in the hopes of quickly identifying the hostess, amidst the crowd of women inside, with just one knowing glance. She would know who this woman was.

She stood smoking and conjecturing: the woman would be tall and long; she'd have an urbane fluency that caused those around her to lower their eyes or clear their throats not knowing what the right thing to say was; the type of woman to turn an act into an event; she'd command attention by those who didn't even have reason yet to admire her; she'd make a woman who was confident feel a bit graceless suddenly; she'd . . . A far away flash of another woman called to her; Diana breathed deeply and continued, letting it pass, returning to her fantasizing . . . She'd lay on you her unceasing passion, this woman, and just as you were on the verge of climaxing, open to her without restraint, she would vanish into, what seemed to be, thin air, leaving you writhing in the juices you would swear never again to secrete for another woman . . .

The spasm of memory of just such a woman gripped her. "How many fucking years does a woman have to grieve before the pain subsides?" she asked herself. "How many years until I let her go?!" The scent of Christina was always upon her.

Cigarette gone, she shook the ashes of the memory from herself, ascended the driveway, leaving the gray-blue night to disappear behind the massive closed teak door.

Oh, the sight was a pretty one. Women were poured into the house, sliding intentionally or not into and out of each other's way. An atmosphere redolent with women's voices, women's bodies and women's scents. The female aroma permeated the house, the backyard, the neighborhood. And just to listen and watch—what a joy—to feel the swell of the female melody, a current rising within the portals of this home.

The woman who simply loved women, for better or worse, stood at the entrance, and allowed herself to be swept away in the beauty of the sight. The memory of Christina put aside, she shifted with eagerness to the present moment. It was necessary, as this was the stuff that survival was made of. Diana relaxed into it. She leaned back against the door watching and smiling. The only prerequisite for this evening was the shedding of inhibition.

Powdered, perfumed female bodies, white or softly tanned gold, passed in front of her, women with a smile or wink or welcoming kiss for her. Was there enough time to take all of this in, she wondered? Ah, to remain a spectator all night, not moving for fear of losing the grand perspective! What a treat! She thought momentarily of the bi-monthly academic parties derisively, and then about Lila.

The hostess must have custom-tailored this party to suit her tastes. Orchestrating this party, this private hunting ground to consummately please Diana, as the women here, for the most part, were overwhelmingly pretty, and this, like a candy store to Diana, a woman who loved to love women. More than anything. Not a slut, not dangerously promiscuous, just simply a woman crazy about women. So who better to throw a party for than one truly appreciative of a female gala event of this sort? So where was this elusive hostess, thought Diana, getting down to the business at hand . . .?

"No one gets away with just watching, Miss Hunter. If it were allowed don't you think we'd all be watching instead of playing?"

Here was Renée: extraverted, fun-loving, sincere, a party-goer and thrower from birth, with a terrific knack for mixing the right women with the right women for just the right kind of good time. She was best at this, other people's parties, because there wasn't that strained edge to her actions—her parties had to be perfect—other's could be passably excellent. They embraced with a kiss and a tender hug, Diana explaining that she had only just arrived.

"No excuses," Renée responded, accepting her excuse, "I've met a wonderful Jamaican woman that I want you to meet," she said tugging at Diana to move with her towards the backyard.

"Already?" questioned Diana in a mock moan. "Let me at least get a drink or smoke a—"

"No, no, no . . . this woman I want you to meet while you're still straight enough to remember her name."

"Matchmaking?"

"I do believe you two would match wits well," Renée offered, as it was her stock in trade to know such things.

"Thanks for your concern for my pleasure, Renée, I can only hope to return the favor some day," Diana said being led through the living room by Renée to the glass sliding doors that opened to the great female out-of-doors. Wall-to-wall women. No sooner had she stepped onto the grass, then Maria Lanning was by her side. This night would be full of enjoyable distractions.

"Welcome Diana Hunter, guest of honor," Maria said a bit too enthusiastically causing a few heads to turn. She continued more quietly, "Was it malaria that kept you out of circulation, or just an aversion to a good time?"

"I am ready to accept any punishment you deem fit, Maria." As Diana hadn't called her since their initial wild encounter.

"Whenever you are ready, Diana," said Maria referring to a followup encounter.

"Whenever you are ready, Diana," said Renée, speaking of the Jamaican woman. She left Diana and Maria alone.

"Give me a few moments to fit the punishment to the crime," Maria continued, smiling, kissing Diana on the lips.

"Having a good time so far?"

"So far I am having a better time than I've had in months. Where do you think all these women came from?"

"I shouldn't be the one you're asking as my invitation didn't even have the name of the hostess on it," Diana hinted hoping for a clue from Maria.

"Don't feel left out, it's been the talk of the party—no one knows who's hosting. It seems that no one is!"

"It seems to be running fine all by itself," Diana said searching the backyard for the hostess anyway.

"A couple of the more curious of us went searching the house, and came up with a dead end. Seems this house is a furnished rental for visiting executives and such . . . no one lives here. Pretty clever, huh?"

"And quite the happening, I see."

"You don't know the half of it . . . it's going to turn into an evening in Sodom and Gommorah if it doesn't slow down," Maria laughed. Diana scanned the room, searching around the women, through them— should she even bother trying or just enjoy?

Maria had cornered Diana against the wall and leaned her body into her. "You know you look wonderful tonight, sweety," she whispered, taking her sweet time with the 'wonderful' part. Diana's snug knee-length skirt in cream white, her silk camisole in cream white, and her snakeskin high heels, and oh, the teasing slit up the back of the skirt spelled sex to Maria.

"What is the good word, Diana?"

"Lust, honey, lust," she responded putting her hands around Maria's waist.

"Care to join me later in my apartment?" Maria said easily but hoping for a yes.

"Don't take it personally, but I think I'll hold out for the hostess to show up. I do owe her something, don't you think?"

"You're wasting your time, she won't be showing up tonight. I'll be willing to wager. She obviously threw it in your honor not intending . . . wait a minute, it's not your birthday or anything?"

"Not for a while."

"Then, as I said, this is probably a gift to you for something spectacular that you must have done or will be expected to do," she said with a seductive wink, "if you catch my drift."

"Explicitly. But I have no idea what thing I could have done to deserve something like this."

"Then your touch is more potent than I imagined. You must have unknowingly pleased the daylights out of some woman for her to go to all this . . . expense," Maria said, and backed up a bit from her.

"I imagine you're right, but who—?"

"Not to worry, for tonight your only purpose should be to enjoy. To consume. You think you can handle that?"

"Alone?"

"Alone," Maria answered reluctantly, knowing that that was Diana's choice, not hers.

"I'll try," Diana smiled, kissing Maria on the lips, an intimate kiss, and made her way into the backyard thankful that Maria didn't push the matter any further. There was still the better part of the year left in Scottsdale to play with Maria.

Tonight Diana Hunter was after something else.

A group of three women stood talking in intimate whispers by the bar. If Diana wasn't mistaken, their faces were a bit flushed, so their talk must have been racy, and Diana decided to intrude, gracefully, and have some fun under the transparent guise of approaching the bar for a drink.

"I can only hope that I'm interrupting something worthwhile!"

All eyes turned to Diana.

"You most certainly are—" said the brunette.

"And we commend you on your timing, you lovely stranger," said what seemed to be her lover, a redhead. Both stared at her.

"Good," said Diana authoritatively. "Now, you tell me what I've missed so far," she said staring at the third woman, a blond.

"Well . . . if you're sure you want to get mixed up in all this." Diana nodded, smiling at the two lovers, "Yes, I am sure," in all feigned seriousness.

"These two girls here, Sarah and Vivienne, are trying to engage me in a . . ." she lowered her voice and leaned in towards Diana, "—in a ménage a trois for the evening.

"Girls! I was prepared for the worst, but this is worse than even I imagined." They all threw their heads back, except the blond, and laughed at Diana's mock horror. The blond, with a tinge of a southern accent was silent, serious. The redhead, Vivienne, said, "Our intentions were honorable, really," and extended her hand out to Diana.

"My name is Diana Hunter." Causing the three to open their eyes a bit wider to survey the party girl in whose honor they were invited.

"So tell us," Sarah questioned, "what is the occasion?"

"I haven't a clue . . . I mean it, I couldn't begin to tell you . . . But that is another topic, what interests me is that—," turning to the blond, hoping for the name.

"Babs," the blond offered.

"—Is that Babs here, a southern girl, is unaccustomed to northern girls' degrading and sinful ways. Your casual—"

"We were simply offering some of our northern hospitality, Diana," Sarah explained.

"Intimate hospitality," Vivienne clarified.

"I see," Diana said surveying both girls, and putting a protective arm around Babs' shoulders, "I can see that I got here just in time. Now you tell me," she said to Babs, "do you want to spend the night with these two? They obviously like you a lot."

"I don't know. What do you think?"

And Diana, who certainly had a way with women said, "I myself," knowing that Babs would probably do as she advised, "think you ought to have a drink with these girls and get to know them better. I mean, do you know exactly what they have in mind for you? Exactly?"

"Well . . . not exactly. I mean not the . . . details."

"Then why don't you find out," Diana responded.

And Babs did just that, turning to the women with: "Exactly what do you expect from me, tonight?" she said puffed up with Diana's assertiveness.

"You mean in detail?" Sarah asked smiling.

"That's exactly what she means, lover," Vivienne said.

"Well, we planned to make you the center of our joint affections tonight," Sarah said diplomatically.

"In the biblical sense?" Diana asked, lighting a joint and offering it to Babs.

"Very much so," said Vivienne, "and Sarah and I have our own special ways of pleasing a woman when we do it together."

"Details," urged Diana, the perpetual voyeur.

"It wouldn't be proper for them to say, not ladylike . . . I guess I'm satisfied with what I hear."

"So you accept?" asked Diana with a congratulatory look thrown to the two women in waiting.

"I think so. But you're right, I'd like to get to know them better."

"I think it's only fair," Diana laughed, "and I wish you all the best. But you make sure to take especially careful care of Babs, you hear? She's not familiar with our northern ways." And to Babs she advised that if she needed any help sorting things out later in the evening not to hesitate to come find her.

Renée was once again at her side—what an eye this woman had for timing. "Enjoying, sweetie?"

"Immensely. It's been a while since I've seen so many women in one place. It's almost overwhelming."

"Almost? And just think, if it wasn't for you, they all wouldn't be here."

"Still, I wish I knew what I've done—"

"Who knows, maybe you'll never know . . . Maybe one day you helped a rich old gray-haired lesbian across the street or something."

"Please, Renée, I'm looking for ideas not grief." They both stood looking out among the gorgeous sea of faces, bodies, legs, covered and uncovered. Oh, if time could only stand still. If heaven were only like this. To spend eternity like this . . .

And it seemed that the party had not even begun to heat up Renée said, informing Diana that coming up was none other than a wet tee-shirt contest!

"No! No, I don't believe you!" exclaimed Diana.

"Don't blame me. You put a group of women who are nineteen or twenty-two, or some such ridiculously young age, together and this is what they come up with. I can't say as I won't watch this childish event . . ." Both laughed, knowing that they'd watch, they'd watch all right.

"Margo," Renée called out to a woman passing who could have been a model. She approached. Black hair, soft hazel eyes and the most sparkling infectious smile on the woman who extended her hand to Diana, staring blatantly into her eyes then to the rest of her.

"I'm Margo Reed." Indeed, this was a black woman hard to ignore.

"Make sure you don't miss anything." Referring to the way Margo was taking her body in with her eyes, "I'm Diana Hunter."

"The celebrity this evening—" Margo countered.

"No more than you, Margo," Renée said turning to Diana, "the infamous Margo Reed is a fashion model in Jamaica."

"You are beautiful, Margo, and well suited to your career."

Margo liked her easy way, "And you? What have you done to deserve such a banquet of pleasure?" Margo asked.

"This private playground was a gift—anonymously given. You'll have to excuse my ignorance, for I too am in the dark."

"Care for an education?" Margo offered, sensing this woman was far from ignorant.

"Perhaps. Care for a sample first?" Diana suggested.

Margo brightened noticeably. "Always."

And Diana put her arms around Margo, and laid her lips on hers. Her creamy black complexion, and smooth skin felt good against Diana's. They stood there embracing in a kiss as intense and passionate as an anonymous kiss allows you to be. Diana could feel Margo's playful tongue in her mouth as the sounds of the party disappeared while they allowed their tongues to tease and taunt one another. Diana's hands moved from the woman's back down to her bottom and slowly caressed her there through her dress. Margo left her hands on Diana's shoulders pulling her more closely as her tongue grew more demanding in Diana's mouth.

The weed, the women, the darkness of this woman, and the kissing all mingled to heighten the moment that found them still embraced, still kissing, still exploring, still testing one another's boundaries. The female sounds that accompany a passionate kiss emerged. And with Diana's first yielding sound, Margo's hand moved to Diana's back then side then breast. Diana made an effort to push back from Margo, but Margo was determined and unafraid, so Diana yielded further and pulled her even closer, held her tighter and felt her strong hand on her breast. The pleasure of this, Diana was thinking. Their kiss grew more impassioned and there, now, were many women who watched, growing aroused at the sight. None more so than Margo and Diana.

Then the two freedom-loving exhibitionists pulled apart, momentarily. Black and white and hot.

"I would love to sleep with you tonight," Margo whispered.

"Consider it done."

Renée had not moved, having had the best seat in the house.

"I knew you two girls would make nice once I introduced you. Now, I can leave you two . . . unless, you'd like to extend an invitation to me for this evening. Not to play, but only to watch."

Diana was up for it but Margo wanted Diana all to herself tonight and told Renée so. Diana told Renée she was sorry, and she meant it as Renée was a very, very pretty woman, and the fact that she asked to watch gave Diana a whole new light on her. Renée was gracious and diplomatic and gone within a minute or two with a kiss on both their soft cheeks.

Already they were lost again in intimate conversation. "By my kiss, can you surmise if I belong in the intermediate or advanced educational class you offered earlier?" Diana questioned Margo who was wondering what Diana did for a living while she pulled her closer to her.

"We'll see . . . we have further tests for you to take my well endowed friend," Margo answered, lost in the feeling of Diana's generous breasts against hers.

"I warn you that my expectations are high . . . I expect to be taught something tonight that I don't already know."

"Rest assured," Margo replied staring confidently into Diana's eyes, "you won't leave disappointed, and you will leave more highly educated."

"I await my degree," Diana whispered before engaging Margo in another wild kiss.

Diana grew more certain of one thing: the mystery hostess was not coming to this party. She gave up her curiosity, replacing it with the pleasure of Margo that now made itself available.

The two made their way to a massive tree, one of many, to talk, to kiss, to touch, to search and to enjoy. Margo was, as Diana was, sure and in control. They both wanted things from one another; they both took. This last embrace was lovely as it found Diana deep in the throes of a kiss, her hands making their way everywhere, slowly, softly on Margo's body, and with no resistance from Margo, they were free to roam.

Another body miraculously was up against Diana's back, arms around her, lips from behind close to her ear. It was a tall woman that whispered to her from behind. Whispered with a sexy voice:

"I will let this woman Margo have you. Just for tonight. You're not to make a habit of this, doll."

The voice stopped; the body disengaged. It was Jade's voice, Diana thought as she turned and looked. It was the back of the woman she saw walking away from her, Jade's back.

"My Lord, who was that woman?" Margo asked not being able to take her eyes off of Jade.

"Jade Desmonde, my Executive Assistant at the University," replied Diana turning back to Margo, not knowing what to make of what Jade had done, had said.

"You must have made her quite an offer—!"

"That's precisely what puzzles me . . . professionally, I had little room to move with regards to what I could offer her for the position. She settled for crumbs," Diana said shaking her head, bewildered to this day about Jade's commitment to her job, but not about her feelings about her. They were all too clear.

"She must want something?"

"That's what worries me, Margo." That was all that was said about Jade for the rest of the evening, as these two had barely enough time to get to know one another, let alone anyone else.

From the other side of the backyard came, "I welcome you all, dear friends and ex-lovers," from a woman who looked as if she should be named Olga or Frauline Svetlana, a large, hefty, Swedish woman with a laughing temperament and massive breasts, "to the event that I once took part in when I was twenty years younger!"

She lifted the garden hose in her right hand, above her head and some of the audience cheered as they moved in closer. The floodlights from atop the house made visibility easy, the alcohol made their response rousing, and Svetlana made this event a memorable one.

The Frauline accepted the cheering with a large grin, knowing they were cheering for the upcoming event, and not her. She didn't care as she was big, and drunk and having a great old time.

"I have the grand honor of being your MC for what I know will be a worthwhile part of your evening's entertainment."

Even the women inside the house singing together, in surprisingly good harmony, stopped to come outdoors. "For our viewing pleasure . . .," Diana added to Margo, putting her arm around her shoulder as they both stood listening to Olga's booming voice.

Monica and Whitney joined them. "Well, well, well, Professor Hunter," Monica taunted, "instructing some eager student, no doubt?"

Diana laughed and put her hand through Monica's hair playfully, saying, "I see we are a bit cocky tonight, Monica. Has Whitney been expanding your ego with flattery?"

After the introductions were made, Diana leaned over to Whitney kissing her on the cheek and telling her how happy she was to see her. Sincerely.

"Whitney has been complimentary to me, but it was all true. I do believe I am as good as she's been telling me that I am." It was clear that Monica was tipsy; that Whitney was blushing.

From Whitney: "We understand that you don't know who threw this party either?"

"And I can honestly say that right at this moment I don't care."

"Professor, is it?" ventured Margo, teasing.

"Yes, in the company of two esteemed colleagues."

Monica appreciated that reference to her as an equal, and returned the favor with, "A professor, a lecturer, a writer, a good friend, and rumor has it, a lady killer."

"Monica!" Whitney exclaimed.

"Don't chastise her Whitney, what can one expect from a twenty-five year old?"

"A lot! . . . And don't even think of patronizing me tonight, Miss Hunter."

"Teasing, Monica, teasing not patronizing . . . and we see that alcohol makes you a touch more sensitive than usual."

"It does . . . that and the fact that I had a very hard week. I just don't seem to have enough time in a day to do what I need to do for you, not to mention for the other professors."

"I am beginning to believe that being granted a research fellowship is not the blessing it is—"

"Blessing? Whitney it's a curse, and don't let anyone tell you otherwise."

Margo asked her, "Do you have any vacation time coming your way? You sound like you could use it."

"In a few weeks, as a matter of fact," she replied, pulling Whitney closer to her, "Whitney and I are going to pay a visit to Mexico."

Whitney and Monica going away on vacation. It seemed like Diana was learning new things about many women tonight. Whitney gay. Oh my. "For how long?" she asked.

"Until Whitney grows tired of me—"

"For one week," Whitney answered.

"Rumor also has it that we are about to have a wet tee-shirt contest," Monica laughed.

"I didn't know that women did such things," rumbled Whitney trying to be amused.

"Women are surprising creatures," Margo smiled to Whitney throwing her an inappropriate but nonetheless hot wink.

"Don't worry, dear, I won't let them force you into participating," Monica joked and lifted Whitney's hand to kiss it.

"Don't let Whitney out of your sight," advised Diana to Monica, who by this time was growing more interested in the contest than the conversation, and took Whitney by the hand to watch.

"Have fun, ladies," Diana said to them, as they headed towards the center of excitement.

Diana was Margo's center of excitement this evening. They preferred their isolation amidst the gathering of what now looked to be more like two hundred women. A public privacy they both relished.

"It is your applause," boomed Svetlana, "that will decide the outcome, the winner. The stakes are high so decide carefully before clapping," instructed the larger-than-life referee.

There were four girls in the center of the action. Four girls no more than twenty-two years old stood in tee shirts and panties and high heels awaiting the water and the cheering.

"All in good fun," Margo whispered nuzzling her lips in Diana's neck as they stood watching.

Frauline Svetlana loosened the nozzle of the hose, and the slow spray of water began streaming out. The Swede was a straight shot, steady hands moving the stream of water from the top of the girls' shirts to the bottom of their panties, and as expected the audience went wild with excitement. It was the last thing anyone expected tonight, which is what made the turnout for it so successful.

The contestants didn't look any worse for the wear after the sixty second controlled downpour. The water was shut off and the girls stood proudly, straight-backed, breasts jutting out. Audience appraising, delighting.

Who could have asked for a more stunning sight: the girls standing, soaked, hand-in-hand-in-hand, glistening with droplets of water rolling down their thighs into small puddles beneath them on the grass. Dripping wet, every nuance outlined, every curve of their bodies highlighted, every swelling enunciated, every nipple erect.

Margo said, "Now, don't you just want to go up and cup your hands around that wet blond woman's breasts?" It was Babs! and Diana laughed aloud. The sweet, innocent southern girl had put one over on her. She decided to cheer the loudest for her.

"It is a momentous event we are witnessing here, tonight," broadcasted the Frauline, as she too was examining the bodies of the contestants, willing to sleep with any one of them. "And now comes the difficult part—choosing."

And from a woman in the audience: "—That's always the hard part!!" Followed by peals of laughter from the group.

"So choose, ladies, before our contestants catch a chill. Who is it to be?"

The Frauline moved to stand behind the first woman to her right and put her hands on the woman's shoulders. "Contestant #1," and followed by lots of cheering and noise-making which could be heard by the neighbors who were at this minute wondering what in the hell was going on next door. Then #2, #3 and #4, Babs, Diana's favorite.

The audience was far from sober, and they roared, roared with approval as Babs *was* blond, and had a most developed body and an excrutiatingly fabulous pair of breasts. The audience gave a loud voice to their choice.

"You like that young one, no?" referring to Babs, Margo asked. And Margo divulged that she was her choice too, and later walking back into the house after the spectacle was over, Diana explained how it was that she came to meet with Babs earlier that evening.

Slowly the party of women made their way into the air conditioned coolness inside the house. To recline with one another, and talk about things they felt important at the time. Few remained outside by the pool, by the scattered tables, rocks, trees.

And inside, like returning gladiators, the women of the competition were surrounded. They were heralded by almost everyone for their spunk, getting offers to be toweled down dry, to have drinks brought to them. These girls knew what they were doing participating in the contest as they did.

Two couples occupied the sofa, the threesome of Sarah, Vivienne and Babs had the floor by the fireplace, and everywhere you turned there were women talking, meeting, tempting, teasing, necking, by the door, in the hallway, certainly in the various bed/bathrooms, and even in the kitchen where women labored to keep up with the demand for more wine, more this, more that. More, more, more. Everyone was busy attending to something or other, as the hostess, it seemed, had the night off.

Diana and Margo left the party at three for their private tutoring session, with everyone thanking Diana for the party. They simply had to thank someone.

The woman across the street in the gray convertible Mercedes started her engine, gave one long cool easy smile towards the teak door now closing behind Diana and Margo, who were leaving, and was off.

When my senses
are set afire
with a creative
burst of wild,
flaming energy,
it makes me feel
like this is what
I was born for.

The evening was Thursday. The auditorium was filled. The topic was "Living." The audience already well aware that "Living" hardly began to explain what they were about to hear. It was a gross understatement. The speaker, by the way, was Diana Hunter.

She was introduced with the usual polite accolades, stiff compliments, dry anecdotes and uncomfortable formalities. All were expected.

The excitement grew in Diana, as this was her first lecture to Scottsdale University's packed, eight hundred strong, audience since she arrived to take on her duties as lecturer/honorary Professor. The first time is always the scariest, she counseled herself. Relax, relax, relax girl was her silent mantra.

She saw familiar faces in the sea of faces in front of her; Jade, Whitney, Monica, Maria and so many of her students hopefully here to learn, if not cheer her on. None of the faces put her any more at ease, while the introductions droned on. Butterflies made their clandestine way into her stomach as Diana mantrad on.

Then she heard her name called and the applause. God knows she loved that applause. And her circuits switched to "On," all of them, and instinctively she rose and approached center stage to claim her space. She carried herself like a woman who had no doubts about her ability to please eight hundred people. Her bearing confident, strong, feminine.

"I can only hope," she began from memory, as she was not one to be saddled with notes on stage, "that you are all of age—," small sounds of laughter emerged from the mass of bodies, "—because I'll be using some strong language tonight." The faculty members shifted uneasily in their seats. "Words like love, happiness, coping, growth, pain, courage and change." Already the laughter and applause rose to greet her, a good match for her increasing energy. And she was off, doing what she did best, and even better tonight than she had previously, much to no one's surprise.

"If they *aren't* dirty words, then why hadn't I been introduced to them as a child, or a student, or a citizen of the United States? Notice how few people talk about the pain of living, the struggle of growing, the labor of love involved in giving birth to ourselves?"

"How many of you," and she added sarcastically, "and I want *names*, are here tonight because your professors required you to attend?" Diana waited and no hand raised. "For goodness sakes, raise those shy little hands and let me see what we're dealing with here tonight!" Still no hands. "All right, Faculty, I want you to close your eyes, and I mean close them—gentleman in the back row with the red shirt, that includes you!—" and she was interrupted by the flood of dozens and dozens of raised hands, then laughter, then applause.

Diana, too, laughed and applauded the courageous students. Lifting her index finger as an angry parent might she warned the faculty, "Now open your eyes and mark my words: Never, ever, ever ask any student to attend my talk again unless they come soliciting your advice. Then, and only then, tell them that it will be the best they'll ever hear and if they want to come, tell them to come . . . tell them, in fact, that it will be Fabulous!" Laughter. Humor has a way of working almost as well as alcohol in lowering inhibitions and defenses.

"In all sincerity, no one should be in this room unless they choose to, want to—want to hear what I have to say. And if that means only three people show up then those three, willing to learn and change, will learn and change. Hear me . . . No one can be forced to change what they are not ready to change, especially if what they are battling with is giving up a negative obstacle in their path to growth. The more negative the obstacle is, the more hold it has on them; the longer they've been acting counterproductively, the more familiar this behavior is to them and the scarier it becomes to let it go. The familiar, even if it is no longer working in their favor in their lives, is preferable to the unknown. So I say leave them alone; might doesn't make right; change can't be forced. We all know that we hear what we want to hear, and grow only when we are ready to, and change only when we open our hearts in readiness for it, and not one single solitary second before."

"We travel, every one of us, at our own pace. My speed of growing is different than yours. I can't expect you to be ready to change just because I am. I must keep the focus on myself, leave you alone, and," she articulated slowly, "*mind my own business!*"

"And when you feel the urge, or get the itch to change someone in your life, to change them, for what you consider to be the better—stop yourself. Get a hold of yourself, refocus your energies, and let the fixing begin with YOU!"

The audience was identifying with her already, for how many times had they tried to fix their spouses, their friends, their parents, their lovers for 'their own good?' The group found it easy to hear Diana's message—her method of excited rise and fall delivery, her sharp ability to articulate, to arouse, to excite and stir up strangers, was uncanny. Let her loose in an audience, and give her a bit of time and she would 'have' them. She loved talking to groups, and it showed. Each person felt as if she was talking directly to them, that's how effectively she used eye-contact. Her enthusiasm was contagious, her voice melodic, her body language animated but relaxed. Her love of the topic consummate and evident.

"So understand that I am talking to you about changing only yourselves, fixing yourselves. Fine tuning begins at home," she said pointing at herself. "With that in mind, let's take a look at the first dirty word: Happiness.

"Never ask someone you don't know intimately, if they are happy. Ask them how they are doing or what's new, but never if they are happy." She paused to let the simple statement sink in, and pulling the mike from its base on the lecturn, took it out to center stage with her, full front facing the audience. No barriers. "Ask a Yes or No question, but never 'Are You Happy?' What I get when I ask, varies: I get a silent response, followed by staring, followed by some mumbling about catching them off guard, and then questions from them like 'What do you mean by happy?' " She paused, letting the laughter subside. "Or I get, 'You mean happy now, or in general?' they say. Or, 'Happy? Happy with reference to what?' Then they shuffle their feet, and maybe answer with a 'Yes, but . . .' or a 'Maybe, but . . .'

"Now I ask you," she said strongly, "Why is happiness such a dirty word to people? Where in our lives did we learn not to seek out happiness with all our hearts, and not to talk about it with others? Who told us that we shouldn't be pursuing happiness, assiduously chasing it down until we captured and claimed it? Someone," she said lowering her voice, coloring it ominously, "is spreading vicious myths about happiness. And personally I'd like to meet this malcontent and set him or her straight." Ending the sentence with an upbeat to meet the howls of approval and whistles, followed by discussions amongst the audience members.

"I say that this culture of ours looks down on the poor souls who spend their time sharing their joy and abundant happiness with others, for they are usually met with 'Oh, goodness, control yourself,' or 'I'm glad you're happy, now calm down because you're embarrassing me!' These are the subtle messages we get throughout our lives from people who are letting us know that somehow it is unacceptable to be *that* happy in mixed company. Happiness isn't on people's priority list. 'Happy? Well, I have more important things to do in life than worry about being happy!" Diana mimicked. "Do you know that three quarters of the people I have met in my life were not happy, and further, haven't the slightest notion of how to get there!? Astonishing!

"Why on earth is it acceptable to talk freely about your problems, your troubles, your bad situations, your despair, but not your joy, or your rapture, or your glee? Why can we draw up a list of our liabilities in a quarter of an hour, and then have to spend a quarter of our lives creating a list of our assets? Knowing what you are good at, what makes you feel good about yourself, what your strengths are, should be forefront in your mind. In our culture talking openly about your skills, your strong points, is equated with bragging. Why is that?

"Something, somewhere along the line, has gone awry, and by god we're going to get to the bottom of this if it takes us all night!" Her voice rang out reaching a crescendo talking right over the applause. She laughed with the audience; her passion, her commitment to her own message propelling her on.

And this was the tone of the evening with Diana connecting with her audience, seemingly one on one. Telling them never to apologize for being happy, telling them to share it, talk about it, think about it, pursue it. She talked about how to start your day with a positive attitude, setting aside time in the morning to affix your priorities firmly in your mind before leaving the house. She discussed the how-to's of living one day at a time and living in the present moment instead of in the past or future. She talked about focusing on the things in your life that you are grateful for, and maintaining a grateful heart throughout the day. She spoke on topics ranging from getting out of your self-centered self and helping others, to the fear of change, and ways to overcome that fear.

She moved fluidly from topic to topic, point to point, drawing the audience in, questioning them, working with them, making them feel as if they, not her, were the most integral part of the lecture. She spoke to each of them personally with her eyes, with her tone of voice which was conversational and full of life. She was just like them, talking to them as equals. She moved, no, swept across the stage with a levity and buoyancy. She used humor well, slowly, slowly utilizing her craft to reach them, touch them, convince them that hers was the better way of living.

She knew what she was talking about—no one could deny that. She had lived through this way of life, starting the year after Christina left her. She'd been to the bottom, and then worked her way up to a way of life that shone with dignity and grace that bespoke well of spirituality and goodness that starts from within and radiates outward to others. But it always starts from within.

Two and a half hours later she was through. Her dress, damp from the workout, from the thrill of passing the message along to such a welcoming crowd, clung to her body. By the sound of the applause, she concluded that she had been successful. It took almost another hour to talk with all the people who wanted to come up to her, talk to her, thank her. Scottsdale U. had itself a celebrity, and the faculty nodded to themselves that 'Yes, she was worth the money they must have paid to get her here.'

Diana had planted the seeds, and as to how many of the audience members would begin to change their lives was hard to say. She would hear about people's quests, students and faculty alike, in letters, in phone calls, in notes that were always left for her after a speech. It was a slow process, this change business, but there would be a strong handful in the audience who would take on the challenge she put forth tonight. Her work was done for now.

Jade was waiting for her in the hallway outside the auditorium. They stood facing one another at 11:45 p.m.

"My congratulations to you, Boss, on a superb presentation."

"We might launch a revolution here in Scottsdale," Diana laughed, taking Jade's hands in her own, and continuing, "Thanks for your help and support. I was pleased to see you could make it. Pleased to find you rooting for me."

"Heart and soul. You had a lot of fine things to say and I know I wasn't the only one who needed to hear them. Tonight, Miss Hunter, it was I who had much learning to do from you," referring back to their initial encounter, the interview.

"Good. Now I don't have to be so insecure anymore." Diana smiled, and reluctantly pulled her hands from Jade's, their hands having rested too naturally in one another's.

"The sound system was flawless," Jade said taking refuge in her Executive Assistant role, "and we got every word on tape."

"Finally . . . Immortality!" They both moved towards the door.

There was no question that there was something going on between these two women, you could see it, but each maintained control. Reserved, cautious control, regardless of how intense the pull was. Each thought the other beautiful and desirable, and for the first time that entire evening, Diana grew disquieted.

Jade, reserved but relaxed, moved forward. "A drink, perhaps, in celebration?"

This kind of offer Diana would never have refused from a woman of Jade's looks and repute. She wanted to very badly. Oh, what to do, what to do?

Diana moved closer to the door, as the janitor had been eyeing them with an 'I want to go home now' look. They both complied and moved out of his way, out of the building. Jade walked Diana to her car, and they stood there, Diana not knowing yet what the right thing to do was. She was attracted to Jade, always had been, which is what made their working relationship so pleasurable. But what would the repercussions be? What if they began an affair? A relationship? The handwriting for them already on the wall for some time now, however silent they both were on the topic.

Thrilled with the high of performing and the advances of Jade, and never one to turn down an attractive offer, she leaned back against her car and said, "I can't, Jade . . . drinks I mean. I . . . better not."

And Jade knew what she meant. And this moment that found them in the dark, alone, staring hard and fast at one another, unable to do otherwise, the electricity sparking between them would lead a passerby to assume that they already were lovers.

"Understood," is all Jade said, because they both completely understood the situation, and both knew that with time and effort, change was not impossible. After all, Diana had spent the last couple of hours talking about just that topic—change.

"Oh, to just touch you once, Miss Hunter."

"Don't I know, Jade. How often thoughts of us together, damp and yet to come, have come to my mind."

Jade moved two inches closer to the woman she would have as her lover one day: "It will be that way with us. We won't be able to wait much longer."

"I already can't."

"Good, Miss Hunter, relent. It will be a decision you will never regret."

"This I already know, Jade. My body is already yours. It's only a matter of time—"

"Until I claim it."

"You've been easy with me until now . . . I'm afraid that it will take your being rough for me to give in."

Visions of Jade taking her, in the truest sense of the word, stirred her. She could easily lean into Jade and kiss her, stroke her hands along the sides of this woman who excited her so. To have her, to be next to her, to be inside of her.

How wet they both were now. They had achieved the 'damp,' and the 'coming' part was yet to come for them. They held fast to Diana's image of them together that way.

They stood still; their bodies whispering things to one another. Sweet things. Hot things. Dirty things.

They parted friends. Each sitting in her dark parked car long after pulling into her driveway, at her respective home, thinking.

Sunrise
is miles away.
I decide to try
and outrun it.
I am exhausted
and my canteen
is empty.

Destiny had its way again. As always. Coming as no surprise to anyone but the participants who are always eternally too close to focus clearly, too close to gain the necessary perspective in time to change its course.

Since the wedding, and subsequent welding, of Whitney to Harold Stillwell, Whitney secreted the hermetically-sealed jeweled box harboring her one dark truth deep down inside of herself. In fear-filled nights she would find herself awake sweating, and not surprised by it, she'd push the truth down even further into the curtained inaccessible recesses, just in case. To be sure. The guarded secret still enveloped in the thick black cloak of denial screamed out to her from the first night Whitney consummated her wedding vows. Shocked at the lie, it screamed to her to listen.

The screaming on this particular night persisted. So did Whitney's tenacity. She would not listen—but she no longer had the denial to fortify herself with against it. Her strongest armament, her impenetrable shield, was gone.

The images of Monica, the sensations of the slow hands, the soft voice, the eyes that looked into her, deep into her knowing what she was and what she wanted. The evening in her room, their vacation, the loving that went from night to day to night. The risk, its consequences: oh, the power it held over her now.

Maybe she might still be able to hold on, from day to day to deny who she was, what Monica meant to her. And from night to night she could fight not to listen. She couldn't afford to listen. It was a matter of survival. Her internal listening mechanisms must be held in abeyance. She would build up her denial system again, it would help her not to listen. Not listening was key in maintaining her too shear semblance of sanity. And the screaming persisted.

Being a woman who loved women, being a woman who had loved a woman, and then pretending to be a man-loving woman was her full-time profession. It required her total attention for executing the nuances of behavior appropriate to the persona. The relentless daily dress rehearsals sucked the humor from her. They required exacting detail work. Her energy was being dissipated. Her anemic soul tried to rebel. By then it was already too late.

She was left languishing with sorrowful eyes and a void in her heart so vast it was questionable as to whether, even under the most perfect circumstances, she could ever be revived. She was ausgespielt. Played out when she met Monica; when she gave in to Monica. And the screaming persisted.

That day, when no power on earth could infuse her with the strength to maintain her indefatigable denial of her sequestered truth, she slept with Monica. Even though she had taken out insurance—Harold—his presence serving as a safety buffer between herself and her self, giving her the needed confidence to rest easy with this artificial reinforcement, even this was not more powerful than the Truth that she ingeniously suppressed.

Would that someone had come to her, shaken her, awakened her to move on, try again, press forward. Live!

Whitney's living was aborted after the Allisone incident. She parted her legs obediently for Harold, sucking his cock on request, masturbating in private when he fell fast to sleep after obtaining his satisfaction. She was a good wife. Frustrated, frightened, frantic, repressed. How much longer could this go on. The facts of her life becoming obscured by the fiction. She was confused now, losing her grip on the needed denial, trying desperately to avoid the Truth. Her femaleness replaced by bitterness. And the screaming inside her persisted.

The power of denial overwhelmed by the power of a woman forced the hand that held the cards: a hairline crack on the inside mirror of her soul was growing now at breakneck speed. Like tiny rivers, new cracks sprung up spontaneously, unspied initially, and soon close to the point of all the cracks connecting, close to shattering, close to the point of seeing the Truth, admitting it, following it she remembered why she had taken the Oath. Then she heard it, a distant cry, not screaming now, but a piercing sorrowful wail almost. She allowed herself to drift cautiously towards its call. Then, ambivalence. Trepidation. Her prayers for the strength not to listen to it went unanswered tonight. She had her chance, she took the risk with Monica, she was alone with it all tonight. The distant cry turned to a voice then to voices: mellifluous choral voices. She heard them as she vacillated atop that precipice of known and unknown, fact and fiction, sanity and insanity. "Is this not insane to listen to choral voices chanting inside of my own head?"

Her sanity lay with living the lie or maybe accepting the truth, but the truth would mean falling in love, which she already had, and that would mean devastation as her time with Allisone had taught her so well. Or maybe it lay with funneling all of her energy into denial, living in denial again. This was not a moment for maybe's. She grasped the bedsheet in her fists hoping to just lay still, not decide anything, decide tomorrow or later, but not do anything now when everything inside her was spinning, was clouded and was calling to her. Nothing called more seductively than these angelic voices that would lead her to the Truth she had pushed down beneath the weight of Harold, the pain of Allisone. Monica brought her to this but she couldn't blame her. "Not her, but me," she knew, "it's me. I am a coward. I let Monica stir the screaming in me, stir the chorus from its slumber, I wanted her to."

She drew nearer to the voices despite herself, against her will. Her will already abraded down to its core: frayed, sore, useless. As she prayed to stay frozen, nearer still she moved, the golden millisonant tones beckoning. There was danger in the voices of Truth, danger with the man sleeping next to her, danger with the woman who loved her but was not in love with her. All she had to do to make it through this night was remain perfectly motionless, there was no danger in that, but there was no one to help her, to hold her still through this night.

Nearer still she moved, and with it came the forgetting as to why it was she was so afraid of these voices for so long a time. They sang to her, as the screaming that persisted was now silenced. Perfect pitch harmony, she made out, now that she was closer to them, almost able to hear the words. The words but a breath away from intelligible, slipping nearer to the source of the siren song seductive music. At last, at long, long last close enough to the source of her secret Truth.

She uncovered it. Denial gone. She was alone with it. The voices crystallized, the words whispers. The source finally had the audience with her that it had persistently screamed out for night after laborious night. It sounded like a sweet imperceptible hum that could only be felt, not really heard. She lay perspiring. Knowing now everything: having heard the truth, felt it, tasted it even.

She lay still for a long enough time to forgive herself. To make amends to herself. To decide, now that everything was exposed, what she must do as her self-imposed imprisonment had finally come to an end.

The screaming persisted. Harold Stillwell's scream persisted for a full sixty seconds. He was genuinely shattered—thus he and his wife, unbeknownst to him, had for the very first time something in common.

The tears came instantly. The telephone call to the hospital and then to his parents put minutes between him and finding Whitney's note. Still the scholarly penmanship, she wrote:

> As a child I was given a creed to live by: Life is meant
> to search for God, Time is meant to find Love.
> The former I was too spiritually lost to find, the latter,
> too frightened. I am overwhelmed by my failures.

When the ambulance arrived, Harold was still torn, hurt, broken, confused over the questions that plagued him regarding Whitney's note: "Why," he asked himself over and over, "didn't she write Dear Harold and sign it Love, Whitney?" "Why," he droned, "didn't she write something loving, something to me, to me . . . something reassuring?" Needing her approval even now. "Why didn't she say she loved me, or anything about our time together?" he repeated over and over sobbing and blowing his nose.

Little time transpired between his preoccupation with the questions, to the exclusion of taking one last look at his wife before she was wisked away, and his embarrassment. He was standing in the den humiliated by her obvious lack of affection, and the thought of his colleagues' judgmental condescending stares when they read the note. Paralyzed with fear at the thought of now more lack of acceptance, enraged at the rejection by his friends that he foresaw, he crumbled Whitney's note and flushed it down the toilet.

The note published in the late edition of the University newspaper read quite differently. The typewriter disguised the real identity of the author: it was penned Whitney, written by Harold. It read:

> Dearest Harold,
>
> It is my love for you, for my career and my civic duties
> that I write to explain my drastic action. My deep sense of
> loss over my brother's death pierced me so deeply that I
> never recovered. His loss is a constant ache that consumes
> me. I have only enough energy to end my life and join him.
> Accompany him in his walk into eternity. Maybe I can help
> him. Maybe I can help myself.
>
> May God delight in the academic gifts I have distributed
> in this life, and the loving gifts you and I shared in each

loving moment of our wedded life. May God forgive me
my one weakness.

Forever My Love,
Whitney

If it is inevitable,
it will come.
You have no say in it
anymore.
You have already had it.

"It seems that I want you more than I am willing to admit . . . but
I'll not allow it to begin."

"It has already begun, Miss Hunter."

"Then I will not allow it to materialize." Diana was adamant.

This was growing frustrating for Jade. "Don't you see that not acting out our feelings towards one another doesn't negate the fact that it
exists between us." How many conversations like this would they have
to have?

Diana stood up, and poured another cup of tea for herself and Jade.
Waiting on Jade this way appealed to her immensely. She had an urge
to get down on her knees in front of Jade and lay her head on her lap.
Jade wanted that, and more.

Diana started, "It's your face, more and more, I see at night when I
lay down to sleep." Christ, what should she do? She honestly didn't
know.

"Good."

"It's your eyes that follow me on my walks in the park to sort things
out. Sometimes, I just *refuse* to accept the inevitable."

110

"Then you've got your work cut out for you, Miss Hunter."

"Then I think it's time for you to leave tonight before anything more is said."

"It will not be easier if I leave tonight." Jade was right.

"It will be safer—"

"To be sure, but ultimately less satisfying."

Diana sounded angry: "Jade, I will not have this thing with you. I will not so much as touch you for fear of it happening. It will be overpowering."

"It will be even more than that," Jade whispered.

"I know, I know it will."

Jade leaned towards the object of her desire. "Then you must also know that it is what you have been waiting for. It is the only next step for you to take."

"I don't choose to."

"You have little choice in the matter."

"I have all the choice!"

It was Jade's turn to sound angry, "Then tell your feet that, Miss Hunter, as they have already begun moving forward without your consent. I would not be here—I dare say I would not have been hired—if you were not ready for me." Everything Jade was saying was the truth, in all of its unpalatable glory.

Diana was a woman of convictions. She was determined. She had made up her mind. She would not veer far away from it. But the pull of Jade was a bit stronger. Strong enough to make her reconsider. She couldn't help herself. She was being pulled forward despite herself. She had met her match.

And the heat between Diana Hunter's thighs gave name to itself and demanded equal time, and nothing short of satisfaction would do.

"I want you more than any woman I have met in the last six years of my life," Jade said slowly.

"And I you, Miss Desmonde, and I you." Therein, lay the dilemma.

It was an extremely hot half hour that followed their last words to one another. Diana sat at her desk, Jade the couch, and like that they sat without a word and stared deeply into the eyes of the woman that they fantasized about all too often. The tea went cold. Their hearts racing at the thought of what it would be like with the other. Just the look—no words—that spoke articulately of their desire.

Oh, to walk over to Jade, and sit beside her on the couch, Diana was thinking, then to hold her, then to kiss her, then to have her. What keeps me away from her? What keeps me back? Her very body convulsed with a "Yes," and she remained motionless. And, so too, Jade, with parallel thoughts barely moved in that time.

This silent speaking they had grown accustomed to was as powerful as their first kiss might have been. They would never know this for certain tonight, these two women in heat, as they parted company in this heart-yearning, groin-aching, heat-rising silent way.

I rest easy,
reassured,
in the sound
of your voice.
It will have to do.

Diana heard all about it within the hour. The suicide note was barely even published, out on the campus stands, when Jade informed her that Whitney had taken her life. Her first call went to Harold: condolences. Her second, more important, call was placed to Monica. That's why Monica was sitting on the couch with her in the middle of the afternoon, drink in hand. Diana knew that she would need to talk, to be talked to.

Monica had already planned her week out: she was going to throw herself into her work with a vengeance until the shock of Whitney's death wore off, and then, only then would she attempt to deal with, understand it. The suicide note was so unlike Whitney, and to the campus rumor rag no less—this whole situation would take some figuring out.

Diana put a comforting arm around Monica, and hugged her closer, "What is a woman to say at a time like this that won't sound pat, or worse, irritating?"

"Nothing I suppose," Monica said, allowing her grief to surface. "I'm not very good at this myself."

Diana drew her closer. "Were you in love with her?"

"No." A definitive 'no' from Monica. "We barely had time to fall in love . . . if anything, we were deep in the throes of lust." After a moment, lost in thought, Monica continued, ". . . there was that."

"What, honey?"

"There was the vacation we had together in Mexico . . . it was . . ." again trailing off in thought and returning, ". . . and she never let on that whole time about what she planned to do when we returned."

"Maybe she herself didn't know, Monica."

"But something like that you think about, you plan, don't you?"

"Sometimes yes, sometimes no. Maybe something happened when she returned home. Do you think—with Harold?"

"Diana, I don't know what to think after this. If she had just said something, maybe I could have—"

"Don't even start that kind of thinking. It won't lead you anywhere. If she did say something, what could you have done? Either she didn't know at the time or . . ." Diana finished the sentence privately, or the vacation with you touched off in her things she couldn't accept. Diana proceeded cautiously, "Was Whitney in love with you?"

"I don't know, or at least I don't think so."

"And she wasn't, I would venture to guess, in love with her husband. Then other than her work—wait a minute, one more question—was she in love with somebody that we don't know about?" Diana probed.

"She talked about someone to me, in confidence, that she was in love with for something like nine years. Before she moved to Arizona."

"Making sense . . . a woman, possibly, Monica?"

"Yes."

"What happened, Monica?"

Monica raised her finger to her lips. "In confidence, Diana."

It didn't have to be said as it fit right into Diana's initial theory about Whitney. She continued, "Then she moves to Arizona, and hooks up with Harold Stillwell—"

"Really . . ."

"I know, don't say it! . . . Marries him on the rebound . . . and then . . . you."

"I already knew all this."

"Good girl, Monica, then at least you know more than you think. She married Harold on the rebound from this other woman, and maybe on the rebound from her feelings about—"

"Other women. You're right. I think I was the first woman she'd been with since Harold—"

"And it brought up for her all the old feelings about her old flame, yes . . . and about her lesbianism . . . and it probably scared her to death—"

"Literally. She didn't act like a scared woman when we were together . . . physically I mean."

"Probably not until she got back home, and had time to sort things out. And found that she couldn't."

Monica started crying. If she had only sensed something amiss, anything, maybe, no matter what Diana said, maybe she could have helped, could have stopped, or could have . . .

"Baby, baby," Diana whispered to Monica, gently rocking her, "don't do this to yourself."

"It's not just Whitney, Diana, it's not just that . . ." Diana waited for Monica to say what she had to say. The competent research assistant in her arms, capable to a fault at academia, and the strongest support system Diana had professionally at the University, aside from Jade, lay weeping her heart out in her arms. Diana's heart went out to her.

Monica whispered as much to herself as to Diana, "How many times am I going to have to be deserted by people in my life? First my parents—"

"Your parents left you, Monica?"

"Worse. My parents stayed, and made my childhood miserable. I always wondered if my real parents died when I was a baby and these two people claimed me. But why they did, I don't know, because they never liked me. They disliked their own, and only daughter. And this hits me in the same spot—being left behind, being—" and she fell into tears again for a lot of reasons.

Academia gave Monica many things, but love was not one of them. Diana's arms felt wonderful. With her head against Diana's shoulders, Monica was warm, safe, loved. It was not too much to ask in life, she thought, a safe and comforting woman to be with you, to love you. Because Diana was there, had always been there for her ever since they met at the University, her needs subtly began transferring to Diana. In her arms, for just tonight, Monica flashed. God knows, she didn't want to be alone tonight. Monica was a woman who had gotten quite used to living alone creatively. But she was at a loss to do it well tonight. This she knew in advance.

The weeping continued, mixed with feelings about Diana, and mixed with a sinking feeling of forever being alone in the world. I'm not a bad person, she was thinking, why should I end up so alone?

"Why am I so unlucky?" she asked Diana, who just hushed and hushed her.

They passed the better part of an hour this way, the two women. Strength seeped back into Monica, enough so that she was able to stand and assert that she was going to dive head-first right back into her work. For Diana. She would work her problems and feelings out later, but now she was going to do what she thought best—avoid the pain. Diana agreed, after trying to get her to take some time off instead of resorting to workaholism, but Monica had made up her mind. She told Diana that the results of the research that she'd been working on with Whitney's students would be ready by this evening. Late this evening, and that Diana could pick it up around midnight at her dormitory if she wanted. Diana assured her that she would, more to check in on Monica then pick up her work.

A hug, a long nurturing one, and each, not just Monica, sunk back deeply into their work after the "goodbyes" were said.

Diana hadn't slept now for almost two full days, but stopping now to rest would break her momentum, as the research was completed, the results in and the book readied to be written. This book consumed Diana, it would be her first major published work. The success she sought, the notoriety she took off after, was close at hand now, and stopping was out of the question. She was exhausted, and not about to stop now. Tearing through her work, she spent the entire rest of the day like this: a woman possessed.

Thick blood.
Cool fire.
One dark shadow only.
Unveil it.
Kiss me there
where it is most hot.

Diana was being perfectly honest with Monica at half past midnight when she told her that she was tired. "God, honey, either I am getting too old or my expectations of myself have become unrealistic, but I can't seem to keep up with the plans I've made for myself."

"Then lower them," Monica responded with the obvious.

"Don't give me solutions, Monica, give me sympathy!" Both were after comfort and sympathy tonight. It was good of Diana to come; it was time for her to go and attend to her own needs.

And wouldn't Monica have just loved to give her the sympathy she asked for. Here was Diana in all of her exhausted beauty asking Monica to do something she had most recently just begun to desire to do . . . give her gentle sympathy, loving strokes: long luxurious strokes up the sides of Diana's body and down the line of her back. This wasn't the time, but Monica's body was not adjusted to receiving discretion signals, as most of the time she did pretty much what she felt like doing. And now, she knew, with how tired and spent Diana was that Diana could be quite vulnerable to her charms. But that would be taking advantage of her. Well, Monica thought, worse things could happen . . .

And she let the desire for Diana pass through her. Dissipated, for the moment only, as she would have to think this one through. The research project had them working together almost daily: both delighted with the intelligent companionship, both learning much from the other. Their drinks at the end of each late night allowed Monica the opportunity to become much closer to Diana, sharing secrets with her, exchanging confidences, that one might think inappropriate with one's boss. Diana was less like a boss in the traditional sense and more like a good old friend. Their relationship meant a lot to Diana too, and she was the sorriest of all to see her work with Monica come to an end.

And now was the least propitious time of all for their bond to be aborted as Monica needed a friend, a loving friend to help her through the days and nights. She hadn't been in love with Whitney, but the pain of her loss, and now again the loss of Diana's company, was intense nonetheless.

"Look Diana, I've done all the research I am capable of doing for you, so you have no business being here wasting your time. Just think . . . no more marathon evenings together."

"I'll miss them—"

"I know, me too, Diana—"

"Miss Peters, I want you to swear to God that you will be in touch with me regularly. This is no excuse to bow out of my life. I mean it . . . swear."

It was Diana who took the lead in maintaining their contact. Diana! Monica swore with all her heart.

"As for you, Miss Hunter, do something pleasurable for yourself. Head back to your office, and relax. Take the night to sleep until you can't sleep anymore." Masturbate is what she had really wanted to say, but this discretion business kept her from talking that openly to her ex-boss, no matter how good their friendship was.

"You know, your advice will serve me better than your sympathy," said Diana tsk tsking the tiny hovel of a studio Monica chose to live in, "Okay, okay, I'm going."

And with that, Diana gathered up her sweater and research that Monica had compiled for her over the months, and her purse. Especially her purse: for within that leather carrier she had all the drugs she would need to approach the loving arms of unconsciousness tonight. A most key piece of luggage for tonight's journey . . . ah, sleep. After all, she had not allowed herself to sleep for some forty-six hours. And now, she was in the home stretch of getting this book, and all the subsequent speeches that would be borne from the book, ready for final drafts. Oh, the sweet feeling of exhaustion that follows the wild fury of productivity. And she would sleep like a baby tonight.

Monica walked her to the door, stopped, put her arms around Diana and gave her the most sympathetic, female-to-female hug that stirred in Diana what was always on the brink of being stirred.

"Mmmm, you do know more than just research, I see," Diana moaned, as vulnerable to Monica's charms right now as Monica was to hers. She could have slept standing like this.

Again, Monica let the moment pass. As it turned out, she was the strong one, the comforting one. It was her girlfriend that just tragically ended her life, and here she was protective of Diana.

"Listen to me, Miss Hunter, I want you to do just as I said and go right back to your office. Do what you have to do, and get into bed as quickly as possible. Take good care of yourself tonight. You hear me?"

Still with her arms around Monica, she whispered, "Yes, Monica, anything you say." And Diana lifted her head off Monica's shoulder, which took more of an effort than she anticipated, looked Monica in the eyes and said, "Your maternal instincts are quite appealing . . ."

Who knows, they both thought simultaneously. And Monica knew that the moment was now if she wanted it.

Monica took comfort in the fact that she knew where Diana would be for the rest of the evening if she so desired to pursue this thing. Monica was a nice girl, very nice, but maybe in this instance not *that* nice. She wanted Diana, and went the step further by adding that this was probably just the thing Diana needed tonight. Thinking that made her feel much better about her own desires.

Maybe it is just what I need, thought Diana as she gently pulled herself out of Monica's arms.

"Are you certain that you will be all right alone tonight, Monica?"

"And if I'm not certain, you will spend the night?" It was worth a shot, Monica thought.

"I'll keep in touch by phone every hour on the hour!"

"In that case, Diana . . . I'm certain. Go home. Straight to sleep."

"With pleasure, Monica. Call me in the a.m., and let me know how you are doing."

Diana opened the door, and lugged her sluggish body with her dragging feet towards her office, only a short five minute walk across campus. The thought of driving home was out of the question—too exhausted for that.

She was doing quite well avoiding distractions as the campus was empty. Until she bumped into Maria Lanning in the elevator. But this, to be sure, was a sweet distraction. Maria pushed the ninth floor button—Diana's office floor. Coincidence? At this time of night?

Diana surveyed Maria and asked, "Seeing anyone I know?" Smiling at the woman who was pretty even at this late hour of the night. A campus filled with workaholics, Diana thought.

"Could be," said Maria with the slightest hint of the devil in her eyes. Maria continued, "Seems like one of the professors left these—" looking down at the thick manuscript in her arms, "—in my office. Paid for it and everything, and just left it behind. Imagine!"

"Some people!" responded Diana with feigned exasperation. "As if you don't have better things to do with your time than run around returning work to its proper owners." Knowing full well that it was hers.

Knowing, too, that seeing Maria again was just what she had in mind at the time that she left it behind. And, unfortunately, now was not the time. She barely had the energy to make it to her office, let alone get down and wild with Maria. Damn, damn, damn, she thought as a night with Maria would be great fun.

They both exited the elevator, and made their way to Diana's office, with Diana in the lead. They passed Jade's desk, and sure enough there was the wonder worker still working. Diana was not surprised to see Jade, but she did marvel at this woman's stamina nonetheless . . .

"Do you ever stop, Miss Desmonde?"

"Not if I can help it, Miss Hunter. If I might be so bold as to mention that you set a poor example for me to follow." And Jade was right, and reached for her lit cigarette, and wondered who the woman with Diana was. And waited to be introduced.

"This is the ever competent Maria Lanning, who you should go directly to if you need any work done from the campus word processing center. She seems to be the only one who can and will do anything with a smile. She is marvelously competent." Maria took the compliment well, and smiled at the double entendres that abounded in Diana's short introduction.

The implications of Diana's comments did not get lost on Jade either. "I look forward to our working together," said Jade in all earnestness. And had Maria not been so caught up with getting on to the evening, she would have paid more attention to Jade, who being Jade, always deserved complete attention for she was some picture of a woman.

"As a matter of fact," Diana said to Jade, and if Maria were the type to fidget, which she was not, she would have been doing so now, "here is the rough draft of the manuscript. If you can make a copy for yourself, and leave me the original, I'd like you to review it and give me your thoughts. And I don't mean proof it, I mean critique it." She handed the thick thing to Jade.

"There is no hurry, Miss Desmonde, as I am about to go into my office and pass out until tomorrow anyway." This Diana said for Maria's information. Maria ignored it, and counted on her special talents to prevail tonight. Or at least she would give it her very, very best shot, as she was known to be quite a convincing woman when she set her mind to it.

Jade accepted the project. How could a woman so fine looking be so serious about work, wondered the woman of like principles?

"Goodnight, Miss Desmonde."

"Come in, Maria," Diana said and turned to go into her office.

Jade watched them both disappear into Diana's office, behind closed doors. "Well, well, well," thought Jade, and smiled, and dove right back into her work. Or so it seemed.

Diana literally fell on the couch which she knew held such promise for her tonight. She put her hand down on the spot next to her, and looked at Maria who was still standing. "Come," she said and extended her hand to Maria, who took it, and joined her, and kept right on holding her hand. "Let me give you the bad news first, Maria . . . we can't play tonight, doll, much as I, and I do, want to."

"Are you open for discussion?" asked Maria knowing that Diana was not just playing coy.

"No, I just don't think that I'm capable of anything tonight, or at least anything of any value to you."

Diana was overworked and overtired, and that was obvious even to Maria. So Maria decided to play her trump card early. "You know that I owe you one. And at that time I will be calling the shots, Diana."

And Diana said that she as much as expected that.

"My way," Maria added.

Diana agreed.

"When I choose."

"It's only fair," Diana responded and grew just the slightest bit excited as this woman laid out her ground rules.

"And if I wanted it badly enough to be tonight, it would be tonight." This Maria said with the utmost gravity. And she meant every word of it. As she took bondage and discipline more seriously than most.

"If you did, it would be tonight. I know—"

"What do you know, Miss Hunter?" she said seductively, leaning in towards Diana, "—tell me."

"I know . . . that any way you want me is the way I want to be had by you," she whispered.

"I've already chosen the way, but you will need more energy than you have now—"

"I could try," Diana said knowing that the experience with Maria would be worth mustering all her effort.

"You couldn't try hard enough for my satisfaction. And I expect to be satisfied."

"And I want you to be . . . and you will be . . . I mean it!" Diana implored, exciting Maria with coming attractions of her submissiveness and eagerness to please.

"I know you mean it," Maria said touching her fingertips to Diana's cheek, "and it is good that you will leave the details to me. You are right to do that."

Diana moved her lips to, right up to, barely touching Maria's ear and whispered, "I always want to do the right thing by you, Maria."

"You'll learn quickly."

"Only if you teach me patiently the first time." As if Diana had anything left to learn about controlling or submitting in this kind of encounter. Was this ever fun. For them both.

"I expect that you will require little training," Maria said, but two breaths away from kissing Diana.

"Thank you for your confidence in me," Diana said with a warm breath, and Maria wished the moment was now. But it wasn't.

"Then, lover, until the time that I call you—" and with that she licked her lips, lowered her head and kissed Diana on the neck first with her tongue then her teeth. Hard. Hard enough to force Diana to let out the quietest involuntary sound, and lay her head on Maria's shoulder yielding to the sucking lips, the mild pain, the strength that this woman had at this moment. And this was no act. And neither was Maria's kiss. And neither was the knock on the door.

Neither of them moved to stand as societal protocol would most certainly call for. If it was Jade at the door, she would wait to be called in. If it was someone else, Jade would get rid of the intruder—at this hour, really! Some people . . .

And if Maria stopped with the knock, Diana would have been most disappointed in her, because if Maria was going to take control, then Diana expected her to take Control. And she left the decision of answering or not answering the unlocked door to Maria. Maria laid her hands on the back of Diana's neck, and pulled her even closer, and Diana wrapped her arms around this woman who, if she really wanted to, which now seemed as if she might, could have Diana right now. And Diana's body moved with the woman's passionate and forceful body. Her legs spread just the smallest bit, and Diana's body was yielding of its own accord: "You may have me if you want, Maria . . ." Diana whispered, meaning it.

With this, Maria stopped, and stood before Diana realized what had happened. "Obviously you miss the point, Miss Hunter. When I want and how I want, I decide. Not you. Not this time."

"You're right . . . I'm sorry."

"I am disappointed, and not in a forgiving mood," Maria explained as she made her way directly to the door and opened it, seeing Jade on the other side of the door. She turned back quickly to Diana and told her that she would be hearing from her.

A "Soon," from Diana followed, but Maria had already left the office. Replaced, now, by Jade.

"Timing," Diana said while making a pitiful effort at rising from the couch, "is everything."

"I know," Jade replied. After a few seconds, she added, "I do my best to help you, which is what you pay me to do. No?"

"Yes," Diana glared. She was amused but still glared.

"And you do need your rest, Boss," she added flippantly, and exited.

Maria rode down the elevator anxious to make her way home to see what her roommate/part-time lover might be up for. Playing with Yvette was fun and it would do, but no one played as hard as Diana. And for one moment, a serious moment, Maria contemplated coming back to Diana later that evening to have her way with her. That might be just the thing. It might be just what she needs. I'll see what the evening brings, and then decide, she thought, as Diana has this one coming to her.

Shortly after, Jade's work noises ceased and the office lights were killed. Another workaholic gives herself a break. And finally, the ninth floor took the rest of the night off.

And now Diana was completely alone. She felt only the smallest pang of guilt for not taking Monica's advice to heart about avoiding distractions, and getting right to sleep. So much had already happened since she was with Monica in her studio. She was wondering how Monica was this first night with the news about Whitney. She wondered how long it would be until hallucinations from lack of sleep began. Forty-seven hours without sleep now.

She did the only thing she had the energy to do at this moment. She made her way to her purse, to the agents of the angels of sleep. She removed two capsules from her purse and made a straight unflinching line from where she stood by the couch to the bar. Two downs and rum chaser. That done, she returned to the couch, and removed her wide constricting leather belt. Then her heels—her feet mumbled something about being grateful—then lay down, and moaned a moan that only a woman post-labor could empathize with. Ah, it would soon begin. The descent . . .

Forty seven hours—she had extended herself beyond, excrutiatingly beyond, her capacity to manage. She lay at the limit and surrendered herself to the angel of unconsciousness, Finally. Her body and mind falling limply down, and further down. She lay dead still on the couch. With strength she did not possess she unhooked her stockings from her garters. Flushed with both the sheer joy of success and ravaged by the weight of exhaustion. Jubilant, elated and exhausted. Too hollow-eyed and weary to even fantasize one of her usual evening pre-sleep fantasies while masturbating. Too depleted to even fantasize without masturbating. She fell into, what seemed to be, the longest overdue sleep. The tender, efficient work of the barbituates had begun.

And now, as narrator, my work is done. So I will leave temporarily and let the rest of the evening's tale tell itself through Diana's closed eyes . . . only to return to you for the necessary clarifications . . . as is my job to do.

. . . the sensations are so pleasant that this was one dream I didn't want to wake from . . . (a fleeting thought forced its way into Diana's consciousness: was this really just a dream?) . . . this must be an apparition, it couldn't possibly be happening, and yet it felt real, it felt dreamy but real . . . I know the dizziness I feel is real and so is the swelling in my chest, but was this woman beside me before, and above me now real? . . . my eyes can't even focus clearly, and I'm doing the best I can to even keep them open, and the soft hands against my face I know aren't mine . . . I can feel the fingers against my cheek—too drugged to do anything but lay and feel them on me . . . and how did it begin? . . . did I just wake up, did this visitor just come in? . . . how long have these hands been touching me while I was asleep? . . . (unconscious) . . .

. . . the hands, fingertips caressing my temples so gently . . . is this real or what? . . . running the smooth fingers through my hair . . . and lips, lips with a kiss against my forehead . . . and warm breath . . . female breath, and I can't seem to move, much as I want to, or even see who it is or even stay completely conscious for more than a minute at most . . . this must be a dream, I would know if it was real . . . and I hear my name . . . purred in my ear, and it's not my voice, and it must be real . . . god, if I could only pray for the strength to keep my eyes open, At Least That! . . . if only I hadn't taken the drugs . . . (she could just kick herself for mixing the alcohol and drugs two short hours ago which felt like yesterday to her) . . . a soft hand slid slowly from my shoulder down to my breasts . . . oh, yes, if this is a dream let it happen, let it be . . . I won't even move for fear of disturbing it . . . the warm hand, palm soft, cupping my breasts and nothing in me stirs, too weighted down with exhaustion, with sleep . . . I want to drift to sleep . . .

. . . the heat woke me now, the heat of this woman's mouth on mine, the wet lips, the hot breath, and I don't even know if my lips are opening to hers . . . I want them to . . . I am trying to open my mouth, feel her tongue against mine and my body continues to push me to sleep again . . . she took my lips in her mouth, sucking them in too gently until I hear the sound . . . the sound from my throat . . . her hands on my breasts, and I wonder if it is the pounding of my heart that I'm hearing, or hers . . . or the door . . . and one hand stroking my breast and one on the back of my neck raising my head to meet hers . . . her lips on mine again . . . my body limp, limp, dead . . . my nipples sting with how erect they are, and her fingers pinching them, lips kissing, palm massaging, and I feel her tongue in my mouth, and a whimper—mine . . . and I'm convinced now it must be a dream, and the pull to sleep is strong . . . and I feel dizzy and faint . . . and the hands now moving down my belly, across my hips and down my thighs . . . I can hear my own breathing, panting almost, and have no strength to move to focus to even try to see if this was a dream or where I . . .

. . . moving into and out of the black divide of sleep . . . and in that time the woman was not with me but beside me, kneeling, I can almost see her figure kneeling on the floor beside me now . . . no, I don't think I can see anything really . . . my eyes refuse to focus, my body refuses to move, and I am commanding them to do it, and they don't . . . I'm dead weight . . . getting hot with the touch . . . my wilted body drugged beyond recognition is beginning to stir now, beside itself with the pleasure . . . oh, the hands that never stop moving, even as I sleep they must be moving . . . there are breasts against my cheek, and then there are burning hot lips sucking, and the artful hands sweeping across my body returning each time to the place between my thighs . . . and another groan must have emerged from me because I heard it when she touched me there . . . and I heard sounds that were not mine . . . I can't make out the words, just far away sounds of a voice that I'm positively sure wasn't mine . . . she was talking to me, must have been . . . and then the sounds stopped as I felt a tongue by my ear, in my ear . . . wet . . . chills already moving down my back with the sweeping hands, hot firebreath against my neck, and again the pressure between my legs . . . the ever searching, curious hands moving down my belly again and in two swift moves spreading my thighs apart . . . the cool rush of air welcome on my hot cunt . . . and still not enough to keep me conscious . . .

. . . the hand now I can feel lifting my skirt up and further up my thighs, and I can't feel the breathing but hear it by my ear . . and suddenly without warning I feel my panties being pulled down and off . . . and I want to say something . . . I lay willing myself to speak out something . . . with all my might I try to find the force to push out the sound, make a move, say yes or no or something . . . and then I knew for sure that these slow-moving hands were nothing but my dream, my drugged fantasy . . . and I fall again, I think, into the blackness . . .

. . . my breasts exposed to her lips . . . my body exposed as I can feel her hands against my skin, her lips against my skin and this must be a dream but my body stirs and tries to move into it as if it were real . . . feeling the kneading hands, stroking hands all over me, up and down and up again against my skin and I try, I try to concentrate, to find the words, to rip the words from my dry throat, my thick tongue unmoving, my head growing dizzier, my mind begging me to just sleep, to just lay still and sleep as it will pass . . . and I don't want to, don't want to sleep until I know . . . and each moment forward I feel her pressing into me, touching me, squeezing me, rubbing me, and a desire to wail, to let it loose to cry it out comes and goes and comes again and yet I hear nothing . . . but feel everything . . . and it is in one place only that I wish the hands to touch me most . . . and the hands are everywhere but there . . . her lips are on my thighs . . . so slowly kissing as I lay still, all I am able to do, stay conscious and feel the pulsing of my own cunt . . . the more I focus, the harder still my body tugs at me to sleep, aroused or not . . . the energy I barely have, draining, draining and I feel heavier against the cushions below me . . . the clouds I think . . .

. . . wetness there . . . is it mine or it is it hers against me, and her tongue is there close, closer and breathing cold and hot air against me . . . my body is awakening and my mind is not, and I'm feeling the swelling in my chest, and it is anger . . . Damn! . . . why did I take the drugs and why can't I even focus my eyes for a second, just a damn second to see . . . but I can smell . . . I sense my own scent and she reads my mind and in an instant she is there . . . and she is inside me and my body drags me forward into it, and I know I am not moving, it is she who is moving inside of me, both of us listening to my ragged breaths . . .

. . . at the heart stopping second when her thick lips touched my pulsing cunt; at the urgent instant when I balanced between the conscious and the unconscious, holding on; at the moment when my body tried to push itself down upon her lips, tried and failed and kept trying; at the breathless pause when I made my-self stay with her just a millisecond longer, a microscopic drop longer with the woman who was prolonging it, lips sucking me in, white arms holding my legs, bracing down on them; at that feverish fleeting space in time when I felt my teeth biting my own lips just to keep me awake for a moment longer; at that electrify-ing moment when there was nothing but just pure sensation, I felt the orgasm grip me and wrench me, and I watched myself fall again deeply into the seemingly bottomless blackness . . .

I'm gonna act real cool
when you say we're through.
I'm gonna put my feelings
in deep freeze,
and leave them there
until someone else comes along
to tamper with them.

. . . The wild night of dream fantasy was complete. As the sunrise revealed itself earlier in the day, the witches spilled what was left of their brew, silenced the chanting, put an end to the dancing, and disap-peared. It was time now, the morning after, for the waking and the questions to begin.

126

The administrative staff on the other side of Diana's office door was beginning to make familiar office noises. The sun had been up for hours. So had the business owners, cafeteria workers, birds, shopping bag ladies, ninety-seven percent of the faculty, and two point five percent of the University student population. Just about everyone of any importance at all was up. All except Diana.

It was either the nagging drone of her conscience or the hateful tapping of the typewriter that lifted her into dulled awareness when her alarm clock failed her. Not that she had set it or anything.

She faced the first herculean feat of the day: the opening of her almond-shaped, crystal blue eyes. That this was definitely not her bedroom was the first rude piece of reality in line to greet her. So now began the onerous chore of figuring out the where, what, when and how of last night. That proving too difficult, she decided to tackle something simpler . . . like moving. She made her first unsuccessful attempt at rising from the couch. Soon after her second attempt ended in failure as well, she yielded and lay still underneath the weight of the hangover which was already eagerly surfacing. Her mind was blank, and she was trying to piece together how exactly it was that she ended up on her office couch. Too hazy, too confused, feeling drugged.

Her eyes regained partial early morning focus, and she lay staring at her office couch. A massive sofa that abutted one, two, three walls of the room. Bankers gray with tiny white pin stripes. One would have had to steal the suits off the backs of at least several dozen Wall Street bankers to upholster this thing, she was thinking. And the small effort at thinking sharpened her senses a bit. It was then that she remembered.

Last night was real, it did occur, she told herself, it wasn't a dream. She was convinced of that. But who was She? Now that she was able, the images of last night crystallized, and came dancing back to her. Taunting her.

Clothes crumpled, head heavy and hung over, Diana rose shakily after a few minutes of unsuccessful half-conscious stabs at identifying the night visitor. A cool chill ran up her spine spawning goose bumps as a larger-than-life rush from last night darted in front of her eyes. It happened! She could see that it happened. Making her way to her purse then the mirror. The reflection in the glass was as she expected—her thick auburn hair fell to her shoulders all right, but in an alarmingly disarrayed fashion. Where to even begin fixing . . . She settled for running her fingers through her hair hoping against hope to create a look that approached passable. Less disheveled was the best she could do.

Her body still resonating with the sensations of the night before. The mystery. Forcing herself there, in front of the mirror, to remember something, anything about the woman. She could not even recapture the tiniest, telling detail of familiarity about the woman. The slightest clue or nuance even eluded her. Maybe coffee would bring clarity. Yes, the ambrosia of the gods. The caffeine that with the first morning sip cooed that, "everything will be all right." The second promising that, "all is right already." And by the third sip of java, it had Diana believing that nothing is really that important anyway, so why waste time worrying about anything. This was the way she would regain her proper perspective for the day. And if she never found out who the night visitor was . . . well, that would be fine, too. She could live with not knowing; but not without the coffee. Now! Nothing was more important now than this . . . First things first, after all.

The knock on the door startled her—her priorities instantly re-prioritized themselves.—Could that be Her? Her? . . . Diana flashed, as pure adrenalin mainlined into her veins at the possibility of being face-to-face with the Woman. Of course, she thought, this would be the perfect time for the woman to appear. Yes, the morning after. It was time for her to show herself. She moved quickly to the door in anticipation and opened it. A voice met her first before she had time to focus, "I want to know *how* good you feel about pretty younger women?"

Diana was stunned. Lila, it was Lila at the door. But the one night they did spend together weeks ago wasn't a fraction as explosive as last night . . . but then again last night's recall was tinged (heavily tinged) with drugs. And if drugs and alcohol aren't a perception alterer, than little if anything, is. She did well to remind herself of that fact. How could it be Lila? At best, she thought, Lila was fun, but far, far from overwhelming. And try as she might, Diana had to answer every one of her own internal questions before she could begin to answer Lila's.

Entrenched in her own thoughts Diana stood blocking Lila's entrance into her office. Lila mistook Diana's stillness: she fancied Diana caught off guard by her cleverly-timed visit and question. God knows, she had thought carefully about her return to Diana this particular morning. She knew that this morning would make all the difference between them. In this, she was correct—it would. And Diana continued to stand there and stare at her. She is too young Diana debated, too inexperienced, too . . . something. Diana knew intuitively that it couldn't have been Lila last night. But, perhaps, Lila was holding back that first night they spent together. Nerves, maybe. Or with the right mixture of drugs and liquor and lack of sleep, it could have been a powerful effect Lila did have on her last night. Perhaps, then, it was Lila. And what an unexpected turn of events.

Diana, her head heavy with questions, was ready to open the dialogue. Maybe in it she would find a clue. She moved aside, and, Lila taking her cue, entered. Diana shut and locked the door behind her. Then unlocked it. She called Jade on the intercom: "You have my word of honor that I will never ask you this again. I need you to bring me a pot of black coffee. Now. Please." Lila was noticeably puffing up with how intense a reaction she was eliciting in Diana. Diana was almost beside herself, Lila noted. This was even more than she had hoped for.

Motioning for Lila to take a seat, Diana took hers behind her desk. It was safer there. Lila was thrilled: clearly she had meant more to Diana than either of them had thought. The girl with all the cards seemingly in her hand eased back into her chair in this, her crowning moment. The control and power she felt enroute to Diana's office multiplied.

They sat silently staring: Diana in a confused state of disbelief, and Lila in a lordly state of omnipotence.

After a time, Jade knocked twice, and entered with a tray of black coffee, croissants, jellies and honey. Placing the tray in front of Diana, Jade poured one cup only and parted. Diana did not say thank you; Jade did not wait for one.

Pushing the tray aside, and the coffee cup towards her, Diana began. "You are treading on very dangerous ground, Lila."

Lila was baffled. What was Diana talking about? Did Diana mean because I'm the Dean's daughter, or because Diana had more to lose by Lila making a surprise visit to her office? Lila realized that that was it. But the impact of the surprise would have been lost had she called in advance. "I didn't think I needed a permission slip to come see you."

Nope, it just couldn't be Lila. She was too mild. Too passive. That was it, Diana concluded for not the last time though, it just couldn't be Lila. Diana now responded to Lila's initial question. "I feel good about younger women provided they know how to make me feel good," Diana said taking a long sip of the scalding java, and taking another tact.

"Diana, you can't tell me that you didn't enjoy it . . . that I didn't surprise you?"

Maybe it was Lila. Diana answered, "Oh, I was delightfully surprised, my dear."

To which Lila replied, "So tell me, how did I do?"

Now that was really it. That was the end of that. Would the woman of last night ask me that ridiculous question about how she did? No, no, no. She wouldn't ask, she would tell.

"You did just fine, just fine."

"Do you want to know how you did?" questioned Lila.

"No!" The emphatic tone put an end to the possibility of this tangent of conversation going any further. Diana explained, "If you weren't pleased, you wouldn't be here, and if you were, then your arrival here this morning is long overdue."

A wild one, thought Lila. Tough. Just my speed. The woman I want. Getting cocky, Lila added to herself, and I will have her.

It was inevitable. Lila spoke it: "How have things changed for you since you've fallen in love like the common folk?" Being met with dropdead silence should have been enough of an answer for her. But it wasn't. Lila should have packed up her emotions and gone home at that very instant. But she didn't.

More than moderate surprise registered on Diana's face. Her answer to who the mystery woman was *not*, was crystal clear. That it was not Lila gave her relief and another successful reason to trust her intuition. But she was far from home, as she still didn't know the identity of The Woman.

Lila, forever reading what she *wanted* to see in every situation, mistook Diana's silence for an affirmation. A positive sign. Compounding her first wrong move with yet another, she continued, "I'm falling in love with you myself, Diana." The curtain fell.

"Let me stop you now, sweetie, please, before you go any further. You have made the wrong choice with the wrong woman at the wrong time." Why so harsh on Lila, Diana chastised herself. She was displacing her frustrations about last night on this most unsuspecting young victim.

Insecurity swept over Lila, and she responded, "I have no choice." Suddenly she sensed something was terribly amiss, and she could not censor her feelings. Her doubts rose to the surface, and demanded air time, and she was now at the mercy of them. "I am in love with you already, Diana, and I don't have another choice." Her voice timid.

"We all have choices. Endless numbers of choices." Diana's words would have been more appropriate if she were lecturing a class, but not in this, a gentle dialogue between two gay women who spent an enjoyable intimate night together.

"I can't help how I feel." Lila couldn't stand herself; she was shrinking with humiliation. What on earth was going on: first Diana is ecstatic to see me, and now this?

"Can't isn't a valid word," Diana said. Patronizing her. "The word you mean to use is won't."

"Can't may be more accurate thought—"

"Won't is more truthful."

"Fuck semantics, Diana! Knowing what I just told you, how do you feel about it?" She was right, Diana was avoiding the issue.

Finally, Diana softened. For after all, it wasn't Lila's fault for goodness sake. Lila was in love with me, and I better treat her carefully, thought the woman who finally got hold of her better self. You were once in this position yourself a long time ago she recalled, reprimanding herself. She said softly, honestly, "Lila, I feel as I felt after the night we spent together: you're a charming playmate; you're fun; and I enjoyed myself a lot that evening. Honestly, I had a very nice time with you. But I am out to play, Lila, not settle down."

"That's all?" Lila blurted out before realizing what she had said, and then continued, "No! Don't answer that. You're being honest and fair with me." Diana smiled, and Lila went on, "The problem remains though that I've never wanted any other woman the way I do you. I know it sounds clichéd, I know—"

With tender caution Diana interrupted, "It's not going to happen, Lila. It isn't in your plan or mine."

"I know. I didn't expect it, or even want it at first, but here it is. Plans change. People change. I have to admit what I'm feeling."

Diana came out from behind her desk to Lila's chair, and leaned over to say, "Yes, you're right, doll, go ahead and acknowledge it, but just don't entertain it. Look, you wanted to meet me, and you did. You wanted to seduce me, and you did. You got both of your objectives met. Be satisfied, you glutton," she said following the words with a smile, and then with a brief kiss to Lila's lips. Diana took Lila's hand, and led her to the sofa. These last few days were quite the roller coaster filled with surprises, Diana thought. Perhaps, celibacy, she pondered lowering her weary body on the couch.

"But now the true objective has shown itself," Lila countered with a tingle of the kiss still resonating on her lips.

"Ignore it. Some women don't even attain one of their goals—ever. Don't be greedy." At that moment Diana realized that she was not a woman to be satisfied with anything less than everything herself. She softened even further, as honesty had a way of affecting her that way.

Lila was hurting: "That's the trouble . . . that's the problem—"

"There isn't any problem—"

"I want more. Being with you made me want more. Being with you for just that one night showed me how really terrific it could be for me . . . for us. I want to be with you all the time . . . I haven't been able to think about anything else."

"And what do you call that?"

"I call that love . . . for you, Diana."

"I call it infatuation," Diana replied telling herself that this is precisely why a grown woman shouldn't even think about playing around with young girls. It's my own damn fault, she thought. She continued, "And infatuation is okay as long as you don't confuse it with love."

Feelings, hurt, Lila struck out, "Have you even ever been in love to know the finer distinctions between the terminology?" Oh, it would be a long time before Lila would forgive herself for this scene she was putting them both through. Diana understood Lila's pain, and responded quietly, "I don't ever speak about anything I haven't experienced first-hand . . . rest assured."

She was stung with the realization that Diana's words were the same she had mouthed to girls in her life that had fallen in love with her after only one night of play-filled lovemaking. Lila just had never been on the other side of it before. But "No" never sat well with Lila. Here she was in a room with a woman who was telling her "No" in every possible way.

It is time to leave before I start repeating myself, Lila thought. But she had yet to make a choice: to take Diana up on her offer of a playmate relationship or to walk out the door with a degree of self-respect, and not see Diana again. She knew her decision wouldn't make much of a difference to Diana; but it would make all the difference in the world to her.

She winced at her performance this morning. How much she sounded like all the other girls—clutching, grasping. Fuck. This was so unlike her, so out of character. Her insecurities chuckled as she stood. Embarrassed.

"Please strike my last remark. It was uncalled for, Diana, and I hope you will accept my apology for it . . . for this scene."

Diana took her in her arms and gave her a long hug. Apology accepted. "Please don't think I don't care for you, Lila."

Yet another Lila special—a silent exit. But this would be the final one. The saga of Lila, daughter of the Dean, had come to an end: fast, furious, fun and done.

So now, who in the heck was this night visitor then?

Sing me the song of Serenity.
I want to learn the words.

The hour was late, the drive home long and Diana's temperament, unlike the sun, was not too hot.

Only twenty-three minutes passed between Diana's dog-tired feet crossing the threshold of her comforting townhouse womb, to the showered, powdered and pampered body that lay itself down with complete unabashed familiarity on the generously soft leather chaise.

Her sigh made itself known right on cue. Exhilirated exhaustion. Well deserved and well earned, she thought before losing herself in another long suspire. A little piece of heaven she was thinking, as the evening was all hers.

She had the terrain of the long night ahead of her to recreate the incidents of the last night's anonymous mystery visitor—to find the clue to the woman's identity. This was so silly and who would believe that it actually happened to her. It seemed to Diana that she spends a good deal of her life looking for clues; first for Christina, then this party in her honor, then this dream sex thing, and who knows what could possibly be next. It was much more fun than frustrating, as Diana loved, simply loved surprises.

The mail—she had forgotten to pick up the mail . . . Later, she thought, and reconciled herself to not moving one muscle for a long time this evening. Relax, don't move, there is nothing of importance in this day left to attend to, she told herself wisely, so enjoy not doing anything. Relax she said over and over as her brain sent simultaneously those 'you-should-be-doing-something' guilt signals. She was having way too much trouble relaxing tonight. Her body, it seemed, was primed for the next 'surprise' even though she told it there would be no more surprises on this, the least likely of all, evenings home alone.

After a while, during which time she gave herself permission to have a guilt-free lazy evening, she began to wonder about who the night visitor might be. And she had by this time already ruled out Lila this morning, so who was left . . . Hmmm. There was Maria right there at the head of the list, and she hoped there was always a Maria in her life. Full of adventure, full of spirit and imagination, so free of the desire for a commitment. Refreshing. And probably she did it, to let Diana know that she was true to her word to call the 'next shot.' What crazy nerve this woman had to do such a thing, Diana smiled to herself thinking that it must be Maria.

Of course within the domain of the next set of minutes and more thinking Diana decided with equal determination that it just must have been Monica. Diana was nobody's fool, she could tell what was playing through Monica's mind when she told her to "Take good care of yourself," which Diana read as "Let *me* take good care of you." Right now Monica needed a loving friendship in her life to comfort her through her hard time in Whitney's aftermath. After all, Monica saw how exhausted and vulnerable Diana was last night and might have used that information to her advantage. Touché, Monica, for your aggressiveness. And with that Monica became the second must-be-her candidate.

(And no sooner did I get up to get a cigarette and return to the typewriter than Diana uncovered yet a third definitive visitor—Jade.) But, of course, she deduced . . . of all three women Jade in the truest sense of the word had the 'moxy' to do such a thing. Jade would do just about anything, Diana figured, and this would be in keeping with her 'seize-the-opportunity' attitude.

And if only Christina had not left her, Diana thought indulging herself, she wouldn't have to be dealing with these questions about which women took her at all. A more blatant lie you might not hear her tell again—Miss Hunter had not been monogamous in years.

Quite frankly, she couldn't decide who the night visitor was. She knew it was probably one of the three women, it must be, but she didn't have the mental energy to follow it through any further than that. Further than, just getting up momentarily to retrieve the mail, and back again to the chaise.

This time it came in the mail and again with no return address. No postmark, no nothing. Someone came by and dropped it in my mailbox personally! She stared wide-eyed at what were two round trip tickets to California for a four day weekend, including reservations for a rental car and a receipt for a cottage on the beach with two photos showing both the cottage and the Pacific Ocean not more than twelve feet from the doorway doing its spectacular crashing-against-the-rocks routine. Also, a typewritten list of straightforward directions for the retrieval of the car and cottage . . . and this was unbelievable. Unbelievable, California! . . . What was this?

She was dying now for her fairy godmother to make herself known. Another gift from her generous party-throwing, lovemaking, gift-giving friend. "My, my, my." Diana's excitement and glee reducing her to monosyllables. Was this ever too good to be true, or what? And for some time she smiled and laughed and said 'thank you' to whomever it was who had obviously taken such a fantastic fancy to her.

The hard part was yet to be tackled—getting through the next week until her flight to California lifted off next Friday evening. Diana had not developed the fine art of patience yet, and the long week wait seemed overwhelming. She simply could not get through, but she would try, somehow, she thought. What a wonderfully eccentric courting ritual, she was thinking, by someone who would inevitably make themselves known, for surely they would have to before she ran out of ideas, not to mention money. And she cared less, at this moment, for who the gift-giver was than the wonderful release a weekend on the coast would provide. How wonderful . . . she simply must stop using that word anymore tonight.

It hit her: it must be someone she works with. "Someone who waited until the research for my book was complete before giving me this offer. I wouldn't have left town until now, until the bulk of my work on the book was behind me. Who knows my schedule that well?" The same three women named themselves. The game grew more interesting at every turn.

For an evening that promised very little in the way of surprises, this one came through with flying colors. Diana couldn't take in any more, as her fragile circuits neared overload. Relax now, relax.

What better time than now to stop the wild current of activities, the new developments and thinking, thinking, thinking. Now, to let her 'self' out for a breath of fresh air. Breathing deeply, eyes closed, working towards slowing down her system. Allowing her spirit the freedom, for a while anyway, in alpha, to stretch its cramped legs. To let her mind air itself out and regain its proper perspective. To let go, and let the Goddess do her work she does best: to soothe, to renew, to revitalize. Too much happening . . . even though they all are tremendously good things. Getting still and keeping all other thoughts away temporarily was more important than anything in the world at this moment.

Surrounding herself with the white light, the spiritual heat lamp, the release made its way towards her as she opened herself to it slowly, bit by bit. Her spirit took a memorably long breath, and exhaled . . . "The spirit of the Goddess is upon me," she repeated over and over until alpha took her over. Diana passed beyond consciousness with what looked like a smile on her lips.

(California!! Wonderful!)

The blinding stare
of laser light
passing from hazel eyes to blue
swallows my resistance whole,
leaving me shaken,
undressed and wet
in the one
dark shadow
of your smile.

Diana was hurting for some good conversation tonight; she was in good company with those expectations.

They each had their own reasons for wanting to go to an anonymous dive on the wrongest side of town to drink. Neither were alcoholics; but both had the taste of the drink long before arriving, and both the desire to receive the wonderful effects that alcohol both promises and delivers.

They differed only in this: Diana came to forget and Jade to remember.

Jade, to remember how excellent it was with the tempestuous Simone. Simone, who with one rendition of a song, could have an audience crying or cheering or just silent, too filled with emotion to respond. Simone who could have Jade that same way when she was strong, sexual and all-powerful. Simone, who needed more than anything to be looked after, taken care of and loved right up to the point of distraction.

Diana, to forget that it was really as superb as it was with Christina. And hurt as much as she still did with the loss of her. To forget, too, what she'd learned about not bringing the past into the present. Tonight, she *wanted* to bring the pretty images of Christina into the present, and revel in them, still in love with her she was, after all these years. And finally, to never forget to remember what the excellence of love is all about, what things are possible between two women in crazy love.

Both entered the bar alone to get lost for the evening. Both gave off unapproachable signals to the clientele. Both preferring their own company. So it was only a matter of time, alone at their tables, that they would spot each other. Both, in variations on the snug jeans-oversized sweater-heels theme, stared at one another. Diana was not only happy to spot Jade, she was positively thrilled. As thrilled, almost, as Jade was.

Jade picked up her drink, and moved in an alarmingly assertive fashion to Diana's table.

"Welcome, Desmonde," Diana said with genuine enthusiasm as Jade stood over her table, "Sit, doll, sit . . . So tell me, how many drinks do you have in you thus far?"

"Two strong ones."

"I myself have had two martinis, and the magic has already begun," Diana glowed. She had that bad-girl look in her eyes which made Jade want to take her home, to bed, this instant.

"Soooo," she said in a husky voice Jade had never heard on her before, "talk dirty to me."

"I want a raise," Jade countered.

"Not that dirty!" Diana laughed, and raised her glass in a toast, "To your quick tongue."

Compliments always made Jade change the topic: "May I pry?" she asked.

"Never pry, Miss Desmonde, it's not ladylike. You may, however, ask."

"What are you getting drunk over this evening?"

"A girl." Diana was ready to speak of it.

"And you, are you enroute to inebriation over anything in particular?"

"Yes." Just 'Yes,' and just like Jade to leave it this way.

And Diana didn't pry, true to her convictions, merely added, "Good. Unfocused drinking, or action for that matter, is never as productive as purposeful drinking or action. Always have a purpose, Miss Desmonde," she said pausing to sip her drink, and add, "I bet you live by that rule." Yessir, Diana had a bit too much to drink as she was about to grow playful, teasing and intimate all in the same conversation.

"It amounts to this . . . I lived with a woman who was, bar none, the love of my life. For six years, in what I considered to be the most bliss-filled relationship ever invented. Now, keep in mind that at sixteen you think everything you discover is of your own invention. Now, at thirty, I know that everything great has already been thought of or executed by scores of other people."

Jade jumped in, veering the conversation back from the philosophical to the personal. It was clear that Diana was about to talk about 'that' event in her past, and it was imperative that Jade hear it. "I congratulate you on your six years. I was able to invent the quintessential relationship with a woman for only three."

"That, unfortunately, is not the end of the story . . . or come to think of it," Diana paused, reflecting, "maybe that is the end of the story . . . *it is*!"

Jade laughed, "Am I supposed to be following your line of thought, or are you having a divine drunken inspiration right in front of my eyes?"

"Of sorts," Diana replied taking another sip of inspiration from her glass, "What just hit me is that that *is* the whole story. Or at least the most important part of the story anyway. As it turned out, the six years were extraordinarily lovely until the woman turned twenty-two."

At which point Diana moved again slightly off track, and flashed to an image of her comforting Christina one rain-soaked evening after Christina had found out her story was rejected from *The New Yorker*. And that was so like Christina, Diana thought, expecting all of her first attempts to be perfect 'hits'—finding the thought of rewriting or redoing anything a second time, repugnant. Either it scored the first time out or she moved on to other things. Christina had not quite grasped the fine art of refinement. Diana explained that night to her dejected lover that all the great artists and writers redid their work countless times until they stepped into the realm of perfection. And Diana, all the while knowing her words were comforting to Christina, but not convincing. That, Diana was thinking, was one of the sweetest evenings. Diana, a woman who loved to be needed, was probably right.

Jade made an attempt at pulling Diana back into the here and now, with, "Do you rather that I guess what transpired on the day she turned twenty-two, or would you care to share it with me? Bear in mind, Miss Hunter, this is asking, not prying." She smiled at Diana for she recognized and empathized with a certain long-ago, far-away hurt in her eyes. The urge to stroke Diana was upon her without warning. She restrained herself; it was Diana who would come to Jade—asking for it, needing it—not Jade.

Diana, taking Jade's light comment seriously, responded, "I don't expect you to guess, because how could you guess without knowing her. I couldn't even guess, and I knew her—," Diana said, lightening up, leaning over the table and whispering, "—intimately." And winked.

Oh, it was so obvious that Diana had too much to drink already. Not touching Jade grew more difficult, especially at this proximity—body to body, face to face.

Jade, enjoying the closeness asked, "Intimately? Do tell, Miss Hunter, do tell!"

So close in fact that Diana felt Jade's breath on her. It was not easy to be grave and lighthearted simultaneously, but Diana was holding her own. "The love of my live vanished into thin air! Amazing as it sounds."

That was Jade's reaction—amazement.

"It's a true story," Diana said staring into Jade's eyes, looking for something. "So, Miss Desmonde, what should one make of that?"

Jade's question was, "What did you make of that?"

"After all this time, I still don't have a straight answer for that question. And believe me I am not being evasive."

"I never presumed you were, honey, as I have quite a clear notion of what you must have felt . . . what you must still be feeling."

"Honey?" Diana questioned, flirting despite herself.

"Honey," responded Jade.

From Miss Hunter to Honey—that's alcohol for you, Diana thought.

"Does it still torture you?"

God, Yes, Diana thought. "It still does, but in subtler ways now than it used to. Now I never quite know when it's going to hit. It used to be that I felt a wave of panic hit me, and I knew with it would come the vivid feelings for her that never quite died, just kind of . . . took a rest in my brain from time to time."

"Laying dormant?"

"Laying in wait. To attack!" Diana laughed, and continued, "They're subtler, but equally as potent. I've just learned to be a functional woman in pain, as there comes a time to work again, and bring home the bread."

"And to live, which is the part I had most trouble with, Diana," Jade offered.

From Miss Hunter to Honey to Diana all in the course of one evening—the hurdles were being overcome at a fantastic speed.

Jade continued, "The working part I handled well. I threw myself into my work like a tornado, and never stopped. The living part, however, took longer. I left society, I left the world of people for quite some time. If I could not have Simone, I did not want anybody. Some would call that self-destruction, spiting myself that way—"

"I, myself, called it punishment. A semantic difference only, but our means and ends were the same," Diana added, relieved to find a comrade in Jade on the topic that most disturbed her sleep, her work, her serenity. A topic that she simply refused to put to rest. Until she met Jade, and now more and more it was thoughts of Jade that disturbed her sleep, making their way subtly into her life.

It was only a matter of time. She couldn't hold out much longer.

"Tell me, Jade, was this Simone woman beautiful?"

Jade cupped her chin in her hands, elbows resting on the table, lost in thought now. Finally, she said with all the seductiveness she was known to have, "She was gorgeous." How to describe Simone Boulange to someone who hadn't met her. She tried, "She was like a lioness. Untamed. Wild. Famous, no, notorious. And I loved her more than I thought possible; more than I will ever feel again for anyone."

"Jade—"

"No. I mean it! I prefer it that way. There will never be another woman like her, and I don't want to burden anyone else with having to live up to the expectations that were achieved with Simone. It wouldn't be fair."

"I agree in part," Diana said, knowing damn well that she agreed in toto, "but that keeps you forever at arms length from every woman that you meet. No?"

"You mean *you*, Miss Hunter. Yes. I know I could not stand that kind of devastation again. Could you, Diana?"

"No. I do the same thing with the women I meet," Diana confessed, "I'll go so far, seemingly open and approachable up until a woman wants to get too close, too intimate."

"Then what, Diana?"

"Then I leave, or worse I back off, and shut down."

"You leave, Diana, not because of your fear of intimacy, but because of your fear of intimacy with a woman who will not be able to hold you, to satisfy you completely, on all levels."

"Both, perhaps."

"So you do the same thing I do."

Diana laughed. "This is how I know that I am not perfect yet, strive as I might towards that goal—"

"You are protecting yourself, and so am I, and for goodness sake, *somebody* has to protect and watch over us. If it happened once it can happen again; morbid, but nonetheless true."

"At the rate that we are both going at it we won't let a woman get close enough to do anything of any value to us again in our lives. A dismal thought considering we both have sixty good years left in us." Diana made Jade laugh.

"Dismal, but safe," Jade concluded.

Each of them hiding behind their talk: both willing to risk the safety for one another. They wanted one another so badly, in fact, that it was all they could do just to keep talking.

"A toast to safety, Miss Desmonde," and they both raised their glasses to their poor interpretations of letting go of the past, and living their lives in the present. It was a struggle for both of them. Tonight they didn't feel like being healthy and positive, preferring to wallow in the unrewarding memories of things past.

"So where is this woman of the animal kingdom now, Jade?"

Jade was about to say 'flirting' but Simone didn't flirt, she was a taker, a conquerer, so she said more accurately, "Fucking. Fucking some pretty little angel in the sky most likely."

The news hit Diana hard—dead was a far cry from gone. Not that she held on to any realistic hopes of Christina returning, but she felt good knowing that Christina was alive and well, somewhere, and doing what she needed to do, with whomever, somewhere on this planet. And the drinks in her made the news even more tragic. She looked at Jade straight in the eyes, and with what Jade saw as pain and grief and possibly tears, Diana said, "I am sorry," which rung so true from her innermost heart. Diana lifted her hands up to Jade's face, pulled her close, and kissed her gently, softly on the lips, once. Then, released her and said, "I don't think that I could have handled that, Jade. That's beyond my repetoire of coping skills. I wouldn't have made it."

"You'd be surprised at what you can deal with when it happens upon you. I surprised myself . . . And—" Jade decided not to finish the sentence, and then reconsidered, "—And thank you for the kiss."

"I warn you in advance, Miss Desmonde, so you can spend this weekend overcoming your envy," Diana said after returning from the bar to pay the check, and change the topic from past to present. "I expect to return to work next week relaxed and tan."

"Going on a retreat, Boss?"

"Of sorts. I have been invited to California," she said, spying Jade for a clue. For after all she still did not know who the gift-giver was.

"Good. You earned it. I am happy for you. But, I don't recall you mentioning this trip before."

Diana smiled broadly, "I haven't. I didn't know until last week when the tickets arrived by messenger."

"From?" Jade asked interested and surprised and innocently enough.

"Your guess is as good as mine."

"You don't know?"

"I so wish I did." Diana was literally dying of curiosity.

"Then I would say you have a generous benefactor—"

"An anonymous, generous benefactor. And this isn't the first mystery either," Diana confided this news for the first time to anyone, "there's been a party thrown in my honor, there's been a . . ." how could she delicately explain that half-dream evening of sex, ". . . a night visitor . . . a sexual encounter of sorts, and now tickets—"

"An anonymous sexual encounter!?"

"Yes," Diana answered over Jade's laughter, "I know—"

"I find that hard to believe . . . How can you have a physical interlude without knowing whom you are having it with?"

"Believable or not," she said to the woman with the disbelieving ear-to-ear grin, "it happened. Remember the night I returned to my office with Maria Lanning, and you came barging into my office presumably to rescue me, for my own good?"

"I take exception to your choice of the word 'barging,' but yes, I remember," Jade said leaning forward with rapt attention.

"That night, later that night, I mixed some pills and alcohol hoping to pass out. That, coupled with the exhaustion of not sleeping for a couple of days in a row, left me hardly conscious at all when it happened."

"Diana, are you asking me to believe—"

"I'm not asking for anything, I am telling you—"

Talking right through her own suppressed laughter, Jade said gently, "I'm not laughing at you, Diana—"

"Yes you are, Miss Desmonde, but you go right on—"

"Diana, if I had told you this story you would never let me live it down."

"That's entirely possible, and totally beside the point."

"I just find it incredible, that's all."

"Agreed! The point is this though: the trip to California is just one of many incredible gifts."

"My, my, we are the lucky one." Jade leaned back in her chair. It was her turn to be curious. What was the meaning of this California affair?

"In a way, but I am aching with curiosity." Thinking whether she should or shouldn't ask, she decided to try anyway. "You wouldn't happen to know—"

"Why, Miss Hunter, even if I did, knowing what you know about me, do you think that I would tell you?"

Diana was right, she shouldn't have. "No, but one can always hope—"

"Of course, that is your privilege."

"Oh, you are such a stern one, aren't you, Miss Desmonde?"

"Yes," Jade replied sternly, and continued on a different track, "And Diana, it's been the bane of my existence, this sterness of mine. Can you help me? I have no one else to turn to, I implore you," she implored grabbing Diana's hands.

"Yes, yes, you can trust me, you're safe with me now," Diana responded conspiratorially, leaning in to her whispering. "Listen closely now, I can help you . . . but you must listen: Let us get out of here. Now."

Enroute to the cars, Diana contemplated in her hazy, drunken concentrationless way, what it was she felt like doing now, and what, if anything, she felt like doing with Jade. Still treading on the old-threadbare theory, she thought: After all, drunk or sober, I am still this woman's boss, whether I can or can't walk a straight line. Which she couldn't. They walked together cautiously out to the parking lot with Diana's head spinning: they had shared some poignant conversation, they were equals, they were lovers in the most intense sense of the word, never once touching but always, always wanting it. They had not so much as laid one soft hand on the other. It was damn near killing Diana.

Jade helped Diana into her car, placed her gently in the passenger side and got in. "Now what, Miss Demsonde? What is your game plan?" Diana's heart raced being this private and this close to Jade. Jade's sped too. It wasn't easy with Jade this draw that never let up between them. Too attracted to each other for words.

Jade turned to her, touched her cheek and replied, "My plan is to take you home, then drive myself home. Does that meet with your approval?" Jade was smiling, as Diana made an endearingly cute lush.

"What should we do then about this tireless sexual thing that has been going on since the day I hired you?" It was a valid question.

"Let's let it be for now." Tactful. She started the car.

"I am ready—"

"You are drunk, not ready. Let this one go, Boss, for tonight. Please."

But Diana's impulsiveness mixed with the alcohol mixed with her sexuality propelled her on. "Afraid?"

"Don't bait me, boss, you don't need to." Jade gunned the motor, and tore out of the parking lot towards Diana's home. Diana didn't even ask how Jade knew where home was for her.

The second alcohol-induced, divine inspiration of the night hit her: Diana could compete with any woman alive. She couldn't compete with Simone. With the memory of Simone. Obviously, Jade was not going to let any woman get in the way of the memory of that woman, even Diana. She spent the rest of the ride home in silence, working very hard to accept that fact, even though there was no truth in it whatsoever.

And, the heat between her legs became an ache.

Like a Cool Blue Light Brilliance.
Just Like That.
It was Then, I Knew.

Friday came and went in a flurry of activity at the hands of the tireless perfectionist attempting to put it all in order to run smoothly in her four day absence. She worked Jade down to her knuckles. Diana had assumed this day would be the hardest and longest, with the endless waiting for the assigned flight hour. She had miscalculated—too busy fighting the clock.

In the middle of the night Diana arrived in California. She picked up the red BMW waiting for her and took off with the typewritten directions in hand for the cottage in Pacifica.

The wind swept the hair from her neck and the worries from her mind. Relaxing was possible now. Not much of it transpired on the flight to the west coast as she kept a keen eye on the passengers— maybe the gift-giver was on the plane, somewhere, watching her. No such luck.

The sign for Pacifica led her closer to her temporary home. Somehow, she anticipated that the woman might already be at the cottage laying in wait to welcome her personally, which was probably why

Diana was speeding down the freeway. And probably why she checked the closets and the shower stall after she got inside of the cottage. She showered, and began accepting that this was going to be a solo vacation after all.

And in her warm, layer-on-layer clothing, about to go and sit on the beach at three a.m., she felt that this was going to be *her* weekend. Her's alone. To do with exactly as she saw fit. And how it was that one person could be so lucky, and blessed . . . The thought of the Goddess entered her mind, and her heart swelled with gratitude and her eyes with tears, and in the cottage she sat crying with joy for the first time in years since Christina had left her. Cried with joy and consummate relief and love of life . . . convinced beyond a doubt that at this moment it was she who was the luckiest woman in the world. Overwhelmed and tear-stained, she sat quietly, unhurried and serene in her solitude.

Diana loved the water. It soothed her and reminded her in its own majestic way that nature has of making its point, that life goes on and on; that there is little use in pushing the river—it flows. Reminded her, too, of her weekends in est when the instructor repeated, what seemed like a hundred times: "It is better to ride the horse in the direction it's going." And it was true, all of it, all of what she had been learning in these last seven years from mentors, spiritual advisors, teachers, friends, group encounters, Unity classrooms: life goes on with or without you, and the trick is to bend with it, and learn from it. Too simple, almost, to be believed. On this reflection she resolved to try even harder, starting now, as Diana always felt that she could do even better if she just tried harder.

Saturday afternoon she awoke with a light heart to sounds of gulls and waves, and it was as close to a dream as she ever experienced. After a caffeine breakfast, she took a blanket and Buscalia's most recent book up to the cliffs. The ocean below was happy to see her, and put on quite a tumultuous show of spray and breaking waves in her honor. The weather also cooperated; the sun shone its smile virtually ear to ear.

During this day Diana reflected on current events: Whitney's suicide, Monica's ability to cope, and Jade. Yes, thoughts of Jade were no less prominent today than most days. Jade wanted her, this was clear. As clear, now, as how much she wanted Jade. The time of waiting would be over with the close of the weekend. What *was* she waiting for? She didn't even know anymore. Then, it must be right to move forward and act. One affirmative word from Diana and their relationship would begin—explode—loosing all the feelings that bided their time, knowing full well that the two girls couldn't hold out forever.

Images of her and Jade together were convincing. Convincing enough to make her descend the cliffs, seek out a telephone, and call her. And call her, and call her . . . Jade was not to be found. Giving up was out of the question. She stayed in the restaurant with the phone for more than two hours, calling every quarter hour. She was crestfallen not to hear Jade's voice at the other end of the line now when she had the "Yes" Jade so much wanted to hear. She chastised the Goddess for not cooperating in the timing department, and kept dialing. She would get through to Jade. This was not news she could wait until she returned to tell her. This was big news, this Yes, life-changing news. In the second hour Diana grew impatient. Waiting didn't sit well with her, and impatience had a way of coupling itself with excitement, and that with anxiety settled disquietingly in her stomach. Just one "Yes" is all she wanted to say! Just that, as Jade would understand the rest.

And the second hour passed in this fashion, anxious breathing met with unanswered ringing, like the first. She stared down the black and chrome phone, and almost growled with displeasure at it. Someone must bear the brunt of responsibility, and short of that, something, she thought as she beat a path out of there before committing yet a third hour to the trial. Putting her patience skills in gear, she gave herself permission to resume her retreat.

But with her Yes, and her open arms to Jade and to their lives together, whatever the shape and form their heat would take, the weekend's significance multiplied as did the gentle pulsing between her thighs.

Later that day Diana saved for taking an honest assessment of the last seven years of her life: her goals, her accomplishments, her journey. For her, most important was that she learned how to talk with the Goddess. Learned that she didn't have to be polite and find the right words. Any words would do, as the Goddess was never one to stand on ceremony. She learned, and she continued to learn how to maintain the everlasting connection with the positive life force that waited to take her hand at the very moment she extends it. Being positive and having a positive attitude was not a hobby with her, it was her life's philosophy, her career, her every other thought. She learned that living life to the Apex was an acquired art. And art requires practice. And practice, vigilence. Constant vigilence.

Her afternoon was spent like this: chatting and reminiscing with the Goddess. Diana hadn't spoken to a soul all day. This vacation was beginning to look more and more like a spiritual retreat. And that was just fine with her. And equally, if not more fine with the Goddess, as she was thrilled to have one of her daughters all to herself, without distraction, for even a few hours.

It was a weekend of the homecoming for both of them. In fact, for everybody involved in this weekend.

At eight she took time out from reading and thinking for some honest-to-goodness eating. Returning from a tiny Chinese take-out, she took out many things—like stir fried vegetables and soup and something or other lo mein—and laid the white cardboard boxes out on the rocks in front of her cabin in front of the ocean. Saturday night found her without a date. She wouldn't be ashamed to admit it as tonight was hers to delight and amuse herself as she saw fit.

Mostly she ate, and thought, and smoked cigarettes and flirted with the idea of masturbating out on the rocks. No one occupied the neighboring cottages, and she was very much alone. She sat deciding in silence, with her arms locked around her legs watching, watching, watching the waves until she heard her first voice of the weekend at what turned out to be shortly before midnight. Because it was the first voice, and for that reason alone, she was startled just momentarily. The instinctive knowledge, the instant recognition of who the voice belonged to, however, was what made her heart stop. Stop absolutely dead in its tracks.

"Welcome, Miss Hunter," the woman said in a low hushed tone laying her hands on Diana's shoulders tenderly. So, so tenderly. Diana could feel the woman's body against her back—that is how close she stood: the thighs, the firm belly and the hands on her shoulders. How she remembered those long fingers of the hands that slid inside of her on those, the best of the best nights. Diana did not turn around, did not move, did not have to know anything more than this moment. She relaxed, and let her body lean back with a fraction of pressure against the woman who stood behind her. Leaned back into her ever so slightly, and closed her eyes, and let the tears fall in celebration.

She licked her lips to taste the tears that made their way down her cheeks; as she wanted to remember the taste of them to commemorate this unexpected, glorious moment, and everything about it. Everything: the sound of the ocean, the time of the night, the feel and the stillness of the woman behind her, the erratic pounding of her own heart. She had envisioned this scene thousands of times, in thousands of ways, but she never pictured this one—so cool and serene. And right.

The Miracle was upon her.

And as for the woman standing: she had stood watching the woman on the rocks less than one hundred feet in front of her for the last two hours. At least. Mesmerized by the sight of the woman on the rocks who she had dedicated the decade of her twenties to. Diana's tears slowed as the woman's tears began. She had learned patience; she had learned all about pain, about loneliness, and learned all about growth in the time since she was last with Diana. She had learned so many things, too many to recount, and at this second every one of them seemed worth it. Worth the wait, worth the struggle, worth what she might have with Diana forever as a result of the wait. Diana was worth anything.

"I haven't for one moment stopped loving you, Christina," Diana whispered, leaning her head to the side to run her tongue along the woman's fingers laying on her shoulder. And when done, she lay her cheek down on Christina's hand, and watched the ocean.

Christina felt Diana's damp skin, and turned her hand over to cup Diana's cheek in her hand. "I've always belonged to you, darling, and regardless of what happens from this moment on, I always will," Christina murmured, leaning down behind Diana. "Let me stay with you tonight . . . for all the nights that I couldn't."

It had been so devastatingly long since those torrential nights with Christina, Diana reflected. It had been, for what seemed like, for fucking ever since she was inside her with a scalding tongue, Christina thought. The heat between them, the embers that never died but remained on a slow far-away burn, ignited. It was the need to touch that seized them both, just to touch, lightly, the other's body. That moment was forthcoming, the image of it arrestingly attractive to them both, but premature. The beloved soulmates did not move for fear of altering the course of this cherished, miraculous and stunning moment. Both still, both overwhelmed.

Her spirit was bucking, but Diana sat still; Christina's heart was slamming against her chest, and she too was still.

It was forever until Diana slowly rose and turned to face Christina and at once enfolded herself over and over into the warm image of this woman who now stood before her. "You have grown gorgeous in your absence." The sight of the other was breathtaking; they stood feverish, impassioned.

"No more dazzling, my love, than you." With the sound of each of Christina's words Diana grew more inflamed.

"It seems you've done well for yourself," Diana said calmly through the throbbing.

"I've done well for myself, yes . . . and for you, Diana." They moved a bit closer, these two mesmerized spirits.

"Not me, Christina, for *you*, and I don't judge you, baby—"

"For me to be worthy of you," Christina gently insisted, "I had to declare my worthiness so I could ask you to spend your life with me—"

"Chris—"

"No, wait, Diana, listen . . . I couldn't ask you to spend it with me if I was spending all my time being afraid of losing you . . ."

Diana seized Christina's pause to use it as her moment to say, "Christina, I understood after a time why you left—I didn't at first—"

"Didn't you read my note?"

"After the drinking I did that night when I found your note, the next morning I couldn't remember much about it . . . other than you said you were leaving. But that's not important, darling, what is is that *whatever* your reasons were, please know that I always was wanting you to find what you were looking for even if it meant in someone else's arms. Baby, I never stopped loving you from the first time I asked you if you wanted to make out with me in the Girls Bathroom."

Both smiled smiles whet with arousal. Heated, wet lips glistened in the moonlight, waiting.

"Diana—"

"Christina, I finally understood that you must have loved me a great deal to have left me that way. You were never a coward, Christina, and I finally realized that you must have chosen a risk greater than—"

"—greater than anything I'd ever taken on. I was scared to death!"

"Come here, baby girl, and let momma hold you," Diana said tenderly. "It must have been rough out there fighting dragons, climbing up castle walls, and fucking princesses in your journey, you wench," Diana teased, mixing the maternal and sexual.

"There were no princesses," Christina whispered before entering Diana's arms to cry. For her journey was indeed a long one, and not once in that time did she afford herself the luxury and privilege of resting. She had not once stopped seeking to get what she went out there for, not for a moment, as speed was crucial. The longer she took, the longer it would take her to return, into what she prayed to God, would be *open* arms. And now, she hoped and hoped hard, that her journey had ended.

Love, magnetic love, holding them, captivating them so that they were alone on the planet, just them, alone with their hearts almost beating in time, and their bodies both shaking with the overwhelming feelings. Love upon love upon love moved them on further into this night.

The rocks were easily navigable with the two of them. Blanket in tow, they climbed with urgent caution far above the wild Pacific Ocean, a sight only more stunning because of its expansiveness, than the two women climbing up high to watch. Diana was enthralled by the sight of Christina, climbing up a few feet ahead of her: her strong tapered legs, her round ass, her wide shoulders and small waist, her thick and inviting mane of blond curly hair cascading down her back. And again her competent hands with their long fingers which she remembered so well. Damp already from the labor of climbing, wet already with the anticipation of the lovemaking, which would come, as she would, inevitably.

Destination reached, blanket laid, they stood arm in arm, heart to heart in the cool windy California middle of the night.

They stood, they sat, they smoked, they stared out at the ocean, and began to talk:

"What am I to do now?" Diana asked as if she had not already dismissed that question in her own mind for being axiomatic.

"What is it you want to do, Miss Hunter?"

"I know that I don't have to be afraid—"

"You don't."

"And that you *are* back—"

"I am, Diana, I am."

"And that you do want me—"

"As I always have."

Diana thought carefully about this one . . . . "And that you are in—"

"Yes . . . *desperately* . . . *wildly* in love with you," Christina glowingly smiled and replied.

Diana's fingertip reached up to touch Christina's lips. "Do you know that not a day went by when we were together without my sharing all my thoughts with you. You, my little runaway, were my best friend."

"I know. That's what I missed most of all, Diana." They both smiled in a way that two people who have known despair and loneliness intimately, could.

"Some nights," Christina continued, "I sat next to the phone aching to call you, tell you everything—"

"Why in God's name didn't you?" Diana asked incredulously.

"Wait. Think, honey, had I given into the impulse, you would have given me every single good reason to return to you, no? You would have soothed me back to you, made it literally impossible for me to complete what I had already set out to do. I know you, Miss Hunter, and I know the effect you have on me."

"And you could have finished your journey with a comrade instead of alone. What would have been so counterproductive about that?"

"Leaving you would have made no sense unless I returned after bringing my journey to an end, my goals to fruition . . . Please understand that," Christina implored.

"Nightly, Christina, nightly for the entire first year I waited for your one call I was certain you would break down and finally make. You brought me to my knees, my love." And now it was Diana's turn—she was crying with the joy that lay precisely in the place where the pain used to be.

Christina wrapped her gentlest arms around her and cooed to her with lips but a breath away from tearful tremors herself. "Go ahead, darling, and cry, I'm here with you now . . ."

Time had time tonight; it paced itself evenly between the moments . . .

. . . "You were a woman of many talents, Diana, and you had sort of a wild drive . . . to change things, move mountains, make your mark. Not that I even knew where this would lead you or how you would use it in the world, but I knew that it would include a lot of people. A lot of people. And I admired you for it, revered you even, and at the same time it threw me into a deeper insecurity—"

"Chrissy—"

"Let me say it, Diana . . . to be worthy of what I knew you were going to grow into—a leader of people in some capacity. I was forced to regroup. Then I realized that a simple regrouping or change of scenery or a new project to lift my self-esteem was not all it would take. Not nearly close to what I realized I needed. I was scared of losing you—"

Diana started to interrupt. She had a that-is-preposterous look on her face.

Christina held her ground. "—Losing you to someone I couldn't ever begin to compete with: someone courageous, someone secure in what they were and who they were. Someone who looked in the mirror and said without hesitation, 'I Love what I see, I Love what I am.' Mind you, I liked myself. I was a pretty happy woman, but you . . . you were shooting out of your skin with talents that you didn't even know were screaming for recognition. I was not enough for myself, and as a result I knew that it would be only a matter of time before I was not enough for you."

Diana wanted to shake Christina. "You *were* enough!"

"*Then*, I was then. But in twelve months or two years or two weeks the time would have come that *I* felt that you could do better than me. And, Diana, I couldn't live with myself, or you, knowing that. I had to leave before that happened. I had to risk losing you altogether, and it seemed like my only choice at that moment, before losing you in the tiny ways that ruin comes to a relationship."

"Christina, you were everything to me—simply everything!"

"Then, yes, but I wanted you for me forever, and I had not earned having you, and couldn't earn it while I was so close, so intertwined with you and your life. And to me, when I looked at forever with you, a few years away from you seemed small in comparison."

Diana envisioned the scenario that would have taken place had Christina told her she was leaving, and Christina was right: "I would have tried everything in the world to stop you. I couldn't stand to be away from you for one night, how could I have let you go for what might have been endless years of nights?" She continued, "You know, of course, that had you not left me as you did, when you did, I would never have ventured out, and stumbled upon my true calling." Diana had never used that word 'calling' before, but that is exactly what it was, her calling, her destiny. "Had I not lost my foundation—You—I couldn't have reconstructed my life entirely a second time on a sound spiritual one." Diana knew there were no coincidences.

"Tell me about the princesses and the dragons and the castle walls you spent all those years scaling."

"Would you be satisfied with the condensed version?"

"For now." As Diana saw it, some information was better than none.

After lighting a cigarette for herself and Diana, running her hand through Diana's thick wind-touseled hair, clearing her throat and collecting her thoughts, Christina began the verbal outline.

"Year one I spent in night classes at the University—"

"Of?"

"NYU, New York University—"

"So *New York*—" said Diana, about to give Christina a hard time.

"Don't presume, Miss Hunter, New York is only a wild town if you are going at it looking for action, which I was not at the time." Christina was not open for teasing. "Keep in mind," she continued, "that I'm only going to tell you about the activities I took on, not the feelings. I don't want to spend all our time together talking. So for now just the steps that led me back here."

Diana agreed, so Christina continued. "Classes in scriptwriting, filmmaking, sculpture, international studies and psychology. I was hoping psych would help me understand myself better—that was the only reason for that class. The other courses I took on intuition. Even though I spent years, as you well know, writing and had never been published even once, I decided to couple my writing skills with my sense of the visual to create a story with pictures and words. Presumptuous of me to think I could succeed at both without ever having succeeded at the one, but this was a time for taking risks. There was no time for fear. I wasted too much of my life battling with fear to let it interfere. Not that I knew what I wanted to do, or where I was headed, just that I had to try anything—whatever—to make my break from where I was.

"Anyway, that was by day. By night, three nights a week I did volunteer work at the Salvation Army off the Bowery. I dished out food, stacked chairs after the Alcoholics Anonymous meetings, and I was available to talk to when they wanted to talk. My psych course gave me a bit of credibility with the staff. Three nights a week for a year is long enough to find out what I needed to know . . . that giving up is not an option. Ever. Under any circumstances. These people I met, for the most part, would never get beyond the streets that led from the shelter to the corner where they washed windows to the bars. It solidified my commitment to make the most of myself and my life, not to mention solidifying my gratitude."

Christina lit another cigarette, leaned forward into the memories, and continued on, "Year two I lucked into a production assistant job with a blue movie producer. He had a great reputation for artistically erotic movies and a superb sense of the aesthetic. To him they weren't soft porn. He was well respected in the business. More important, I respected him and his work. I worked thirteen hours a day, six days a week by his side.

"The following year he gave me free reign to cast, to help with editing scripts, and to layout preliminary lighting schemes as well as my usual gofer duties. Fifteen hours a day became the norm, and I didn't complain as I knew that I was on to something. I didn't just *happen* to be in the right place at the right time to meet him—it had to be a larger set of implications than that. In the third year I knew it was meant to be. And it wasn't until my fourth year, when I started group therapy, that I began to understand. And never again will I underestimate the benefits of psychology.

"By my fifth year with James, and four excellent movies later I had the confidence and drive to strike out on my own. I had learned all I needed to know, and had made some important contacts in the field. And I had written two very fine scripts that were as ready as they ever would be to put to film. Money was easy for me to get as James gave his name for me to use as freely as I needed. His name carried the weight, and mine the energy and experience. I got the money. And the actors, the crew, the space, which was no easy task in New York City, and was ready. I struck out on my own.

"By February of my sixth year I handed James the completed film and waited for his opinion. He kept me waiting a month which led me to believe he no longer had time for me, or he didn't like my work. In actuality he spent the thirty days peddling my film for a price I had to hear twice to believe. The movie opened in New York at the Art Cinema on 8th Street to shockingly terrific reviews. 'Dressing Up,' put my name on the charts—"

Diana barely got out the question: "You are Leigh Chagall?!"

"One and the same."

"That was a lovely film."

"Thank you, darling, I hoped to God you would think so . . ."

"Then, 'Ladies of Leisure,' 'Mercedes,' and 'Girl Talk' were yours also?"

"Yes, yes, yes! Make sense why all the heroines were all named Diana, Diana?"

"I am astonished!"

"Good—I worked hard for your praise, Diana."

"And you want me to believe that you worked for all those years in that genré, and didn't find any princesses?" Soft sarcasm from Miss Hunter.

"No, I found plenty, but let me remind you that in all those years it was you I wanted, you I was headed back to."

"And group?"

"That continued until 'Girl Talk' opened, and that's when I sent you the tickets, and left the city to come home to you."

"What do you want with me now that you have achieved fame and for—"

"Don't tease me, Diana. What sounds like a fabulous success story was filled with endless dark and cold evenings. Alone without you. Working my way back to you was a fever. It propelled me forward. I've never worked so hard in my life."

"I didn't mean to tease you, lover—"

"Still the pretty liar, Diana?"

"Really, Christina, I just simply can't imagine—"

"Nor could I."

The events having been sketchily recounted made their exit, and on their heels the feelings arrived taking their seats in the spotlight.

"Group helped me to keep on the path during the times when I couldn't remember anymore why I wasn't with you. I was furious at myself for leaving you, Diana, and hurting you, which I know I must have done in my amorphous search for self. Please don't think I didn't know what suffering it might have caused you. It was hell living with that knowledge."

"I tried to self-destruct after you left me," Diana said absently staring out at the water.

"And it hurt, Diana?"

"A lot, momma, too much some nights." Diana kept her eyes focused on the horizon to keep from crying about how much she did, in fact, go after hurting herself for a crime she believed she committed to make Christina go away.

These were two different women than they were when they parted. They were both stronger, wiser. And no less in love. Perhaps more. More than they would have been had their personal tragedies not so changed the course of their lives.

Christina did have the harder path: made the more difficult choices, took the largest risks available, sought the hardest road she could possibly find to get to her goal as rapidly as humanly possible. Speed, speed. "I chose a city to settle in where I wouldn't have the comfort of familiarity or friends. I wanted to do it all alone. And my first year aside from school and my work on the Bowery I thought and planned and wrote and ran and burned for you Diana, and was desperate about the thought of losing you in my attempt to have you forever.

"Nothing scared me as much in what I had to face alone, as losing you did. Nothing loomed larger in my path than having sent you away. And there were times I didn't think that I could do it . . . do anything without *you* by my side. And that reality scared me more than anything I've ever had to deal with—not being able to do my own life without you being there." The urgency with which she spoke, and the thrill of accomplishment caused her cheeks to flush with the rush to hold Diana, love her, tell her every single feeling, swallow her whole instantly.

Then Christina said calmly, confidently, "I learned that I was much stronger than I knew." And, oh, the swelling pride that came with saying such a thing. I AM strong. I am. What a thing to accomplish, to know, to believe about yourself.

"Not stronger than *I* knew," Diana replied.

"I knew that. But I believed that your faith in me was unfounded. That you were being polite, blind to my weaknesses with your feelings for me. None of your reassurances could have negated my doubts about myself . . . nothing, nothing you could have said would have altered my feelings—not even your rose-colored glasses theory."

Diana understood her, heard her well, for she had mouthed those words enough times in her speeches not to believe that yes, there is nothing you can do for someone who doesn't believe it first herself. Diana said quietly, "I do understand that. Now."

"I came," continued Christina, "with the intentions of laying all my worldly spoils at your feet, my—"

"You have. You carry them inside you, they radiate from within you, darling. I can *feel* the strength. You are changed, darling, you have, I think, within you that which you traveled so far to achieve: courage, serenity, victory."

"I do, Diana, and it sits well with me."

"I am proud of you." Actually Diana was overwhelmed with pride if not astounded by it. She had a confession to make: "I never thought I'd lay my eyes on you again, Christina. Ever."

"I did. Every night of every day I wanted and waited for this time, and you know that I was not, am not, a patient girl."

At this the girls laughed with the memory of how often Christina's impatience had gotten them into trouble. The laughter quieted: both humbled by the homecoming.

Diana tried to imagine what it was like for Christina; Christina sat trying to imagine what it must have been like for Diana. "Is there any need to talk of your forgiving me?"

"Don't—"

"I have to ask," Christina said gravely.

"The answer is no. No need for anything but just being with me here and now."

"I can't begin, and I mean not even begin, to tell you how magnificently overpowered I am with your story. With you." And with this Diana turned to Christina in all humility and reverence and said, "I bow to you, Christina. I salute the greatness in you that propelled you to find your truth your way—away from me, and then back to me."

It is as plain as
Black and White.

Margo Reed had the fever of the mission: the Jamaican woman cut across campus with an untamed élan. She moved swiftly towards the Communications Building, towards the ninth floor, towards Jade Desmonde—there was no time to waste for this female in heat.

Last night, Margo was on the Island having a heart-to-heart with her mentor, her mother, when it hit her. Tonight she came to get what she left behind on her last Phoenix visit. Diana's party was no coincidence—it was there she laid eyes on Miss Desmonde.

Since that time, thoughts of Jade just would not let her rest. Her modeling assignments took her to Milan, Egypt, Australia; the exotic scenery, women and long hours could not stop the obsession.

Miss Desmonde intrigued her to distraction. The more she found out about this brilliant amazon, the more she wanted her for herself. Margo swept into town for one reason only: to take Jade Desmonde. With Diana off at some mysterious vacation on the coast, Margo hoped Jade might be ready to negotiate, or better still, to be taken.

Armed with a well-financed smokescreen, a business proposition, she entered the building and quieted her exultant heart: Margo Reed could make a pitch like nobody's business. As Jade Desmonde was about to witness.

Saturday night, international date night, and Jade was at her desk working. In front of her, a proposal she had drawn up utilizing state money to fund a profit-making landscaping business that she mapped out. A business to be staffed by the mentally handicapped adults that were being forced out of State Institutions and into the city streets to fend for themselves. A business, Jade proposed, that would garner not only a profit for the State, but profitable publicity was well. Jade was gearing up for a crusade.

Jade looked up from her papers when the elevator across the long, narrow hallway opened. She lay down her pen only when the dark woman arrived at her desk, extended her hand and said, "Hello, I'm Margo Reed."

"Jade Desmonde."

"I know. I saw you briefly at the . . . Diana Hunter party."

"Yes . . ." Jade remembered this woman's striking smile, her hazel eyes. This was Diana's girlfriend the night of the party. What in the world was Jade to make of this?

Margo Reed, in all of her steamy dark beauty, had the same effect on Jade as she had on Diana as she had on all her women. Jade thought she better keep talking. "Diana is not here. I hope you are not disappointed."

"Not at all," Margo smiled, removed her sunglasses, and continued with deliberate nonchalance, "I came to see you, Miss Desmonde."

The woman told Jade that she had a proposition for her, and then came straight out with it. "I have in mind to open a string of Salons, the first in Quebec, exclusively for women. Women like ourselves."

"How long have you had this on your mind?"

"Long enough to be dead certain that it will be wildly profitable, and welcomed with great enthusiasm. The concept is long overdue, no?"

"How long until we break even?" Jade asked, trying to imagine what it must have been like the night Margo spent with Diana.

"Three busy months."

"I am serious, Miss Reed!"

Margo defended herself, "What makes you think that I'm not?"

Jade said she wanted to know what was wrong with the deal. It sounded too good to her.

Margo smiled broadly. "You mean other than the fact that I need you to leave your job, your home, and your . . . woman, and come work your pretty bottom off with me for the next twelve months? The bottom that you teased Miss Hunter with at her party when you walked away from her so very slowly and seductively?" Margo said slowly and seductively.

The girls couldn't help but smile. Margo kept talking. "I know Diana noticed the way you looked, the way you moved. I want you to know that *I* noticed, as well." Margo had to light herself a cigarette.

Jade had to sit down. The desire to lunge at this woman, and take her down, came upon her in waves. "You come on campus on a Saturday night, and I don't even want to ask how you knew to find me here, to offer me a lucrative proposition, business and otherwise, and tell me that I will have to pick up and leave everything to come away with you to open exotic Salons for women so we can both get rich and famous. And," obviously Jade was not through with her quiet diatribe yet, "I know that if you had enough money and energy yourself, you wouldn't have come to me at all!"

The woman who possessed more than enough money and energy said sarcastically, "Do you want me to withdraw my offer? Apologize for disrupting your evening?!"

It turned into an ache now. She couldn't help herself. Jade was holding herself back from moving into this black, hot magnet of a female. "Margo, I don't know how I feel about all this."

"I am not staying here to discuss your feelings, Miss Desmonde. If I stay tonight, it is to be with *you*. Tomorrow we can discuss the intricasies of my proposition.

The Jamaican arrogance; the Jamaican beauty; the Jamaican sexuality.

Suddenly, Jade needed some time to herself. She was drawn to this sensation in front of her. As she was toward the woman who had helped her feel like living again for the first time in years. Diana Hunter: The woman she threw the party for, the woman she served as night visitor to, the woman she was in love with.

This was anything but a simple proposition. Jade postponed thinking about Margo's offer tonight. She surrendered to the undertow of desire: the stranger inflamed her, dared her *not* to move forward. Powerless against the black magic of the woman, and already wet with the possibilities, she welcomed the adventure. Jade's intuition was mounting: it told her that in countless ways, this was to be a memorable evening.

Margo Reed was banking on it.

You,
Omnipresent
in the Alpha and Omega
of my life,
Eclipse all else.

Victims both of each other's hunger, it was Christina who initiated: "You have never been more beautiful." Placing her hands on Diana's shoulders and summoning her forward. "I shall love you like this for the rest of my life, lover," she whispered before moving closer to lay her soft cheek against Diana's.

Oh, how Diana wanted her, wanted to eat this woman whole, and she said nothing, just stood shivering beneath her layers of clothing, shaking with the heat and the cool wind and her dancing heart.

She slowly caressed Diana's cheek with the downy soft of her own, and moved slightly to kiss her ear, lick her lobe with her tongue. Diana heard her breathe, the sound of her lover aroused, the lover she could never seem to let loose, let go, forget.

She had Christina in her arms, that close, and it was still hard to believe this Miracle. Christina's tongue slowly and deliberately made its way encircling Diana's ear first, then into it, teasing, wetting. Diana pressed herself against Christina to let her delicate tongue wet her gently, quietly. Slowly, slowly the temperature rose between them with the hot breath, the wet tongue, the fingers that ran through and through Diana's hair.

The cool wind on the cliffs felt good on their slow burning bodies.

Diana's hands wanted to move, of their own accord, beneath Christina's leather jacket, beneath her shirt to feel her breasts, just to cup them in her hands for a moment, a second, to press against them. Full and fleshy and round and her hands wanted this with all their heart. With arms around Christina, she pressed her close, too close as if in a flash the apparition of her might disappear. The closeness, the tenderness, the breathing mixed to begin the flush.

Then, what each had fantasized countless times, in endless solitary nights, happened: they engulfed one another in the kiss—this, the first kiss—that was so long overdue. Wake-up, fireburning kisses that tore into Christina's mouth, seared her lips with Diana's hunger, the steamy hunger that grew in them in their absence. The yawning abyss of their appetites pursuing their sustenance here on the rocks, on the cliff, by the ocean in the quite, black night. Breath smoking with passion, lips sucking in lips, tongues touching tongues, and mouths wide open welcoming the wet, the quenching. Hungry mouths, red-hot with years of seething energy yet to be loosed, scalding tongue to tongue, plunging in, exploring, sucking in. Standing, throbbing with their fevers, they kissed the kiss of life into one another. Teeth biting, lips wetting mouths, arms locked, hands engulfing one another, taking it in, taking it in, trying to swallow the dream they longed for and now held so close.

Sounds of pleasure, moaning sounds, waiting sounds, tasting sounds, wet sounds of unabashed passion in the cool night wind, mixing well with ocean sounds, waves slapping the rocks sounds, all sounds waiting for the trembling moment to take its next step . . . And they were powerless to release one another; they could not, their mouths would not stop drawing in, licking, wetting, sucking as it grew more and more inflamed between them.

Skin damp, body pressing, rocking next to body, they moved to each other's rhythms they knew so well. Time heals but never forgets: they knew the smells, the sounds, the tastes, and bathed themselves in it this night.

It was more Diana wanted when she pulled gently away from Christina to bring her down to the blanket with her so they could lay on one another, next to one another, lips to lips, breasts to breasts. Diana shuddered with the pleasure and let her hands go, the hands that ached to explore Christina's body, to touch her in her most hot places. Waiting grew harder. "Let me, let me," Diana implored, "take your breasts in my mouth . . . let me see them please, darling." She unzipped Christina's jacket, and unbuttoned her shirt ever so slowly.

It was cold on the cliffs, and neither cared, as they would survive the chill of nakedness blanketing themselves instead in the tempetuous heat that radiated between them. So painfully slowly Diana was unbuttoning her shirt, watching, waiting to see the breasts she fondled with such familiarity years ago.

And on her back, below her was Christina waiting to be touched, to be seen. "Yes, Diana," was all she said over and over, and then, "I want you to see me, to take me."

Shirt opened and spread apart; Christina's breasts exposed to her lover; and Diana reeling inside at the sight of these two full, round beautiful breasts that awaited her lips, her hands, her mouth to cover them. Hotlicking her dark nipple tenderly, first one then the other, so

161

slowly, as slowly as time seems to pass when you sit and watch it move from second to second. That is how slowly Diana's tongue moved across Christina's nipples, one to the other, to the other, wetting them, licking them with fingertip caresses, barely, just barely touching them. Caressing them with fingers, grazing them easily with her cheek, looking at them, at Christina exposed to her like this. Biting them with a gentle pressure, nipples between her fingers pinching them, the friction, the slowness stirring Christina, making her want to cry because it was real, it was upon her as she prayed it would be all those quiet and dark lonely nights without Diana.

Breathing became more pronounced, more irregular for these two women in heat. The longing took the form of holding, pressing. Christina asked Diana to suck her breasts in her mouth, to suck them in, to press them hard and have it all, to take her, to be taken by her. An inflammatory ease made Diana move slowly, savoring the tastes, the smells, reminding her of the nights when she had Christina in just such a way, with just such a slow urgency. But, of course, whatever they had, ever, did not begin to compare with how big this was now between them. Her hands circled Christina's breasts, her lips kissing small tiny kisses on her chest, her neck and back to her mouth to suck the very life out of the woman she had not seen in years, and her hands never changing their langorously steady pace.

They had time, all the time in the world tonight, and Diana's deliberately slow moving hands explained that to Christina. Diana laid now on top of her, embraced her, held her unsated body in her arms, and gave her tears time to rise and fall, as they lay like this—still—until Diana once more lay her pillow soft lips against Christina's and began to take her in full-mouthed again. Christina acquiesced, no, she melted easily into Diana's strong arms and her strong body and her insistent mouth. They moved as one, these two, in their rising arousal.

Hands massaging Christina's full breasts tenderly; moving on hands that were searching, holding, pressing and her mouth kissing, tonguing her to move on, move on further still. One move towards her spread legs, Christina knew, would shake her to orgasm, and Diana, it seemed, having something entirely else in mind. Diana, unhurried, savoring each moment as if it were her last. She had learned well that it *might* be her last with Christina, and that she could never be too sure, too sure about anything anymore. A lesson she would not soon forget, if ever.

Diana's breathing lay heavy on hers, her lips full on her lips, her hand resting full on her breast, and they thought of nothing else but this one, very focused moment. The world was nonexistent for them as

Diana's hand moved down over Christina's taut belly. And then a slight sound from Christina with the moving hand, or was it the wind suspiring with the sight of these two, and then Christina's pants zipper sliding imperceptibly down under Diana's fingers. Christina's belly exposed and joyous with the long forgotten touch. Exploring hands, lingering hands across Christina's stomach and up again to tease the breasts, and down again closer still with each sweeping stroke to her crotch, the tight pants holding the wet lips still, and she knew that Christina wanted her there, as she was undulating, her hips undulating under Diana's hands and Diana's words telling her that it would not be now. "Not now, baby, you don't want it so soon." And Christina agreeing and wanting it now all the same. Sweet hands stroking up and down her body and stopping when Diana lay her lips on Christina's with quick kisses, loving kisses to her closed eyes, her cheeks, her forehead damp with the suspense. Gently, all this time so gently, and tenderly, until—

Until the savage kisses came. Suddenly the savage kisses with the lips that were after blood, sucking hard, her tongue now commanding its due after their eternity of enforced waiting, the anger at the absence, her hands pressuring, squeezing and hurting, and red nails digging into the woman willing to yield to it all for the woman she desperately loved. Diana was overwhelmed with the urge to hurt, the power of the conquerer, the fury of all the time wasted between them.

"Have me, baby, take, take what you want, I'm yours," Christina responded to the pain, to Diana's newly awakened urgency.

"You've been mine, always been mine, Christina," Diana growled between the kiss to her lips and then the one to her neck which she knew she wanted to leave marks on the surface of her skin. And neither cared. This was not a time to care about such things. This was a time to take, to have.

And what they did not say with their mouths could not be said, as the kissing was articulate, the tongue to tongue, breath to breath, mouth the mouth, heart to heart moving as one in the dance known to women in love. This, the dance of the sparks.

The bodies moved together pushing, pulling, tugging, resucitating one another from their eight-year-long sleep.

Diana released herself from Christina's arms, and put a space between their bodies. In a barely audible underbreath, she instructed Christina to remove her jacket and her shirt, and lay, like this, half-naked.

There was no resistance for Christina to overcome, the sound of her lover's voice like welcome liquid to her dry throat. Anything, she would do anything Diana asked of her.

The woman in heat drew Diana now on top of her semi-nude body, but Diana preferred to remain on her knees between Christina's spread legs. There she undid her own shirt buttons to release the breasts that held her hard palpitating heart captive, her beating heart beating, beating, beating in crazy anticipation. Removing the clothes that separated her breasts from Christina's mouth took but seconds. Lowering herself, her breasts, onto Christina's mouth easily, she heard her own moan at the contact, of the wet lips, hungry mouth with her own stiff nipples from the cold, from the contact, from the high. Below her, Christina sucking warm breasts, she lost herself in the sight, in the feeling. Christina kissed Diana's breasts with her lips, her hands, her heart. Diana's own heart quickening with each caress. Diana on her hands and knees over her lover, her large breasts grazing the woman's cheeks, brushing them against Christina's baby soft face, the face she so desperately tried to forget for so many years. Christina took each of the breasts in her hands, caresses growing forceful, and now pulling Diana down full upon her own body, breasts to breasts, both women laboring to maintain regular breathing, and failing. Both clothed only from the waist down, fondling, feeling and fluttering hearts from the waist up, they lay like this amidst the sweltering kisses.

They were endowing each other slowly, reviving each other's heart to pound, and blood to rush as it was meant to, as it always had when they connected this way.

Only a handful of minutes balanced between them and what was to come. It would be soon. Soon, they would be inside of one another's rapacious bodies, soon. They wanted that, at once, at once, but neither moved to make it happen yet. Diana's breath even hotter than Christina's touched and touched her neck again and circled her ear and brushed her jaw—just her breath making contact. The smell of Christina, the incense that aroused her passion, meeting her at every turn daring her not to grow wetter.

They were approaching the fine line between wanting to be inside of one another and needing to be. Inside, deep inside. Christina's thoughts were already deep inside Diana's body even though her long fingers remained still massaging the silky skin of Diana's back, and her mouth continuing to search to find Diana's.

Hungry girls.

"I lost my heart to you when I was sixteen and it has never stopped, much as I tried, much as I wanted it to," Diana sighed and moved down to Christina's body to find her breasts again, to get lost in them. And when she shifted and lifted her eyes to look at Christina she found her fondling her own breasts which sent a tremor of heat between Diana's thighs. Lifting one of Christina's hands and placing it between her own legs, on the material of her pants that held back her pulsing, she said, "I burn for you here, Christina." And Christina's hand moved easily against her there, stroking the cunt that was wet for her, the cunt of the woman on her knees who never stopped wanting her. Every second of the eight years was worth this one single moment.

Christina released herself and moved up to her knees, too, in front of Diana, inches apart, both admiring, adoring. Tormented now with the need to penetrate, Christina lifted Diana's body to her feet, and she her own, and without words they removed the rest of their clothes. There in the still blue-black backdrop of night, with only the waves to witness, they stood naked, supple, soft bodies next to each other, submerged in what was nothing less than exhilarated ecstasy.

"You are a breathtaking sight," Diana appraised aloud, after a subliminal groan emerged from her at the sight of her lover's body clothed only in a long mane of honey-white blond hair that waved and curled its way down her strong back. Swept away with the blinding vision of beauty in front of her, she led them to the furthermost part of the boulder upon which they stood, so they could see the ocean more clearly and feel the sharp, gray cold stone beneath their bare feet. The blanket behind them now, there they were, choosing to freeze and burn and press and reel with all the turbulent feelings and sounds and smells of this miraculous California night.

It was Diana who knelt down in front of her lover, mouth to thighs, lips to lips, and there she waited for Christina to spread her legs for her. And Christina did, while laying her hands on Diana's shoulders with a gentle pressure to guide Diana's head closer, pressing it closer to her own body, saying 'Have me now,' with her hands. Christina could barely feel the torrid hot breath on her, but Diana would not be forced: she kept an inch of distance, wanting Christina to feel only her breath, not her tongue. Christina insistent; Diana patient and breathing in of the scent that intoxifies; brushing her fingertips against the soft hair of her lover's cunt that invited her in, saying 'Come, my love, come, you've been away too long. I've waited for you.' Yes, Diana could almost hear this. Knowing Christina wanted Diana's tongue on her most, Diana let her lips touch only her soft triangle of blond hair, then her tongue did touch her flesh, the flesh of her thighs, the insides of her tight thighs. She kissed her lover below, above, around but not on, not on top of her fire. Yet. Diana's lips and tongue moved tenderly kissing, sparking tiny embers to light moving her lips down to Christina's knees, her hands holding Christina's legs firmly in place.

This sight for Christina, seeing Diana on her knees, naked below her, was unmatched, tormenting her beyond her capacity to wait any longer. She stood shivering, trembling, aroused as Diana caressed the backs of her knees and her thighs with sweeping hands up and down her strong legs, always moving closer and closer to their heated destination. The scent of Christina's arousal convinced Diana to move even more slowly still.

Christina moved her own hand down to her pussy and stroked it once for Diana to see, saying, "It begs for you with wetness. Please . . ." Feeling her own come on her fingers, so wet with passion. Then moving her fingers to Diana's mouth she said, "See how much I want you." And Diana's lips tasted her lover's wet heat. Sweet-tasting come arousing her further, she let her hands roam up Christina's body to her breasts, to her waist, to her back and then bottom to feel her lover's waiting shaking body.

Diana's lips found her lover's fingers again and sucked the taste of Christina into her mouth. There, on her knees, licking tenderly the hand that held the cards for so many years. Diana's hands exploring, Christina's body slightly swaying with the urges that more urgently demanded sating, and Diana's mouth taunting, teasing, kissing her everywhere but there, where she most wanted to be kissed. Every fucking place but there, and she knew she must wait.

Cool, windswept minutes passed, and Diana brought her hands around Christina's body to cup her round ass, to part her firm cold cheeks, to move her curious, anxious fingers into, close to, next to, on top of her anus, wet, too, with come. Then with an unexpected pressure she drew her close, and Christina pitched slightly with the pleasure and the pressure, and tried to stand straight again despite the arousal which was growing heavier inside her, on her.

Her legs spread further, instinctively, her flashes multiplied, and then Hit—Diana's mouth was upon her, her fingers pulling back and exposing the tiny blond curls, the swollen lips. Oh, Christina was so good to wait, for she was swollen and red and soon to be feverishly aching for the inevitable moment. Diana tasting of the come that glistened even in the darkness, and Christina concentrating on standing still, on watching Diana kissing her, on balancing herself with her hands on Diana's shoulders urging her on. "Yes, Oh Christ Yes," her body pleaded for her to Do It, Do It to her.

And Diana was doing it, pleasing her with the slowness, not giving into the instinct to have her come immediately, as she knew Christina would, given the chance. Diana's lips sucking in the swollen lips tenderly as her hands held fast to Christina's ass, holding her here in place, while her tongue made its way to inside this woman she held so dear. Her fingers replacing her tongue, sliding easily into Christina, who after craving just this moment, was wrenched forward a bit, losing control, the feelings taking her in, taking her away, her nipples rock hard, her clitoris throbbing, Diana's fingers entering and exiting, penetrating smoothly and deeper and deeper into the woman who opened wider and wider to her with spread legs. The tempo between them captured both their bodies with Diana's fingers inside Christina and her other hand on her ass pushing her forward, rocking slowly, rocking her with the rhythm, deeper and deeper, tongue inflaming her on and on. And rocking together the both of them, in measured motion, each thinking the same thought: Now, Now, Now!

Now, the moment was now, as Diana's mouth lay full upon Christina's clitoris, her tongue, too, full upon her summoning her to the Ascent. Now.

"Please me, Hunter . . . come now . . . I beg you, lover." With that Diana braced down with masterful hands and hot mouth burning with the need to engulf, relentlessly rhythmic over and over rocking and penetrating until Diana's skin raw from the stone beneath her knees, Christina above her riding in tempo to the motion, riding the crest of pleasure feeling the swell, awaiting the crash, fingers reaching now deeper into her, reaching into her lover to find it, to find it, and then, finding it to grip her very center, to grip it hard there and hold it fast. She did this, now, yes now, when Christina shook with the scream that was her climax in the hands and mouth of the woman on her knees, the woman who set her body now literally aflame with love.

Both women vibrated with the scream. Damp bodies, Christina's pulsing still, she lowered herself cautiously with weak legs down to the stone, too, in front of her lover, close enough for Diana's fingers to remain inside of her. She threw her arms around her lover's shoulders, and still racked with tremors, the afterspasms of orgasm, she wept like a baby.

God, how they loved one another at this moment; it was beyond comprehension, it was beyond words, and that is why Christina wept so, because there was nothing more she could say. The release she had waited eight years to earn was upon her.

It was later when the tender kissing between them turned hard again, the hard turned impassioned, the impassioned to impatient, and Christina laid Diana down on the strong bare stone that would scrape her back as it did her knees. With sunup but two hours away Christina whispered, "Let me love you . . . let me love you raw, my love." Studying Diana's beautiful ocean blue eyes, her thick long lashes, her pink lips puffy from the kissing, her creamy complexion, olive and smooth. And the auburn hair, fetching as it lay about her on the gray-black speckled stone. Diana alluring; Christina bewitched. She began.

Easily she lifted Diana's head to her own, murmuring, graphically murmuring what it was she wanted to do, would do with Diana. She spoke in a voice subdued and smelling of sex, of lust, of the much awaited conquest of girl over girl. "Let Momma love you, baby; she knows what you want," she explained between wet kisses to Diana's neck, to her face, to her shoulders, "Momma's back now to take good care of you."

Each was the mother and child to one another, the lover, the confidante, the protector, the master of the other from moment to moment. They sucked strength from one another; the ebb and flow of their roles slid easily between them.

Diana yielded completely to the woman who would have her now, whose anxious hands slid over her chest, her breasts, her belly and then the top of her thighs as gracefully as befit a woman lover. Long, longing strokes up and down the smooth surface of Diana's damp body with words that cooed promises of delights, of pleasure upon pleasure, all followed by the request from Christina for Diana to turn over, on her stomach.

The brittle stone mattress hurt her flesh, and Diana did not speak of it. Whatever the cost she would do as Christina asked. Christina asked her to part her legs; and she lay there naked, face down, on the rocks with Christina beside her. And what felt like the gentle kneading strokes of a masseuse were upon her back bringing with it a relaxed descent into arousal. The stone against her breasts were ice; Christina's hands, warm. Christina could feel the tension of arousal beginning along Diana's shoulders and back, her muscles growing taut but yielding, forever yielding to her touch.

Nothing, absolutely nothing, had changed between them.

And with each pressure of Christina's careful hands, Diana's body pressed more stridently against the rocks. The signaling of the coupling of pleasure and pain. Christina massaged up and down the length of Diana's body, saying, "Let me soothe you, lover, and get you ready to be taken."

Diana thinking, let me be taken.

"I will have my way with you my love, and you will want it."

And this was true. And the mixture of the hard rocks and soft hands excited Diana, and she spread her legs a bit further apart. Christina's hands moving from her shoulders and back down to her bottom, pushing Diana's belly against the rocks. Hands sweeping across Diana's body, skin tingling with the touch, and Diana's arms extended at her sides . . . Christina kept her hands moving, relaxing the body that submitted without question. Hands moving down below Diana's ass, to the tops of her thighs, down her legs and back up again. And a kiss, then two, wet kisses from Christina's lips, on her back and then down her spine inch by inch until her lover's lips rested on Diana's ass. Tongue searching, tasting, and Christina cooing to her as tender hands spread the cheeks, leaving Diana face down and vulnerable. Diana grew excited and Christina's words and tongue whet her arousal further. "Oh my salty baby, I can see how beautiful you are," Christina said, gazing at her lover's exposure this way, with legs spread.

And Diana lifted her hips an inch, maybe two, from the stone so Christina could know, saying, "I want you to see me, I want you to watch me as you make me come, Christina." To that the woman replied, "I will . . . I will watch you as I am watching you now." Breathlessly, overwhelmed by it all.

She lowered her head to breathe out soft breaths against Diana's bottom. "I will go inside of you from behind . . . you know that."

"I want you there," Diana replied in a whisper, and lifted her hips up again, giving in to her quickening pulse. And Christina's tongue against her skin, there, from behind, making Diana vibrate, making her purr, making her want it all the more.

And the woman on the top, Diana realized, was the gift giver, the hostess, the night visitor. There was no longer any mystery, there was only love, there was only love, there was only for her to give. To give it, whatever she was asked, to Christina. It would be months before Diana discovered that Christina was the gift giver of the California tickets only. The mystery would be alive again for her; her search would lead her correctly, then, to Jade.

Christina's never-stopping hands rubbing flesh, massaging flesh, holding, pushing, pressing, deliberately inciting and Diana's hips in turn stirring, stirring. The cool wind and Christina's hot breath upon her and the tongue wetting, and breath cooling and again and again this endless teasing that went on for minutes, long, long minutes with Diana's racing, palpitating heart.

Envisioning what this must look like, Diana grew more aroused—the sight of it, the sight was what aroused Diana most, then the feel of it. Diana wanted to get on her knees now with her bottom up to Christina's lips, and she would do just that when Christina asked for it. For now she readied herself against Christina's massaging strong hand, long fingers, pulling and pushing her slightly forward and back down again, lifting her gently up and then down against the stone beneath her, with that rhythm, that rhythm of their bodies which would lead them closer, together, closer to it. Then the fingers moved to where Christina's mouth was, wetted with her own saliva they touched lightly upon Diana's opening and then moved in slowly, excrutiatingly slowly.

Diana heaved her body up and told Christina how very much she wanted her this way, from behind, inside her, loving her that way, watching her. And with the words Diana raised her body further back into Christina's fingers, taking them in more deeply and pleased at how easily Christina fit into Diana's most private places with two fingers and then three and then the pain that twinged replacing the gentleness, and the sweat that came to her brow, and upper lip and the body that was already damp, making it damper.

And Christina and Diana were together moving, the motion of in and out and in had them rocking with Christina behind her, one hand inside of her where she was welcomed, celebrated there, and the other hand around her on her waist pulling her towards the pressure of her fingers. And the pressure, and gentle pumping and the woman softly rocking in motion, in unison, and the grace of their movements and the feel of the fingers arousing her perspiring body. The fluid, easy rhythm hurting and not hurting, bodies dancing in a sweet swaying, nipples erect, hands feeling, Diana moaning and all the while Christina talking her through it telling Diana what she was seeing, what she was doing, what she was seeing while her fingers were buried deep inside of her lover, engulfed in the sweetness that was the best Christina ever wanted to have with anyone.

"I'm right here with you, baby," Christina cooed still talking. "I want you so much," she whispered gradually increasing the speed and the pressure and Diana's sounds, her moans grew louder and stronger and more insistent for the rocking was rubbing her knees raw and inciting her beyond her capacity to wait any longer, not one second longer, and she called out Christina's name over and over, and then with the last one she lifted herself to her knees with Christina behind her and lowered her hands to her aching cunt and began slowly to masturbate herself telling Christina that she wanted it this way, to let her, let her come now. And Christina said, "Yes, Yes, but slowly, lover, only if you go very slowly, and I promise to be gentle with you now."

Diana touched herself in the place that was ripe for touching, running her fingers smoothly, purposefully over her clitoris that was only a breath away from orgasm. Christina held her lover tight and firm in her arm, and kissed and licked her shoulders from the back, and seconds, only seconds passed before she sensed that Diana would come she pulled Diana's hands away, deliberately removing them from their hotbed of arousal. This wasn't fun, this wasn't pleasurable; Diana wanted to scream with waiting, so close, so close she was to coming.

"Now, baby, back down and stay on your knees but bend way over for Momma, let me fill you, all of you." Diana leaned over with her head resting on her folded arms on the rocks, poised for the woman to take her.

With her free hand Christina slid her fingers into Diana's excessively wet vagina and filled her full with her. Diana, time and time again between the muffled moans, pleaded with her to, "Please let her come," and Christina pressed on, insistently into her most treasured lover. Diana was filled with her lover, in all her open places, wet beyond her own comprehension.

And the roles, in a single instant, reversed—Diana pulled herself away from Christina's hands, moving out from under her, and turning, she grabbed Christina with her strong arms and hands. Christina was propelled to the ground now underneath Diana who pinned her shoulders down, as Christina was obstinately refusing to be had again. Not now, not now she implored Diana, but Diana was determined, and put all of her weight on Christina's shoulders and held her down despite Christina's bucking body. "Lay still my love, and spread your legs," Diana said.

Christina, who was far from receptive or docile, spread her legs for Diana. Defiantly. "Wider, for me, lover, spread them as wide as they will go. Now." Christina did, but still tried to release herself from Diana's grip. But with each of her moves Diana bore down harder, pushing Christina's back into the grating rocks that dug deeper into the soft flesh of her back. The pain was too much for Christina, with more arguing, more fighting like this she would be bleeding, and before long she acquiesced. Diana moved between her legs, and Christina lay still on her back as Diana lowered her lips, her mouth, to arouse the already aroused Christina again . . . to orgasm. Her hands stroking the thighs, Christina's hands pushing Diana's head into her, between her spread legs.

Within a single minute in time Christina succumbed to the climax again. "I didn't want this."

"I did," Diana whispered seductively and then tenderly lay her body on top of her lover. Christina's heart was still racing, and the afterglow, again, was upon her.

They stood when Christina said she was able. Christina moved herself in front of Diana, face to face, and said, "Now," staring at Diana without humor, "Now touch yourself, lover, and I will watch you. This is the way I want it."

Diana leaned back against the side of a massive boulder that hung over the cliff. She supported herself, her back against the cold rock, and lowered her hands, first to spread her swollen lips and then rubbing herself, almost too gently at first to be felt. Softly, slowly her lean fingers moved against her own skin while she spread her legs further apart for Christina to see, standing open, lips exposed, daring Christina to stand still and watch without touching or approaching. She began the serious stroking which would lead her very soon to her orgasm. Christina could see her breasts moving and Diana's body began to shudder slightly with the impending release. Already, she was about to come.

Christina lost the dare willingly, not wanting to play that game, she approached. She got down on her knees in front of her lover and without prelude slid her fingers into Diana with one fluid move. Her other arm she put around Diana's back to protect her from the cold of the boulder, her hand pressing her forward and back again. Christina's face laying softly against Diana's belly, kissing her there, whispering into her skin. Then, her mouth moved down to it—licking and sucking now with a soothing motion over and over, a bit stronger and stronger, a bit harder and harder, and still easy and female and softly back and forth and back and forth rocking her towards the climax that would make Diana unable to stand unassisted. Christina letting her hot breath tantilize, titillate even further, still rocking and letting her tongue stroke and stroke and stroke. The heady scent embracing her, her fingers moving deeper still into Diana, her tongue laying firmer on Diana's exposed lips.

Diana watched it, was dying for it as she was so close, urging bodies moving, throbbing with the desire and the love and the bond and the persuasive gentle fingers bringing the Rise . . .

When finally the tongue upon Diana brought the wave to crest, the heart-jolting orgasm . . . the spontaneous urgent cry resonating within her long before she let it go, long before she took a breath . . . Crying out Christina's name in a carnal groan that emanated from her deep recesses, the cry that Christina would hear for days to come . . . The Climax, the cry forcing her against the boulder for support for her trembling knees, standing there, breathing long deep raw breaths, not being able to take the air in to fill her fast enough, she stood bare, exposed and powerfully overcome. Vulnerable. She flashed to something Jade had said, "that she wouldn't be able to stand the pain of devastation again, of being left," and at this moment Diana knew that she would not be able to either. She had exposed it all to Christina, down to her core. Naked, and yet it seemed right to her, to give it to this woman again. This woman who leaned in against her, her arms around her telling her in a soothing whisper that it was all as it should be, that she was safe now, nothing would hurt her again. Hushing her and hushing her and bringing her down, bringing her back. Hushing the fear she knew Diana was feeling.

Before Christina knew how it happened she had Diana's ring on her finger: a large solid gold ring, the band, the bond affixed on her finger. The initials of the woman she had always loved, DH, engraved for her on her body now. Diana didn't notice the tears, but she did notice the joy, the rapture. Oh, Diana had earned this moment. This release was hers. Love was around her. She was all of happiness, and sadness and love and Christina was here, she was here now, holding her, loving her. They were all one—the two on the ground, the One that was not.

At this exact moment when dawn was breaking, the women swept through with exhaustion, smoldering still, Diana had her flash of inspiration: it was freedom she was feeling, and deliverance.

And unless you were right up close to them you couldn't hear Her thought: 'Between the folds of my spirit and my soul, inhaling deeply of you both.' And unless you were right up next to them you couldn't see the steam.

Clip or photocopy the coupon below to order.

ORDER NOW

A THIRD STORY
by Carole Taylor
ISBN 0-917597-06-0

_____ Enclosed is $7.95* plus $1.05 postage ($9 ppd.)
_____ Charge my   MASTERCARD   VISA   (circle one)

ACCT. # _____ EXP. DATE _____

Signature _____

NAME: _____

ADDRESS: _____

CITY: _____ STATE: _____ ZIP: _____

Send your order with full payment to: LACE PUBLICATIONS
                                       POB 10037
                                       Denver CO 80210-0037
*Colorado residents please add 29¢ tax per book ordered
Thank you.